TROPIC ENVY

A LUKE ANGEL MYSTERY

NATE VAN COOPS

Skylighter Press

For Marguerite Van Coops and Marilyn Bourdeau, two women who inspire me to create from the heart.

ONE

FREE FALL

FALLING out of an airplane is the number one stunt Americans associate with thrill-seeking.

The cocky call it "jumping" to claim a sense of control, but let's be honest, gravity reigns undefeated.

For a pilot, jumping out of a perfectly good airplane is akin to buying a ticket aboard a cruise ship because you're excited to try the lifeboats.

The most frequent reasons I'd worn parachutes in my life thus far had been because A: Uncle Sam had told me to, or B: I was doing aerobatics in an airplane that the Feds might ramp check, and I had to play by the regs.

Now I had occasion C.

Hank Martin's eighty-sixth birthday.

The old man had declared that if George H.W. Bush had done it at ninety, then by God, he certainly could manage at eighty-six. He wasn't about to be outdone by any politician, especially an Astros fan.

Hank's wife, Maddie Coleman-Martin, looked me dead in

the eye and said, "Luke Angel, I'm trusting you with this one. 'Cause Lord knows, I'm not going."

So here I was, along with a half dozen other friends Hank had roped into the celebration.

We lingered on the turf at KZPH—Zephyrhills Municipal Airport—waiting for our jump with Skydive America. They operated a fleet of planes that included a pair of DHC-6 Twin Otters, a Pilatus PC-12, and a Cessna Grand Caravan. We'd all signed liability waivers longer than The Constitution and were now waiting for our chance to board.

"How come you aren't wearing one of these funky tracksuits with your parachute?" Tyson asked, comparing his purple-and-teal jumpsuit to my tactical pants and Archangel Aviation T-shirt. The youngest mechanic on my crew was also Hank's grandson, so his attendance had been mandatory.

"Jumpsuits are optional," I said.

"What? They never told me that! Here I'm dressed like I got sneezed out of a nineties Taco Bell, and you look like your normal self."

"The jumpsuit keeps your clothes from getting scraped up on landing if you skid in on your ass."

"So you're saying I'm gonna suck at this."

"You'll be fine."

His eyes widened. "Wait. Then how come none of them look like neon clowns?" He pointed to two members of our group walking up in trendy black jumpsuits with sleek helmets under their arms. The guy was tall, lean, and handsome, with a bright smile on display as he laughed with the stylish blonde beside him. Despite the heat, they looked like they hadn't shed a drop of sweat.

The guy's name was Jason Evan Brooks II, and he was a corporate pilot I'd known for years. He asked everyone to call him "Brooks." He'd been chief pilot during the era Hank had been running the flight school but had since moved on. The twenty-something young woman beside him was new to me, though clearly a veteran skydiver. Her rig was top-notch, and her jumpsuit was embroidered with the initials SJN.

"Who's that?" I asked Tyson.

"You don't know?" He arched an eyebrow.

"You must be the only one." This comment came from the vicinity of my right elbow, and I looked down to discover the petite figure of Nina Yee had appeared beside me, also dressed in a teal-and-purple rental jumpsuit—though hers might have been a kid's size. She'd worked the front counter at the Bayside flight school since high school, and had been training there for years on the side. "That's Sierra Noble," she explained. "She's got more social media followers than Tom Cruise."

"Sounds implausible," I said.

"Well, if you base it on *engagement*," Nina clarified.

"You've lost me."

"Shit, man. Bet she's gonna film this whole jump for her YouTube channel," Tyson said. "I'm gonna be in a tier one aviation influencer's video for the first time in my life, and it's gonna show me wiggling around on some dude's front like a chest hair. I knew I shoulda taken the solo jump training."

"Don't worry," I said. "Based on the ratio of female jump instructors I've seen here, there's a fair chance you'll be strapped to a woman's chest. Like a GoPro. Or a papoose."

"You're not making this better, man."

"And you're being sexist," Nina added, "Suggesting it's a woman's job to hold babies. Also, using the term 'papoose' might be cultural appropriation. I'm not sure. I'd have to check."

"Should I just leave the parachute here and jump from the plane without it?" I asked. "Save the internet the trouble of cancelling me?"

"Probably," Tyson replied. "Good thing you're not on the socials."

But he stopped talking when Brooks and the influencer in question joined us.

"Luke. Thought you only landed in water these days," Brooks said. "Somebody fish you out of a lake for this?"

"I was all for celebrating on a beach with a margarita, but when the big man says jump, we jump. Literally, it seems."

"Oh, that's right. He's your landlord too, isn't he?" Brooks asked. "Heard you were still squatting on his yacht."

"I've had worse setups." I turned my attention to the blonde. "Hi. I'm Luke."

She extended a hand. "Sierra. You're the one with the Grumman seaplane I've heard about. Is it a Goose?"

"Mallard," I said.

"Brooks told me you have a charter service out of Albert Whitted with it. That's *so* cool. Those big radial engines? And from an airport with so much history. Talk about nostalgic."

"He likes getting his passengers there an hour later than necessary," Brooks said.

"And deaf," I added. I gestured toward the Pilatus on tie down. "You flying us up there today, Brooks? You're rated in a PC-12, aren't you?"

"I've moved up to the jet," he said. "Unless these guys want to give me my 2K a day. Then sure, I'll fly it."

"Must be nice," Nina said.

"Hi, Nina," Brooks grinned at her. "You'll get there one of these days, kid. You're on the right track. I'll save a spot for you to ride shotgun in the PC-24 anytime you like."

Nina blushed and pushed a strand of hair behind her ear. "Okay."

Sierra studied Nina. "You ready to be a rule-breaker with me?"

"Who, me?"

"The state of Florida still has a law that says it's illegal for women to skydive on a Sunday. Today, you and I are going to be outlaws. And I'm going to highlight the antiquated sexism in my video and see if we can get the law off the books. Maybe we'll get some other women fired up about it too. And the quality men, of course," she added. She elbowed Brooks. "Right?"

Brooks popped a mint into his mouth. "Hell no. Let's keep all these pesky women home on Sundays. Sounds perfect."

Sierra swatted him.

"Speaking of quality men, have you met Tyson?" I asked. "He's a bit of an influencer too. I'd bet he'd love getting fired up with you."

Sierra gave Tyson a smile. "Very cool. Have I seen your content somewhere?"

Tyson just stared for a long moment, then finally some words came out. "Yeah. I mean, I do some reels of . . . plane . . . stuff—"

Just then, a tall female jump instructor walked up and tapped him on the shoulder. "You ready to get cinched up? I need to get you into your tandem harness."

Tyson groaned.

"Okay, I guess we'll see you guys onboard, huh?" Sierra said. She gave me a nod and winked at Nina, then she and Brooks headed for the plane. They were soon laughing about something.

"I think I'll go chuteless with you," Tyson said. "She was probably recording that whole thing. I'm dead. It's over."

I slapped him on the shoulder. "Don't worry. We're about to jump out of an airplane. We'll have fun or die trying."

The rest of our group headed our way too. Hank looked good, hooked into his tandem harness and sporting a cheap pair of rental goggles. At his age, he didn't rely on fashion to maintain his style. He could have made a cardboard box look distinguished. He was going to be strapped to Tom "Ripcord" Wilson, my senior mechanic and the most seasoned skydiver of the group. He'd logged over three thousand jumps in his forty-odd years in aviation. If any of us were going to struggle, it wasn't going to be Rip.

The Twin Otter they were using today taxied near and we loaded in. One other face I recognized in our group was that of Chase Dempsey, one of the Bayside Flyers flight instructors. He'd given Tyson some of his primary instruction, and we knew each other in passing from the airfield, but I didn't know him well. He held a Celsius energy drink in one hand and was lugging a cooler with the other.

"You need a hand with that?" I asked.

"Sure."

I felt the weight of the cooler. "You must be thirsty."

"It's a long ride up to thirteen-five. And Rip swears by 'em."

"You don't have to tell me," I said. Our hangar fridge at work was continually stocked with various brands of energy drinks thanks to Rip's enthusiasm for caffeine.

Thirteen-thousand-five-hundred feet was the target altitude we'd climb to before jumping. Aviation regs stated that flight in a non-pressurized aircraft above twelve thousand feet for more than half an hour required the use of supplemental oxygen, so thirteen-five was about as high as the pilots of the aircraft could get us and still have adequate time to get back down below twelve thousand before the thirty minutes was up.

There was supplemental oxygen aboard in the form of small portable tanks, but most people didn't need them for such a brief climb. Even so, I took a spot on the floor near Hank and kept an eye on him as we ascended. He may have believed himself undiminished by age, but if he had a health complication on this flight, Maddie would have my ass.

Tyson sat on my other side with his eyes glued to the Otter's jump door. Huddled on the floor of the plane in a circle, things were getting real, and the idea of jumping out of an airplane hits harder once you're inside and contemplating your exit options.

"Doing okay?" I asked.

Tyson's eyes stayed wide. "Yeah. No problem," he shouted back over the noise of the engines. "This'll be cake."

Chase opened the cooler. "I propose a toast. To the man of the hour!"

Hank raised a hand. "The birthday boy. That's me."

The open cooler revealed a mix of energy drinks and sodas with a few waters and seltzers thrown in.

"You forgot the beers," Brooks said.

Chase offered the cooler to Hank and Rip first, then we each took turns choosing something. I settled for a Sprite.

Chase lifted his Celsius. "To Hank. The reason so many of us have jobs in this crazy, awesome career."

"Hear, hear!" Sierra shouted.

"You are all my proof I did something right in life," Hank shouted over the noise.

"You may be old, but you've got cool friends," Brooks said.

"Who you calling old? In a minute you're gonna see this old dog's still got a few tricks in him yet."

Our drinks met in a salute in the center of the circle for the cheers, and even the jump instructors joined in.

Above ten thousand feet, we jostled into our exit positions. Sierra ended up next to me. She'd donned a pair of sleek-looking goggles but was having trouble getting them to go on inside of her jump helmet. The helmet already had a visor, so the goggles seemed redundant.

"Double wind protection?" I asked.

"They're a prototype," she said. "Friend of mine gave me a pair to promote for his startup. But I didn't realize they'd feel so bulky inside the helmet. I'll have to tell him. You want to try them? They give you in-flight data."

"Like what?"

"Look and see." She handed over the goggles and I slipped them on. She wasn't kidding. They were smart lenses and mimicked a military-style heads-up display with altitude information, ground speed, and even an artificial horizon.

"Hang on," I said. "Is that traffic?"

Even though I was looking at Sierra, there was a virtual dot in the distance showing as an airplane.

"It projects the traffic data from the app on my phone. Cool, right?"

"Amazing."

She pressed something on her phone screen and a little camera icon appeared in my peripheral vision.

"You can be my bonus cameraman today." She reached up and adjusted them on my face. "Just don't lose them. Pretty sure they're like five grand."

"Noted." It was a fancy upgrade from the altimeter already mounted to my wrist, and probably overkill, but having options never hurt.

Next I knew, the red jump run light was on and we were shepherded toward the door.

The light turned green, indicating the aircraft had reached the jump zone.

The tandems were due out first.

I slapped Rip on the shoulder. "You two all set?"

"Totally chill, man," he replied. "Feeling Zen to the max right now."

"He's the calm one," Hank said. "I'm pumped!"

Rip pointed to me. "Remember, there's no AAD in that swooping rig. We all pull at five thousand. Scenic cruise down."

"Got it," I said. "No worries." The AAD or Automatic Activation Device came standard in a lot of other rigs, but at least I had a manual reserve should I need it.

Chase and his instructor went out first.

Behind them, the woman jumping with Tyson guided him to the open door.

"Hang on, I'm not sure this is a great ide—aaaaaaah!" Tyson shouted as they vanished out of the plane.

Nina and her instructor went out silent but smiling.

Hank and Rip reached the door next. Hank gave a big thumbs up, then a whoop as they went out. Rip threw up a pair of "hang-loose" Shaka gestures as they fell.

Next came the solo acts.

"Ladies first," I said to Sierra and let her go ahead of me.

I found the sight of human bodies hurling themselves into the wind was giving me the same rush it had the first time I'd made a jump. These friends weren't wearing fatigues, but the sensation was the same.

Sierra went out, then I was at the door, heart pounding. The trick is you just keep walking.

I gave one last pat to the straps of my chute for luck, then stepped out into open air.

Free fall would only last about a minute.

But a lot can happen in sixty seconds.

TWO
JUMP SCARE

THE THING you don't anticipate the first time you free fall from an airplane is the noise. We might have left the high-pitched whine of the aircraft's turboprop engines behind, but traveling at one-hundred-and-twenty miles an hour through the atmosphere is the auditory equivalent of confronting a chainsaw with your face. Anyone who's ever raced down a freeway on a motorcycle can tell you with some accuracy how the velocity of the air can siphon tears from your eyes and relocate your cheeks to your temples.

Sierra's fancy goggles were doing a good job of cancelling out the tears issue, but without a full-face helmet I had no way to avoid grinning like The Joker on my descent from on high.

Sierra wasn't far ahead of me, spread-eagled for maximum wind resistance and using the angle of her outstretched hands to further direct her fall. She'd mounted an Insta360 camera pole on the back of one wrist, and it had to be recording one hell of a view.

I tracked my way toward her, joining her pursuit of the rest of the group. The figures of Rip and Hank were doing some circular head-down rotations, and beyond them, Tyson's instructor had done a good job keeping Tyson flat and maximizing time for us to catch them. There was a chance we might even join up as a group if we timed things right. But a black streak shot by me and plummeted past, helmet down and arms at his sides for maximum speed—Brooks tracking away with his own ideas of how a free fall should look. He flew in front of Sierra and turned a somersault for her camera.

Showboat.

The altimeter reading on my goggles already read below ten thousand feet. At terminal velocity, a thousand feet flashes by every five seconds. Another reason our group would pop chutes at five thousand feet. It would give us a chance to recover from the adrenaline of exiting the plane and to relax and enjoy the phenomenal view for a few minutes before the ground welcomed us home.

You couldn't talk to each other in free fall—too loud, too far apart. But I got a wave from Nina and a thumbs up from her tandem instructor. Seemed like Nina was doing well for a first-timer. Sierra was close by too. She gave me an enthusiastic peace sign and a whoop. If she was hoping for a good shot of herself from my goggle-mounted camera lenses, she'd nailed it. It reminded me of my duties as a secondary cameraman.

Tyson and his jump instructor had fallen too far away for me to get a good shot of them. I'd never catch them in free fall, but Hank and Rip were close. Scoring a decent shot of the birthday boy for Maddie would show her the bravery her husband had exhibited. I directed my body that way to capture whatever I could before we all hit our rapidly approaching moment of popping chutes. Getting a shot as Rip deployed the pilot or drogue chute would be especially cool.

I gave Hank a wave and tried to get Rip's attention, but he wasn't looking my way. His head was nearly flush against Hank's.

Trying to say something? It was an odd angle. Hank's expression of concern was understandable—most student jumpers aren't exactly a testament to calm—but his smile was missing entirely, replaced with a grimace of fear. Most tandem instructors will use a drogue chute early, helping to keep the fall stable, but Hank and Rip's angle was strange, canted farther head down than normal, top heavy. It made it even harder to see Rip's face.

A parachute popped. Tyson's instructor deployed their chute, and the pair swung upward with the newfound lift. I looked up and caught the moment Sierra's chute came out too. I put a hand to my own pull handle. It was time.

But Rip and Hank were still falling.

Rip was the most veteran skydiver in our group. He no doubt felt comfortable opening at a lower altitude, but the odds that he'd do so in a group like this were slim. He was the jumpmaster and team leader. And he had Hank to think of.

Something was wrong.

The altimeter reading on my lenses whirred past four thousand feet.

Come on Rip, pull the pilot chute.

The rig was equipped with an automatic activation device. For a tandem jump, it ought to activate around two-thousand feet as a safety precaution, maybe eighteen-hundred depending on the density settings for the day. But there was no reason to rely on that.

My chute that I'd borrowed from Rip didn't contain an AAD. More reason I needed to pull now in case my main chute had an issue and I required time to deploy the reserve. But Rip's drogue chute wasn't even out yet.

Pull the cord, Rip. Come on!

I might be a hazard if I got too close to the pair, arrive at their position at the moment the AAD activated and only cause an interference, but I was already committed.

Arms extended, I reached toward my friends. Hank saw me, eyes wide, terror on his face. He extended a hand, like I could catch him midair, save him from his fate.

But I wasn't reaching for his hand, I was searching for the pull handle on Rip's big tandem chute.

Come on. Deploy.

In my mind, I wasn't talking to Rip anymore. It was clear he was out of action. Something was seriously wrong. But I wanted the damned AAD to go off. Twenty-five hundred. The wind was flapping their jumpsuits at high speed, a thousand little pops and cracks reaching me in the wind as we fell.

Deploy goddammit. Deploy.

Two-thousand. I could touch Hank's outstretched hand.

Eighteen hundred. Nothing.

Shit.

I collided with them, Hank grabbing at my clothing, fingers desperate for purchase.

"No, Hank!" I shouted. The wind ripped the words from my mouth. I didn't want Hank's hand on my arm; I wanted that damned handle. I knocked his arm away and spotted it. The red cushion handle tucked securely at Rip's hip, but his hand nowhere near it.

I wasted no time. I yanked the handle, deploying the pilot chute that would pull the main chute free of its container and arrest their fall. I wanted to see it happen, but there was no time. The collision with Hank sent me spinning, tumbling away— writhing like a cat in midair— desperate to get my back aimed toward the sky.

Eight hundred feet.

Let it be enough.

I pulled the handle on my rig and my pilot chute deployed, then the main, and I felt the upward yank of the harness against my chest and groin as I swung vertical and beyond.

Thank God.

The main chute had worked.

But I wasn't out of danger yet.

The extended free fall had taken me out of the landing zone. The ground was coming up fast, and it wasn't just any destination; it was the active runway of the airport, and a small plane had just touched down on the runway.

See me.

Stop your plane.

But they wouldn't see me in time. There was no control tower here. No one to warn the pilot of the rogue parachutist careening toward them on an intercept course. But this parachute came with controls, so it was time to use them.

I pulled on both toggles, pulling harder on the left side and cupping the chute to pivot my body in that direction. Turn, turn turn! No time to be delicate. One choice. Hard contact with the ground or death by propeller. As I turned into the wind, the ground rushed up to grant my wish.

I'd executed some flawless flares in the Army, with graceful landings that looked like I'd just shifted to a casual stroll. This wouldn't be one of them. I hit feet first, and I even ran a few steps, but wildly off-balance, my momentum carrying me forward with all the grace of Wile E. Coyote about to run off a cliff. Then I tripped, hit the ground with my shoulder, and somersaulted. I went end over end in a tangle of lines, half-strangled by my parachute. The impact punched the wind from my lungs as I crashed to a stop in a cloud of dust.

I lay on my back and wheezed to gain my breath as dandelion seeds and agitated grass flies swirled overhead. The air didn't want to come. Even spitting sand from my mouth proved impossible with my dry mouth and no air in my lungs.

But I staggered to my feet the next instant anyway, because in the near distance, Hank and Rip were streaking in for a landing.

Hank got his feet up as he'd been taught, bracing for impact, but Rip was dead weight behind him and they struck hard in a violent heap.

I cringed at the impact.

I clawed at the straps of my parachute harness, fighting out of it, my eyes locked on the pile of parachute canopy settling over my friends.

My breath finally came.

"Don't be dead. Don't be dead," I gasped.

The harness relinquished its grip on my body—I yanked the goggles from my face, and I ran.

THREE
WHUMP

HANK WAS alive and cursing like Samuel L. Jackson on a plane full of snakes when I ran up. I found him pinned beneath the limp form of Rip who had fallen on top of him. Their parachute canopy lofted in the wind, tugging at the pair.

"Help me, Luke," Hank shouted. "I can't move."

The fact that Hank was bellowing gave me some assurance that he wasn't in immediate danger. My tactical combat casualty care training came rushing back, and I ran a mental checklist.

Rip's tinted goggles made it hard to see his eyes. My friend had come in limp as a rag doll, his feet dragging behind him. So I took Rip's head with both hands and pushed the goggles up to his forehead.

His eyes were open. Hazy, but moving. Chest rising and falling.

Thank God.

"Rip, what's going on, man? Can you hear me, buddy?"

"Just . . . chillin' . . ." Rip mumbled. "You good?"

Was he in shock? I checked him quickly for visible injuries. There was nothing I could easily identify.

"Can you tell me what day it is, Rip?"

"Taco Tuesday."

It wasn't.

Hank was straining. "I can't move my arm. Can't breathe right."

I shifted Rip's weight off of Hank as best I could, then pulled out my phone and dialed 911, continuing to check the two men while the dispatcher responded.

"Yes. I'm at Zephyrhills Municipal Airport, east side of Runway One, midfield. There has been a skydiving accident. Two males with injuries. They landed full canopy but came in hard. Tandem jump. One geriatric, possible rib fractures, labored breathing. He was the passenger. Hank, can you move the fingers on that hand?"

Hank wiggled his fingers but winced as he did so.

"Possible fractures to the right arm. Circulation appears good, conscious, alert. Second man is late fifties, altered LOC, no visible injuries but pupils dilated, pulse is fast—but he did just jump out of an airplane. I've got them stationary in a safe location east of the runway. Requesting EMS and you'll want to tell the driver to look out for airplanes when crossing the runway. This place is still active. There's no control tower to redirect incoming planes."

The dispatcher confirmed a few more details and told me Emergency Medical was on its way. I put the phone away and tended to the two men, gingerly getting their harnesses separated.

By then the other jumpers were on the ground. Tyson and his instructor ran over first. The instructor had introduced herself earlier as Jackie or Jess or something. She pulled out a phone and started talking to someone at the jump school. Tyson went straight to his grandfather.

"Holy shit, Grandpa. What happened?"

It was a good question.

"Give him some room," I said. "Ambulance is on the way."

By the time the EMTs arrived, there was a crowd around the two men. A couple of golf carts, concerned skydivers from the jump school, and more than a few looky-loos. Rip had found his feet and stood, no noticeable injuries on him, but he was confused and swaying.

"Do you remember anything about what happened up there?" I asked him.

"We jumped?" he replied, looking skyward. "I'm sorry, man. I'm feeling über shaky. Is everybody okay?"

I made him sit back down. He couldn't recount anything from the jump or even the ride up.

A paramedic pulled me aside once the men had been assessed. "We're giving them both supplemental oxygen to treat possible hypoxia, and we're going to transport them to the local hospital. AdventHealth isn't far. We see nothing here suggesting we'll need Level I or II trauma care. Are you the emergency contact for either man?"

"I'm Rip's—I mean Tom's—employer. Hank is a friend. I've got both of their info. Hank's grandson is also here."

"You're welcome to follow or ride along if need be. Do you have a vehicle?"

I didn't. Four of us had flown up in the Cessna 185. But it was a problem I could solve. I went to talk to Tyson.

"You think you could get a ride home with Chase or Sierra? Or you could take the 185 back yourself, and we can find an alternate way home. Your grandmother will come up, no doubt."

"She's already on her way. I just talked to her. So I'll hang with you. He is *my* grandpa."

"All right. Good."

The party was over.

Chase, Brooks, and Nina conversed quietly among themselves. Sierra broke away from that group and walked over.

"Everybody going to be okay?"

"Seems like it so far. We got lucky."

"Lucky they had *you*. I saw what you did. That was incredible. Did you actually pull their main chute for them?"

"Their AAD failed for some reason. No idea why."

"You saved their lives."

I had. And it hit me then how badly this day could have turned out with a few minor changes.

"Hey, do you by chance still have those goggles I lent you?" she asked. "I know there's been a lot going on, but I figured I'd grab them back."

I felt my head. They weren't there. "No. I think I must have tossed them in the grass on the run over here after I landed. Somewhere . . . that way." I pointed to where my rig was still lying in the grass beside the taxiway. "Sorry."

"Not even a problem. I'll find them," she said. She patted my arm. "We can handle putting your chute away too. Take care of your friends."

Then the EMTs were ready. I climbed into the ambulance with Rip. He was awake and looking more alert, but the oxygen mask on his face made speaking impractical. So I squeezed his hand instead, and he laid back and stared at the ceiling. I looked out the rear window of the ambulance and watched the scene outside recede in the distance. Nina, Chase and Brooks joined Sierra on her walk toward my downed parachute canopy.

Framed in the window, I felt their camaraderie. Ease returning. Relief. Tragedy had been avoided. Barely.

My left hand was shaking. I made a fist to stop it from trembling. But then I felt the pressure on my other hand. Rip, squeezing it. He stared at me, then raised his right hand, thumb and pinky finger extended. Shaka.

"Yeah. All good," I said. "Just another day in paradise."

And it was.

Unless one of these people had just tried to kill him.

FOUR

CHECKRIDES

WHEN I WALKED into Hangar 4 the next morning, it was to the sound of clapping. Reese, Tyson, and even Elsbeth, my bookkeeper, had made it in ahead of me and welcomed my arrival.

"That's not necessary," I said, dismissing their applause. "But thanks."

It had been a late night. The medical staff at AdventHealth had been top-notch, but good care isn't always fast. I'd stayed late and slept past eight this morning to compensate.

Tyson had already filled the rest of my crew in on what had happened to his grandfather. Hank had sustained a wrist injury involving a fracture of his radius. His ribs were bruised but not broken, and he'd also thumped his tailbone pretty hard and was dealing with that, but otherwise was okay.

"How's Rip?" Reese asked.

"Recovering," I said. "But confused. Nobody seems to know exactly what happened. Frank is keeping an eye on him this morning and he said he'd keep me updated."

My father, Frank Angel, had moved in with Rip, helping to

pay the mortgage on a bungalow over near Mirror Lake. The two men had hit it off working at the hangar lately and had taken to being bachelors together. Turned out, skydivers and ex-drug smugglers made good roommates. Who knew? For now, I was just happy there was someone to monitor Rip as he recuperated.

"The doctors didn't tell you anything definitive?" Elsbeth asked.

"Possible oxygen deficiency. They ran some tests. We'll see what comes back. But for now, he's supposed to rest and hydrate. You can all send him some encouraging messages. I'm sure he'd appreciate that."

Reese walked over and handed me the Detroit Tigers hat I'd given her for her heroics in Mexico a few months back. "That was some real Magnum shit yesterday. You earned this for a while."

I laughed and stuck the homage to Tom Selleck on my head. "All right. Everybody back to work. This place isn't going to run itself."

And we tried.

But my crew weren't the only ones talking about the weekend's excitement. By lunchtime, Tyson and I had retold the story several times to curious visitors. But it was only when Diana Longoria came striding across the ramp and directly to my toolbox that I knew the news had reached all corners of the airport.

Diana ran a nonprofit called Sunshine Relief Services that did hurricane response and other charitable aviation activities. Her brow was glistening from the walk over in the heat, but she looked good, all dark curls and long legs in a skirt that might also have been shorts. It left a lot of real estate to admire in either case. She fixed me with a stare from under long lashes, her lips playfully parted.

"You. Are something else."

"Hi, Diana. Always good to see you."

"Maddie called me. Hank is *so* lucky. I don't know what we would've done if Hank—I don't even want to think about it, it's so awful—but you. You're a goddamn hero." She walked directly around my toolbox and wrapped her arms around me, giving me a powerful squeeze.

"Oh. Okay. Hank would have done the same for me. You work out? That's a hell of a grip you've got."

She released me. "Never skip arm day. And yes. Hank is a national treasure. Like Dolly Parton, or Snoop Dog. But you? You just earned gold stars for life, mister. What are we doing to celebrate?"

"We?"

"Yes. I've been tired of waiting around over there in my office for you to come take me out. So apparently, I have to take *you* out. And celebrate."

"Tempting. But totally unnecessary."

She cocked a hand on her hip. "You already have plans? Is that darling ex-wife of yours cooking up a party already?"

"No. Cassidy is back in Boston for the time being. Busy flight schedule."

"What's the story with you two these days? Anything . . . residual?"

"We're business partners. That's it." I tried to keep my tone from revealing my frustration about that fact.

"Where I grew up, we had a term for that kind of situationship," Diana said. "It's called: You snooze, you lose. So if Cassidy isn't going to take you out and celebrate you for being the brave hero you are, then it leaves it to me. *We're* going to dinner. Champagne for me. Beer for you? Whatever you want. You earned it, big guy."

"I *could* go for some dinner."

"I can't tonight because I'm super busy and over-committed and popular, but tomorrow or the next day? Definitely by the weekend. Look forward to it. It's going to be amazing and you'll love it. I'm even gonna buy a new dress. It's gonna be short. Get excited."

"Copy that. I'm already excited."

"Better be." She gave a toss of her hair and a wink, and she was off, striding back across the ramp like a conquering goddess. I watched her go for a moment, then caught Tyson staring from where he'd been working on changing the muffler on a Mooney. His eyebrows were threatening to join his hairline.

"Daaaammnn," he muttered. "You're taking Diana Longoria out now? What even is your life?"

"She's just being nice."

"That girl's—"

"—Fine as hell. Yes. I know your general feeling on women."

"I mean she is though, right?"

"He's not wrong," Reese said from somewhere behind me.

I turned around to find her munching an apple and looking the direction Diana had disappeared.

"You too?" I asked.

"What?" She took another bite of her apple. "I'm in a committed relationship, but we can all enjoy the scenery, can't we?"

By mid-afternoon, it was too hot to do much of anything. I had fans in every corner of the hangar going full blast, but it was just turning the place into a convection oven. Elsbeth had gone home, and Tyson was on his third ice pop from the freezer. His tongue was dark blue.

Even my dog, Murphy, had abandoned me for the air-conditioned confines of my upstairs office. He and my hangar cat, Blackjack, were lying on the floor up there having a staring contest, no doubt wondering why the humans were so stupid as to still be mobile. Reese was the only one who didn't seem to mind the heat.

"People pay good money to sweat like this in yoga classes," she said. "We're getting it for free."

That rosy assessment aside, I made an excuse of needing to settle a parts bill with Bayside Maintenance and took off on the golf cart for a joyride.

The crew over in the Bayside maintenance hangar looked just as sweaty as we were, though their hangar got better airflow. I kept going because I wasn't ready to abandon the relative wind I was enjoying from the golf cart's acceleration, and there was some sort of hubbub going on over at the flight school.

I walked in to find a crowd in the lobby. It was mostly fresh-faced young people with carefully messy hairstyles advertising their membership in a generation more hip than mine. Several were lounging on the airport couch or in armchairs, and a few more were just standing around staring at the television on the wall. They gave me a wide berth as I moved my sweat-drenched self through the group.

I expected to discern some cause for the gathering on my way through, but instead of a sports game or trending movie as a draw, the TV displayed a ground track map from FlightAware. The familiar outline of Pinellas County was overlayed with a neon flight path and a little airplane logo that had evidently done several turns and possibly a hold. Riveting viewing it was not. Despite this, the young people around the room were chatting and snacking and treating it like the Super Bowl.

I walked over to the flight school rental counter where Nina Yee was perched behind the computer glaring at a Jeppesen test prep guide.

"Hey," I offered.

"Oh, hey! Luke." She pulled herself from her reading. "How are you? How's Hank?"

"A little banged up, but he'll recover. What's all this?"

Nina looked over at the group near the TV. "Oh, yeah.

They're having a viewing party. Sierra Noble is taking her ATP checkride. Those are her groupies."

The Airline Transport Pilot certificate was the top tier of ratings for general aviation pilots, and necessary for many higher-paying commercial jobs. So Sierra earning hers would open a lot of doors.

"People do checkride watch parties now? That's fun. Supportive bunch of friends," I said.

"Not everyone gets them. Don't worry, this place will be a ghost town when I do my exam."

"Oh that's right. You've got a checkride coming up too." I eyed her textbook. "Instrument?"

She sighed. "Third time's the charm, huh? I think Chase might give up on me if I fail it this time."

"Instrument ratings are no joke. That's a lot of new content to learn. You'll get there."

"I don't know. I'm starting to think maybe this career isn't for me. Chase says the airlines aren't even hiring anymore. He's an instructor with sixteen hundred hours and even he can't get a break. What hope will I have if I take this long to even get through my Instrument and Commercial ratings?"

"You're young, you're smart. You've worked in aviation for years. I gestured toward the groupies. "Sierra is evidently making it just fine. What's she got that you don't?"

"Um. A flying budget. Her own Bonanza. Three hundred thousand followers. An avionics sponsorship. An engine sponsorship. A multi-engine instructor rating. She has gorgeous hair you could put in a shampoo commercial—"

"Okay, I can see how *some* of those might help. Minus the hair thing. You've already got stellar hair."

She fingered the strands of her own mousy locks and made a "pffft" noise.

"You know what? No one has ever offered to put me in a

shampoo commercial either, and look how badly I could use a shower." I took off my hat to display my sweaty head.

"Yeah. You *should* do something about that," she replied. But she had found her smile again, so I counted it as a win. "Did you actually need anything?"

"Just enjoying the A/C."

"Okay, cool. But next time, can you bring your dog?"

FIVE

OLD MAN SYNDROME

A LATE AFTERNOON thunderstorm unleashed fat splattering raindrops five minutes before I'd intended to leave the hangar. By the time I had the hangar door halfway down, the drops turned to a steady drumming, cancelling any hopes for a dry walk home. And since I'd failed to put the top back on my Jeep, driving wouldn't do me any better.

So I waited, trudging back upstairs to my office and organizing a pile of work orders for the following day. Tyson had forgotten to clock out, so I sorted that, logging him an extra half hour beyond what he'd earned. He was a good kid. I figured he'd earned it that way. He and Reese had made it out ahead of the storm and would be safely home by now.

Murphy stared at the door longingly but didn't budge from my side while the thunderstorm was booming. After a nearby lightning strike set the roof quivering, he crawled under my desk and laid on my feet. Blackjack, my cat, was just waking up. She stretched atop my desk and set to work giving herself an aggressive tongue bath, then stopped abruptly and stalked into the hangar in search of vermin to destroy. Her crooked tail waved like a war flag on her way out.

The rain brought the temperature down.

By the time the storm cell had rained itself out and blown northwest, the world outside had dimmed. The sun wasn't all the way down yet, but the light in the hangar had changed, a warm golden hue tinting the walls.

The sky was clearing. I locked up the hangar and toweled off the driver's seat of my Jeep, then repeated the process in the back seat before helping Murphy up. Nobody loves the smell of wet dog.

There was a direct path to the road I could take, past the charter company and the avionics shop to a gate that led onto Eighth Avenue SE, but I wasn't ready to leave the airport grounds just yet.

I missed my plane.

Because of the space limitations at Albert Whitted Airport, hangars were scarce, especially since a particularly damaging hurricane season had drastically reduced our hangar count. It meant that a big Grumman seaplane like my Mallard stood no chance of gaining a hangar and had to slum it outdoors. The ramp and wash rack in front of my hangar were already in high demand, so *Tropic Angel* was currently on tie down on the Taxiway Charlie ramp. The open space was exposed to the elements, out of sight from my hangar, and a farther distance to travel than I liked, but it came with one perk. It sported a helluva view.

Albert Whitted Airport is nearly surrounded by water. The port of Saint Petersburg fronts the southern edge of the property, Tampa Bay abuts the eastern perimeter, and the Yacht Basin surrounding Demens Landing Park is another watery view to the north. The only terrestrial neighbors to the property are west and northwest, the latter of which is the Downtown Saint Petersburg waterfront with its steadily growing jigsaw puzzle of high-rise condo towers.

In my time at the airport, I'd witnessed a dozen buildings crumble and rise again, reborn as taller, more expensive structures. It was only the flight path for the final approach to Runway 7 that held the high-rise expansion in check to the south —much to the chagrin of real estate developers citywide, eager to reimagine the shape of the waterfront and the corresponding sizes of their bank accounts.

For now, the dam had held. Citizens had voted that Albert Whitted Airport was to remain an airport "in perpetuity" so that city residents and the subsequent generations of their children would always have a place to learn to fly.

The south side of Runway 7 was the spot for locals, and the most fortunate of these lease holders abided in the north-facing hangars that looked out at the ever-evolving city and the thin demarcation line represented by the chain-link fence of the airport's northern edge. It was a view that invited contemplation, often from the comfort of a hangar lawn chair angled toward downtown. That's why it wasn't at all surprising to me, even at that hour, to find one of the hangar doors open and the figure of Bud Truman seated in a chair enjoying just such a moment of quiet contemplation.

I steered my Jeep in his direction and rumbled my way past his hangar before cutting the engine and hopping out. Murphy followed.

"Someone's working late," Bud offered.

"Curse of being the boss," I said. "How's life on Skyline Boulevard?"

"Hot and wet until a few minutes ago, but the circumstances have much improved."

He had his battered leather satchel briefcase out and a laptop sitting on a tool cart beside him, along with a file of documents.

Looked like a government website on the laptop screen. Besides being a retired airline pilot and flight instructor, Bud was also a designated pilot examiner for the FAA, the guy responsible for passing or failing applicants on their pilot exams. The job was niche, and extremely difficult to be selected for. But once you were in, the pay was excellent.

"Heard you had a star ATP applicant today," I said. "She pass?"

"You know I can only reveal the results of an applicant's exam to the applicant and the FAA." He gave me a knowing look as he took a stack of papers, straightened them, and slid them into the satchel. "But I suspect Miss Noble's future in aviation will be bright."

"Not a shiny paint, no horsepower situation then."

"That girl knows her stuff. Probably flies an approach better than I can," he replied. "Flight decks today are nothing like when I came up. It takes some reeducation. Hell, even the paperwork is all different now. It's all about 'download this,' 'upload that,' and using digital signatures for endorsements." He gestured to the laptop. "It's getting so you need to take a course in computers before you can teach someone how to fly an airplane anymore. You'd better take heed. Don't get old and useless like me."

"I'd say you're doing fine." I wandered around his hangar and admired the vintage airport signs, nostalgic paintings, and family WWII memorabilia he had on the walls. His aircraft was a home-built RV-8. He hadn't built it himself, but had purchased it from someone who had, and years before, I'd done the pre-purchase inspection for him. It had a stylish paint job, was fully aerobatic, and was the kind of plane that existed for the sole purpose of having fun.

A formidable bank of tool chests and workbenches lined the walls. Bud was also an airframe and powerplant mechanic in addition to being a pilot, though he rarely worked on any planes except his own. That and the classic Harley Davidson roadster he kept in the corner. As man-caves went, plenty of toys were on display, and each of them was kept in pristine condition. It was evident why the line guys referred to this place as the "Taj-MaHangar."

"Yours is one of the only airplanes improving the view out here," Bud said, nodding toward *Tropic Angel.* "That's an era when they knew how to build a beautiful aircraft. Is she flying enough?"

"I have a charter at the end of the month. That should keep the oil flowing."

"Better find some more. These birds need to stay airborne. Sitting around is what kills 'em. Same with old farts like me."

"*Tropic Angel* will be flying long after you and I are gone, if I have anything to say about it," I said.

"Good. That's what I hope this new crop of pilots figures out. They get so tied up in their own careers, bouncing from one captain's seat to another, that they forget that we're not the stars of this show—we're the custodians."

"Of the airport or the airplanes?"

"All of it. The future of aviation."

"Deep thoughts on tap out here tonight."

"You get it."

"I do. But I usually do my deep thinking on the boat. You can almost see it from here." I pointed across Demens Landing to where the mast of Hank's catamaran protruded from among the thicket of other sailboats. "Your chair might have the superior view. But just barely."

"We'll have to enjoy this time while we can," Bud said. "Since the world's going to Hell in a handbasket."

"Considering that phrase has been around for centuries, I suspect Hell might have a while to wait."

"You're not worried about the state of the world? Kids

spending all their time on the internet and unable to focus on anything but themselves?"

"Sometimes. But old men have fretted about the irreverence of youth since the dawn of time. I think it says something about our inability to let go of our relevance as we age. One way or another, the world *will* find its way on without us, and our way of doing things, and that can be hard to cope with."

"Easy for you to say. You're still young. But I get your point." He stared off at the skyline. "Speaking of my fellow old farts, how's Hank? Heard he banged himself up fooling around with you and the youngsters."

"You know Hank. He considers aging to be a contact sport."

"Good for him. I mostly 'contact' my doctor these days. Turpin says I need to smoke fewer cigars. Told her she could have my Cubans when I'm dead."

Gabby Turpin was the medical examiner most of us used for our flight physicals. She had a Cessna 182 on the field.

I eyed the stub of cigar in an ashtray near his computer. "We all need at least one vice," I said. "But maybe you can trade the cigars for tacos. We still need you around here."

Bud harrumphed.

"How's Nina doing?" I asked. "I ran into her at the flight school today. Said she has her retest scheduled with you."

"Don't get me started on that fiasco."

"She was studying. Seemed determined."

"It's not Nina that's the problem. It's that shit-for-brains instructor of hers. So damned set on landing his next job, he's been phoning in his instructor duties for a year. I don't know what they've been doing in all the hours they've been flying together, but it sure as hell isn't working. I have half a mind to report him to the FSDO and get his instructor's license revoked. His students deserve better."

The Flight Standards District Office was where our local

FAA inspectors were based. Mike would certainly be interested if an instructor was shirking his responsibilities.

"Did you advise Nina to try another instructor?"

"I implied it. But she's the loyal type. He tells her I'm being hard on her and *I'm* the bad guy, when he's the one setting her up to fail."

"Maybe I can talk to her. There are plenty of excellent instructors at this airport."

"You should. She's on my schedule this week. But if she doesn't make it this time, maybe she'll be ready to make a change."

Murphy barked from the back of the Jeep. He'd evidently peed on his quota of weeds and had climbed his way back up.

"You're being summoned," Bud said.

"Dinner time is sacred."

"Don't worry. I'll keep watch over *Tropic Angel* for you a little longer."

"Good. Let's take her for a spin next time I see you." I climbed back into the Jeep and started it up. Murphy nudged my shoulder with his nose. "I know. I'm going already."

When we reached Gate 6, I looked back and got a wave from Bud. Airport guardian on duty.

All was still right with the world.

SIX

BREEZE

IT WAS eight-thirty in the morning when the white Nissan Maxima with government plates pulled up in front of my place of business. I waited until the driver had climbed out before yelling across the hangar.

"Oh shit, it's the feds! Everybody scatter!"

Tyson fumbled an oil filter into a bucket and looked up with raised eyebrows.

"They've sent the meanest one!" I continued. "Hide your torque wrenches!"

Inspector Mike Gonzalez from the local FAA office walked over shaking his head.

"Don't know why you still do this every time I show up."

"I want you to be able to go home and tell your kids how feared and respected you are at work."

"My twins are fifteen now. They fear nothing, except maybe having their phones taken away."

"I've heard landlines are making a comeback."

"Is it the cords? So parents can choke their teenagers with them?"

"Could be. How's Mindy?"

"Beleaguered. Counting the days till school restarts."

"Tell her to send the boys here. I'll put them to work sweeping floors."

"Be careful what you wish for. She'd take you up on that in a heartbeat. Is Rip here?" He scanned the hangar.

"Not yet. Will be soon though. Says he's feeling fine and wants to work today. I told him to start with a half-day. Evidently he's choosing the latter half."

"Good. I was hoping I might have time to speak to you alone before he gets in."

"Anything serious?"

Mike shrugged with his mouth.

"Talk upstairs?" I aimed a thumb toward my office.

"Probably best."

We climbed the stairs to my office. Blackjack welcomed us and rubbed some fur into Mike's pant legs until he sat down and tried to pet her. Then she played hard to get.

"She only loves you when it's inconvenient," I said.

"I have one at home the same way," he replied.

"What's the word from the local office? Must be important if they sent you out unscheduled."

Mike pulled his phone from his pocket. "Are you on social media?"

"I'm not. But Tyson keeps me up to date on the latest and greatest short takeoff and landing competition videos. He follows all the big aviation influencers."

"Surprised he didn't alert you to this then." Mike scrolled on his phone and tapped something.

"To be fair, Tyson's not officially awake till break time," I said. "We get him at full power around 9:30."

Mike handed me the phone. "That's a video posted early this

morning. From Sierra Noble. A local aviation influencer. I gather you know her."

It was the skydive from Sunday afternoon. A shot from Sierra's chest-mounted GoPro, her 360 camera, and the additional footage from the goggles camera I'd been wearing. Mike sat in silence while I watched.

It was well-edited, showing quick snippets of our group on the ride up, the energy drink cheers, then the parade of jumpers diving out. Free fall.

The camera angles were great. A panorama of the sky over central Florida from Sierra's wrist mounted 360 degree selfie stick cam. The shots highlighted the free fall down, a few of us almost joining up. It was set to music that gained intensity as it neared time to deploy chutes. Then the film went almost exclusively to the goggles cam from my point of view, tracking toward Hank and Rip. Hank's stricken face appeared in the frame, then I was pulling their main chute for them. My subsequent impact with the ground was captured too. It didn't show the aftermath with the paramedics, but there was a shot of Hank and Rip both standing at the end that proved they'd survived the ordeal.

"Pretty cool editing," I said. "She did a nice job."

"*You* did a nice job. You saved two lives."

I shrugged. "A bullet dodged."

"We had a call from Skydive America on Monday. They walked us through the incident. We're looking into the faulty AAD issue. But we'll need to talk to Rip too."

"Are you suspicious that it might have been tampered with? I had that worry myself."

"No one is implying anything. We're simply investigating."

"The doctors couldn't find any cause of his fainting spell," I said. "Possibly the heat or the altitude, but I don't think that really explains the loopiness. But he's been fine since, so we're grateful for that."

"He's on your 135 charter certificate as a mechanic," Mike said. "Plus he flies for the biplane rides company. Both businesses have mandatory drug screening programs."

"You need us to do a 'for cause' drug test? Is that what you're after? He's not on any drugs, Mike."

"I'm not saying he is."

"The hospital already ran a bunch of tests."

"It's just procedure."

I frowned. "I'll ask him."

"You'll need to insist."

I puffed my cheeks and then blew the air out. "You're going to be *so* disappointed when you end up with nobody to bust again, buddy. I feel bad for you."

Mike sighed. "Why does everyone think I'm only out to bust balls?"

"You should slam your fist on my desk and demand to see our cable tensiometers."

"Why? We both know they're going to be calibrated."

"But I could *pretend* they aren't right till the moment you see them, and we could have this dramatic moment of palpable—tension."

Mike groaned. "Did you just set me up for a tensiometer joke? That's dumb on such a niche level."

"I want you to feel like you're close to nailing someone, Mike. I want it for you as a friend."

"Well, since you asked. My FSDO manager *did* send me with a reprimand. For *you*."

"She did?"

"She'd like you to stop referring to me as Darth Inspectorus in your emails."

"Ah. But does she know *why* I call you that?"

"No. And we're going to keep it that way."

"I bet you still have the screensaver I sent you. On your computer. The one with the big FAA logo on the Death Star?"

"She made me get rid of it."

"Damn her. But very on-brand for The Empire."

Mike stood. "I've got to go over and talk to Bud while I'm here. See how our latest crop of pilots is doing. Let me know when you get the drug test results."

"Fine. Tell Mindy I said hi. I'm going to send her some Princess Leia hair bun tutorials on YouTube. Spice up your love life."

"You say that like she hasn't worn them already."

"Whoa. You scoundrel."

I walked Mike back downstairs, and he spent some time petting Murphy before climbing back into his Maxima and driving away. I met Reese at her toolbox.

"What was all that about?" she asked.

"Due diligence. And evidently the jump from Sunday is on the internet."

Tyson piped up. "Oh damn. Did Sierra post her new vid? That's right, it's Tuesday. I totally forgot to check it." He had his phone out in an instant and walked over with it. Reese leaned in to watch when he swiped to the video.

"Beach Sierra," Reese said, noting the profile handle. "That's cute."

"Too bad she flies a Bonanza and not a Beechcraft Sierra," I said. "Then it would really fit."

"Close enough."

"Dude, it's already got over twenty thousand views," Tyson said. "It's not even brunch o'clock."

"Is that a lot?" I asked.

But he was absorbed in the video. "Oh maaan, she got me screaming like a goat going out that jump door."

"Still looks cool," Reese said. "You can't be uncool while skydiving."

"I don't know," Tyson said. "I might be the first. But check this out. She got shots straight from Luke's POV. That's some *HALO* shit."

They watched to the end.

"Badass," Reese said.

"Dope on a rope," Tyson agreed. "I gotta watch it again."

Just then, the sound of an engine reverberated from the hangar walls. The throaty rumble of a Continental IO-550.

"Holy shit, that's her," Tyson said.

And sure enough, Sierra Noble's white-and-blue-and-gold A36 Bonanza came rolling into view. She taxied to the edge of the hangar and shut down.

We walked over while Sierra climbed out and stood on the wing, beaming at us. "Hi, guys. Guess what? You just earned yourselves a new maintenance customer. Think you could fit me in for an annual inspection?"

I smiled and gave Sierra a thumbs up. She climbed back into the plane to gather her things.

Reese rested a hand on my shoulder. "Buckle up, boss. Archangel Aviation just showed up on radar."

My smile faded. "Whose radar?"

"Everybody's."

She got back to work, and I was left to ponder her comment.

Everybody.

I generally liked people, but on a selective basis.

Trying to please everybody was asking for trouble.

But it looked like trouble had just breezed in my hangar door.

SEVEN

RIP

IT WAS lunchtime when my father, Frank Angel, drove into the parking lot in the gold Plymouth Scamp he'd found on Ebay. It was a '70s era project car but had only set him back 5K so he treated it like a treasure.

When Rip climbed out of the passenger side, I was there to meet them.

"Our hero is mended," my father said, gesturing to his roommate. "Have I earned my nursing badge?"

"Head inside, Florence Nightingale. I'm stealing Rip for a quick errand. We'll be right back."

"He just got here," Frank said.

"You are relieved of duty. Pretty sure there are some of Elsbeth's chocolate chip cookies left on the break table if you hurry."

"The ones with the sea salt and those big chocolate chunks?"

"Make sure you save one for your patient."

But Frank was already headed for the hangar. "It's every man for himself when there's snacks involved."

Rip gave me a quizzical look. "What's the errand?"

I jerked my head toward the Jeep. "Hop in. I'll drive."

We were headed up First Street when I told him.

"You're kidding me. Already? I just had bloodwork done."

"Mike says it's procedure. They've been under extra scrutiny with the calls from Skydive America and now this video thing."

"No kidding. I saw it this morning."

"You follow Sierra's content?" I asked.

"You don't? It's good stuff. She's not hard to look at either. Was that her plane I saw out front just now?"

"She brought it to us for some TLC. But what are your thoughts on what happened on Sunday? We haven't had much chance to talk about it."

"I'm totally fine, man. I was probably just dehydrated. Doc told me to lay off the energy drinks. Says I need more water and electrolytes. She's got a point. I've been mainlining the caffeine pretty hard. I need to cut back."

"I won't argue there. But how do you explain how you were after? No offense, but you were nothing close to your normal self. You couldn't even remember the flight up."

Rip shrugged. "It was an off day, man. But if the doc says I'm good, I'm good, right?"

I frowned. But this was typical pilot behavior. Never admit to an ailment.

"Did someone tamper with your AAD? Who was around your gear that day? Did you see anyone messing with it? One of the other jumpers maybe?"

"Nah, man. Everybody's chill up there, dude. We all look out for each other."

"Except your parachute failed, Rip. You know how rare it is for those to malfunction? I've been thinking about this, and if someone had it out for you, if they could've rigged it so it wouldn't go off, messed with the settings—"

"Luke. No way, man."

"I'm serious. Is there anyone up there who has a beef with you? If there is, tell me and I'll go up there and—"

"No. No, stop. You're barking up the wrong tree."

"In what way?"

"It was me, man. It was my fault."

"How so?"

He stared out the window for a long second. "I might—*might*—have let that battery go a little too long. I'd been meaning to replace it, but it's just been on the back burner for a while. You remember I bought that new wingsuit rig two months ago? Plus, I have to maintain that old swooping chute that you used. Had to have *that* reserve repacked to have it ready for this week. And the AAD on my camera rig—which is still up to date mind you—I use that the most up there. I *always* keep that one current. But you do three-hundred plus jumps a year, this shit adds up."

I tightened my grip on the steering wheel. "The 'shit' will be hitting the fan when the FAA finds out. Did you tell anyone this?"

"Nah. Maybe a few of the guys I jump with, but nobody who would rat me out. There's no regulatory requirement that says you *have* to use an AAD on your own chute. It's more of a guideline."

"It was a tandem rig, Rip. With *Hank* in it. Here I am thinking someone was up there trying to kill you."

"I know, I know. I was going to get it replaced. I swear it hasn't been expired long."

"How long?"

"June. Maybe April. "

"Goddammit."

"I know. It figures, right? I've had that thing for over ten years. Jumped hundreds of times with it. Never once have I needed a damned AAD. The *one* time I let a battery lapse and this shit happens." He gestured to the sky and then let his hand fall in his lap. He glanced over at me. "Hey, you're not gonna mention this to anyone, right? I was planning on heading up there this weekend, see if I can iron things out."

"Skydive America is already cooperating with the FAA on an investigation. They'll look into the AAD issue. You'll have to explain yourself."

"Those guys are cool. Everybody knows me up there. They're not gonna throw me under the bus. Just don't say anything to Mike, okay? I'll get it straightened out."

"Are you asking me to lie to cover your ass?"

"No. I'm just saying—asking—that maybe you don't say anything . . . yet. You know I'd have your back in the same situation. Please, man. Just give me a couple of days to set things straight."

I swore again.

Rip was an exemplary employee. Amiable, took direction. Never late or absent without fair warning. Hell, he'd taken my own felon of a father in as a roommate and carpooled to work with him every day until Frank found a car. He was the last person in the shop I'd ever imagine having issues with. The guy was an airport treasure.

"Fine," I said. "You handle things with Skydive America. They're your people. I won't go out of my way to bring it up with Mike, but if he asks directly, I'm not going to lie to him."

Rip put his hands up. "That's all I'm asking."

We'd reached the collection lab. I pulled up in front of the glass double doors.

"Go pee in your damned cup," I said. "That'll give us at least one point in our favor with the feds."

"You got it, boss," Rip said, and unbuckled himself. He slid out of the Jeep. "You coming in?"

"I'll park and see you in there in a minute."

"Roger dodger."

I found street parking for the Jeep and paid the meter. By the time I made it inside, they were ready to see Rip. For his sake, I hoped he'd be all clear. His admission made me rest easier that the incident with the AAD hadn't been malicious, but *something* had happened to him on that free fall, and my gut told me that altitude and dehydration weren't it.

I knew crossing my fingers wouldn't help the test results, but I did it anyway.

Then we'd wait and see.

EIGHT

PHOENIX

"TELL ME THE IDEA AGAIN?" My ex-wife, Cassidy, peered from my phone screen. The view out her hotel room window was of the Phoenix Sky Harbor Airport. I was on my boat. Hank's boat, more accurately, but the place I called home. I was watching stars while Cassidy still had daylight.

"Sierra wants to shoot a video with *Tropic Angel*, all of us in the water somewhere. People jumping off the wings, what have you. She thinks it would make a good add-on to the skydiving video she did and showcase the company. Maybe draw Archangel some extra charter business to keep the Mallard flying."

"You're already viral. I've had four coworkers send me that skydiving video today."

"But no one connects that to the business yet. She says if she gets her Bonanza's annual inspection done with Archangel Maintenance and shoots a few videos with us, it will drive people to our website. She tagged some guy who loaned her some smart goggles in the video this weekend and apparently his company's sales exploded."

"Wow. Good for him. What's in it for her?"

"Don't know. Maybe she'll lobby for a maintenance discount. Could be she's just being nice. I guess we'll see. You think I should do it?"

"We'd be stupid not to. It's free publicity on a scale we'd never manage on our own."

Cassidy was an equal partner in Archangel Aviation, so I'd been obligated to run the idea by her, but part of me wondered if she'd shoot the plan down.

"You're on social media," I said. "Is this what people are doing these days to advertise?"

"Influencers with Sierra's amount of followers can typically charge for placement in videos, so you're getting a deal. Don't worry. I don't think it requires acting skills."

"That's a relief. If anyone comes at me with a camera, I'll make Murphy intervene." My dog picked his head up from where he was lying on the foredeck. "Yeah, I'm talking about you," I said.

His tail wagged twice, then he laid his head back on his paws.

"I'm sorry not to be around for any of this, but it sounds like you'll have plenty of help. Anything else pressing to relay?"

"Not much. Oh. I got asked out."

"On a date?"

"Don't sound so shocked."

"By who?"

"Diana Longoria wants me to take her to dinner."

Cassidy's eyes narrowed.

"What? You disapprove?"

"No. I'm honestly surprised it's taken her so long. She's had her eye on you for a while. What did you tell her?"

"She didn't leave me much choice in the matter. Evidently she's not used to argument. We're supposed to go out sometime this week."

"Fun."

But it didn't sound fun the way she said it.

"You have anything else to say about it?" I asked. "If there's some reason I shouldn't go out with her, tell me."

"No. You should. Diana's . . . great. Just be careful, okay? Seeing someone at the airport. She's got the non-profit. We run into her at Maddie's events. If things don't work out it will get weird, right?"

"Airport romance is how we got started."

"And look how that turned out."

"We've still got time," I said.

"Luke."

"What? You know how I feel about this. The day you come back and decide to stay, I'm going to be here."

"I know. But you shouldn't put your life in a holding pattern while I figure out my issues. It's not fair." She exhaled. "You deserve better. Maybe that'll be Diana."

"I'd say it's up to me to decide what I want."

"You want all the people you care about to live happily in St. Pete with you and fly out of Albert Whitted Airport forever. Diana fits that bill perfectly. So there you go."

"Is that such a terrible thing to want?"

"Not everyone can live on a boat downtown and take their dog to work and bathe at the beach after hours. Not everyone wants that."

"Maybe more should."

She stared at me hard through the phone screen and sighed. "I need to go shower. You should let me go."

It was hard to tell if she meant the call.

"Goodnight, Cass."

"Goodnight, Luke."

And then she was gone.

I clenched my jaw and tossed my phone to the deck. Then I leaned back in my chair, stared at the glittering sky, and sighed.

Awash in the glow of the downtown city lights, I only got a fraction of the stars I could view from inland or out in the gulf. But Jupiter and Venus were there. The constellation Aquila was visible too. The Eagle. Its brightest star, Altair, was one of the nearest bright stars to Earth. Under seventeen light years away. Close. But even with the fastest spaceship humans had ever built, it would take over two-hundred thousand years to reach it. More than enough time for our entire human civilization to appear and likely disappear. Impossibly far.

Like Phoenix.

I got out of my chair and Murphy popped up and shook himself. "Bed," I said. "Early start tomorrow. Water day."

I picked my phone off the deck and saw I had a text from Diana. It was a photo of a red dress with a smiley emoji.

I texted her back.

>>> We're doing a beach video shoot in *Tropic Angel* tomorrow morning. Want to ride along?

Little dots appeared almost immediately. Then the reply.

<<< Asking me to ditch work for the beach? You're a bad influence.

Then a moment later, <<< I'll find my bikini."

"Sounds like she's in," I said to Murphy.

His tail wagged.

I had a feeling that if Diana had a tail, it would be wagging also.

What the hell. Maybe I could do with a little wagging too.

NINE

SPLASH

I HAD *Tropic Angel* preflighted and ready to roll by 6 a.m.. Sierra Noble climbed aboard at six-thirty along with a wiry-framed camera guy wearing a neck scarf. An ascot? Something like that. It accented his shirt's multicolored vertical stripes. Diana arrived shortly after, also looking beach-ready, an American Flag bikini top showing through her barely there beach coverup. Her jean shorts showed off her dancer's legs. She pushed her gold-rimmed aviators up her forehead to address me. "When you said beach day, I didn't realize you meant the break of dawn."

I offered her a coffee from the flat of Kahwa Coffee options I'd brought in. She accepted one, then pecked me on the cheek before getting on the plane.

Evidently, I was forgiven.

Tyson had a hard time keeping his mouth from hanging open as he made his way up to the copilot seat.

Once we were in the flight deck, he jerked his head back to the passenger cabin and gave me a look. "I mean, dammmmn, right?"

"Keep it together, Don Juan."

"I don't even know who that is."

"Then you should read more."

"Read? Who's got time to read when you keep fillin' planes fulla hotties around here."

I made my way back through the cabin to make sure everyone was settled and to secure the boarding door. Nina Yee had made the invite list too, along with her shaggy-headed flight instructor, Chase. Sierra claimed she wanted to include as many of the participants from the original video as possible, though we were notably missing Rip and Hank. Brooks was due to meet us out on the water with his boat.

Murphy was along this time too. He panted happily from one of the divans, and Sierra scratched his head with her manicured nails. She said he'd add an element of charm to the shoot, and I agreed.

The cabin smelled like sunscreen. I didn't mind. It was a beautiful day for a flight.

I had *Tropic Angel*'s radial engines rumbling in minutes and taxied out to Taxiway Alpha for a run up. Enrique, the camera guy, made me do several things twice during the run-up checklist so he could capture them from different angles, but eventually I got him to buckle up and stay seated.

The destination was Egmont Key, a short hop to the mouth of Tampa Bay. The island, which was only reachable by boat, featured long sandy beaches, a lighthouse, and the ruins of Fort Dade. You could get to it on a ferry too, but our way was faster.

"November One Eight Eight Tango Alpha, you are cleared for takeoff on Runway 7 with a right turnout to the south," the tower controller said.

I repeated back my clearance and rolled onto the runway. The feel of the throttles in my hand still gave me a thrill no matter how many times I'd pushed them forward. Something about the growl the engines put out as they revved to full power. We picked up speed, and *Tropic Angel*'s tires broke free of the surface, the aircraft's big wings pulling us into the air. Tyson retracted the landing gear for me, and we made a right turn over the shimmering bay. The tower gave us a frequency to contact Tampa, but we wouldn't need it, staying low and clear of their airspace, a sea bird doing sea bird things.

The Skyway Bridge already flowed with morning traffic. Saint Pete had been discovered in recent years, and the roads showed it. But we had clear skies as we crossed Fort De Soto and its miles of sandy beaches. The shallow water was blue-green and dotted with patches of seagrass. I spotted several manatees bobbing in the shallows, and a huge school of stingrays was feeding offshore, dappling the water like a layer of brown leaves.

I set up for an approach that would bring us in on the bay side of the island. The gulf side was pretty too but got choppy as the morning progressed. As it was, I was looking at mostly calm water with gentle swells—an easy landing surface for *Tropic Angel*.

Sierra had mounted her Insta360 on the bow cleat of the Mallard so it had a killer angle of our splashdown. In a matter of minutes, we were nosed up to the beach. Tyson climbed out the bow hatch and dropped the anchor so I could shut down.

We adjusted for drift, and soon my passengers were eager to exit.

"Let's get wet!" Chase shouted.

"Not yet. We have to get the exit shot," Enrique insisted. "Remember we are shooting 'stylish adventure lifestyle.' That's the brand. Showcasing the life our viewers can aspire to. Always classy, never trashy."

"And inspiring young women to become aviators," Sierra clarified. "Let's not forget the core demographic."

"Sure your core demographic isn't drooling old dudes with hard-ons for airplane chicks?" Chase asked.

Enrique gave him an appraising stare. "Which one are you?"

"Chase is just trying to be funny," Nina said. "Pay no attention."

"He said classy, not trashy," Chase replied. "I guess that leaves you out."

Nina reddened.

"I invited *all* of you," Sierra explained, "because we represent the next generation. The ones who are going to *change* aviation for the better."

"By highlighting more old laws about women skydivers?" Chase asked. "Really edgy stuff. How does anyone tell you and Malala apart?"

I wondered for the first time if Chase might be high.

"Okay, let's get this shot," Diana said. Edging her way through and forcing Chase to sit back down. "Where do you want us, Spielberg?"

"Yes. *You* I can work with," Enrique said, sizing her up. "You are fit, girl. Is that Stella McCartney?" He pinched the fabric of her beach coverup.

"It is! Thanks for noticing."

"Slay, queen. I love it. I'm putting you up front with our star."

Enrique shot another withering glance at Chase, but then snapped into director mode, assigning positions.

Over the course of the next hour, he had us in and out of the plane. Sierra and Diana hit it off well and posed together atop the Mallard's wings, laughing and chatting while absorbing the sun's flattering morning light. My role turned out to primarily consist of doing simulated plane chores with my shirt off. Tyson tried to follow suit but was instructed to put his shirt back on and smile with his eyes, not his teeth. Neither of us knew what that meant.

I also got filmed on the beach playing with Murphy, but once my dog shook seawater all over Enrique and his camera equipment, his moment in the spotlight was over.

Chase did a backflip off the right wing that Enrique found visually engaging, but once Brooks showed up in his thirty-foot center console bay boat, Chase was largely forgotten.

Brooks was well-sunned, athletic, and had a smile you could put in a Crest commercial. The bronze-skinned beauty he'd showed up with also got attention. She seemed not to speak any English, but laughed and smiled a lot at all of Brooks' jokes.

Tyson and I convened on the beach with Nina, who had also found limited success as a model.

"I knew I shouldn't have bothered coming out here," she grumbled. "Bet I don't even make it in the video."

"I thought you looked good on top of the plane," Tyson said. "You found your balance eventually."

"I should have stayed home. I'm supposed to be studying for my checkride this afternoon. Chase said he'd quiz me on oral questions while we were out here, but I don't even know where he went."

Chase had found a beer in a cooler on Brook's boat and wandered off into the shrubbery with it ten minutes earlier. I hadn't seen him return.

"You ever think about flying with one of the women instructors at Bayside?" I asked. "I heard Sari is fantastic."

Nina wrinkled her nose. "No. I'm almost to the end of instrument now. And Chase has been my instructor since primary. I don't want to have to start over with someone new."

"I always encourage my students to fly with other instructors," I said. "Get a fresh pair of eyes on their status, catch things I might have missed. We're all human. Never hurts to get help from another point of view. I mostly do tailwheel instructing these days, but if you want to do a lesson together sometime, let me know."

"Thanks," Nina said. "I just need to get through this checkride with 'Bust 'em Bud.'"

"He's tough," Tyson said. "On my private ride, I was shakin' so bad I thought I'd set off the crash sensor on the ELT. Did he make you print out your digital logbook on paper? He wouldn't take my iPad logbook as proof. Made me print that shit out like we in the Middle Ages."

Nina shifted her feet. "Yeah, I don't have my own ForeFlight subscription. Chase lets me use his iPad. But I had to make paper copies of my *paper* logbook. Bud said he wanted to file them in his cabinet for a year in case the FAA headquarters burns down or something."

Tyson shook his head. "FAA finally gives us digital paperwork, and the old boy out there filing away a forest of trees anyway."

"You showed him you were prepared and organized," I said. "That's all an examiner really wants to see."

"And a pile of cash," Nina said. "Let's not forget that."

"For real, though," Tyson said. "Examiners be rollin' in it. I'd love for someone to pay me eight hundred bucks to sit around and watch somebody else fly for an hour."

"Good to know I'm draining my bank account so he can hire someone to wax his Harley," Nina mused.

Tyson shook his head again and squinted into the sunshine.

I checked my watch. "Speaking of making money. We've got planes to fix. And it sounds like we need to get Nina back to study. Who thinks we can wrap this up?"

Out on the water, Brooks and Sierra were laughing about something aboard his boat. Diana caught my eye and blew me a kiss.

But everyone was already glistening.

The temp had gone up another ten degrees since we started. I hoped Enrique had a camera filter that obscured sweat, because no matter how cool he tried to make us look, nobody stays that way long in a Florida summer.

Whatever else this day had in store for us, one thing was guaranteed—it was going to bring the heat.

TEN

LAST GOOD DAY

A THUNDERHEAD WAS BUILDING to the north. Come late afternoon it would unleash its fury, but for now I appreciated the shade.

The hangar was still preheating.

Tropic Angel sat at the wash rack directly across from my shop, drying from the hose-down I'd given it after our morning dip in the gulf. I'd donned a fresh shirt after the excursion but I was already damp again.

"I like airplanes, but I don't know how much I enjoy living in Florida right now," Sierra said. She'd hung around after the shoot to discuss maintenance items she wanted tackled on her Bonanza's annual inspection. We'd parked ourselves on stools in front of a fan near my toolbox.

"Have you been doing your flying elsewhere lately?" I asked.

"Some. I did my initial training at Embry-Riddle because my mom insisted I needed a degree with my ratings, but then I went out west for some mountain and canyon flying training. I wanted winter flying too, so I did an Alaska trip to learn skis and Tundra tires. Bush pilots up there are incredible with what they can do on ice. I got to do some float flying in the summer too and got my single-engine seaplane rating."

"That's quite the resume."

"Still need my multi-engine sea, so if you know a guy . . ." She tilted her head toward my Grumman Mallard and gave me an exaggerated wink.

"Flight instructor, new ATP rating, plenty of flight hours. Seems like the world's your oyster. You have a specific career you're headed toward?"

"I'm still trying to figure that out." She moved a strand of fan-blown hair back behind her ear. "I've had a couple of offers from avionics companies to be a brand ambassador for them. Seems like my channel is getting popular enough that it might make a real impact."

"I'd say. I mean, you've definitely got Tyson hooked." I gestured toward my youngest mechanic. He was over at the sandblaster cleaning spark plugs while wearing headphones.

As we watched, the song he was listening to must have changed because he straightened up and pulled one earphone loose and shouted, "Oh yeah. This is my jam right here. Dance break!" He then proceeded to gyrate for several seconds. He ended with a spin move, then pointed. "Reese!"

Reese and the rest of us in the hangar were listening to an entirely different genre of music over the hangar speakers, but she dutifully started dancing. She swayed back and forth, threw her hands up like she was in a club, waited for the beat to shift, and threw a finger toward me. "Bossman!"

I sighed and slid off my stool, did my standard moves. A little Latin sway, some shoulders, did a left-to-right arm wave to spice it up and then pointed to Frank. "Dad!"

"Still no!" Frank shouted back.

"No worries, I got the rebound," Rip yelled. He mimicked

catching a ball and then took it straight into a dance move that looked like a sped-up twist, mixed with the mashed-potato.

"Um, what did I just witness?" Sierra asked.

"Dance break," I said. "Every employee gets to call one per day if they hear a song that gets them grooving." I shrugged. "Makes the time go by. You have to forgive my dad. He's still new." I cupped my hands around my mouth and aimed toward Frank. "Evidently hasn't found that STICK UP HIS ASS yet."

My father shot me the middle finger.

Sierra was smiling. "I want to play."

"Rip!" I shouted. "Pass it over to our girl."

Rip did a spin, then faded back to chuck an imaginary football through the air. We all watched its invisible arc, and when it hit Sierra's outstretched arms, she broke into a wiggle and some dips that got a cheer from Tyson.

"Damn! Hell, yeah. That's what's up."

Sierra was still grinning and dancing when we were interrupted by a plane engine. A silver-and-lime colored Cirrus SR22T spun around out front of the hangar at high power and then shut down. Its three-bladed propeller had barely stopped spinning when Murphy ran up to the back, tail wagging.

Brooks let the passenger-side gullwing door of the Cirrus glide up and looked out at us. "Whoa now. No claws on the paint," he shouted to my dog.

"Murphy, sit," I said. "And my dog obeyed for half a second before his butt was back up in the air and his tail was wagging again. It became clear what had piqued Murphy's interest when we were met with the sound of barking and yipping.

"Oh my gosh. Are those the puppies?" Sierra rushed out to the plane.

The back of the Cirrus and the copilot seat held animal crates. Each one had small dog noises coming from it.

Brooks climbed out and walked around. I met him at the

front of the plane. "Hey, chief, you have an extra quart of oil I can nab from you? Want to top this baby off real quick."

"Sure," I said. "Which viscosity?"

"You would know better than me. Can you fill it for me too? That'd be awesome." He slapped me on the shoulder. "Can't get the puppies dirty." He held up his clean hands, then winked at me and walked around the wing to join Sierra who had climbed up and was cooing at the animals.

I observed the scene for only a moment, then popped the oil door open on the engine cowling. The viscosity rating was written right on a sticker placarded inside the door. I walked over and snagged an appropriate quart of oil from the shelf, then made my way back.

"Can't believe you get to do this. What a sweet cargo." Sierra had one of the puppies out of its crate and the little fur ball was aiming furious licks at her face. "I want to volunteer to fly puppies between shelters. You're inspiring me."

"I can make room for a co-pilot if you want to come along for the ride," Brooks offered. "I'm just doing Jacksonville and back."

Sierra checked her watch. "Really? Maybe I will."

"Get you out of this sweat-fest," Brooks said, gesturing to my hangar. "Hey Luke, you should try one of those newfangled things they call air-conditioners. Heard they're all the rage."

"I'll get right on that," I said. I untwisted the oil dipstick on the hot engine and checked the oil level. It was still full.

I frowned and screwed it back tight.

"Look how cute this little guy is," Sierra said, extending a puppy toward me. "Couldn't you just eat him up?"

I tussled the fur on the top of the dog's head. "They have water in there?"

"Yeah, let's spill water bowls all over the interior of this million dollar airplane," Brooks said. He gave me a smirk. "Don't worry, this thing *does* have AC. They'll be fine."

He took the puppy from Sierra and stuffed it back into its crate, then shoved the crate into the rear of the plane to make room for her. "Good news, little guys, you get a flight attendant for the trip."

Sierra climbed into the copilot seat and I handed her the spare quart of oil to stow somewhere. "Save that for later."

Once they were buckled in, Brooks restarted the Cirrus. The TSIO-550 engine was powerful and loud. It put a lot of torque to the propeller which in turn blew a tornado of propwash behind it. Brooks seemed blissfully unmindful of this fact as he turned out toward the taxiway, and I got a faceful of wind and ramp dust as they taxied away. I squinted and shielded my eyes. Sierra gave us a wave from the copilot seat and then they were gone.

I wandered back to my toolbox and picked up the checklist of maintenance items for Sierra's Bonanza that had blown onto the floor. We'd only discussed half of it.

"Guy needs to learn to aim that thing," Reese said.

"Nobody's perfect," I said. "But at least it's for a good cause."

"Hope one of those puppies pees on him for Karma," she said.

I laughed. Murphy came over for some attention, so I gave him a good petting.

"Don't worry. You're a good dog too, buddy."

Then I got back to work.

ELEVEN

RED AND BLUE

BUD TRUMAN CRUISED by on a golf cart with Nina Yee in the passenger seat around 2:30 pm. The glum look on her face would've been appropriate for a trip to the gallows. She clutched a flight bag with her headset on her lap. Evidently, they were headed to an airplane somewhere on the Taxiway Charlie ramp for the checkride, because a little while later I tuned a radio to the tower frequency and caught Nina's takeoff clearance.

Good luck, kid.

Bud would probably make her shoot an approach into Clearwater or Sarasota airport and put her through some simulated instrument conditions the whole time. There was a danger of actual instrument conditions if they waited long enough. The clouds continued to build to the south and west, one storm cell having rained itself out already, but another growing in its place. The towering thunderheads often stretched above ten thousand feet and pummeled the landscape with lightning for a neighboring twenty miles. Not the weather I wanted to be flying in, though I wouldn't have minded the breeze.

Around the hangar, we worked and sweated.

I retreated to my hangar office once or twice for a blast of air conditioning while making calls to customers, but I always ended up back on the shop floor. In the Army, I'd never respected officers who wouldn't endure the same conditions as their squads, so as the boss of a maintenance shop I operated the same way. Work together, sweat together. Made the end of the day a shared accomplishment.

Rip had put in a full day. No issues that I could spot.

Others in my crew had kept an eye on him too, especially Reese. She was a keen observer and if there had been anything amiss in his behavior, she would have flagged it immediately. No results had arrived from the drug test yet. So far so good. But the situation nagged at me.

I cut everyone loose around four-thirty. We typically did a "clean-up-time" session at that hour anyway, but today the place already looked tidy. I did a walk around and yanked a couple of trash bags from cans and tossed them onto the back of a golf cart to run to the dumpsters. Murphy heard the noise and came trotting over. Never one to miss a golf cart ride. As I refilled the trash cans with new liners I spotted the distant figure of Nina Yee running across the scalding ramp toward the parking lot, her flight bag jostling at her side.

Was that a run of joy or exasperation? It was hard to tell at this distance. Then she was out of sight. Had she passed closer to my hangar, I might have offered her a ride to her car, but by the time I had my trash cans sorted and had the trash loaded onto my golf cart, she was out of sight and likely already to the parking lot. I puttered around the hangar a little longer, tidying odds and ends, then whistled for Murphy to hop aboard the cart.

The closest dumpster was in the opposite direction, so we rode off and I made my contributions. It wasn't a far detour out to Skyline Boulevard and the hangars on Taxiway Charlie, so I headed north from the dumpster and cruised out that way, curious if I could catch Bud as I had the night before. But when I rounded the curve at the end of the taxiway, Bud's hangar was already closed. Places to be, I guess. I waited a moment just to see if he was still around, but no one emerged from the hangar, and no one would linger inside long with the door closed in this heat.

"Bud? You in there?" I shouted from my seat in the golf cart.

But no response came from inside.

"Smarter than us," I said to Murphy. "We should get home too."

A boom of thunder added a point of emphasis and Murphy pressed against my leg.

I turned the golf cart around and wended my way back along the taxiways to my hangar, closing up and climbing into my Jeep for the brief journey home.

Home was Demens Landing marina on the far side of the airport and Hank's fifty-foot catamaran. It was close to being the largest vessel in the marina and should have been kept somewhere with more suitable docks, but Hank insisted on keeping it in view out the window of his condo in Bayfront Tower. From his living room, he had a clear view of Albert Whitted Airport, the pier, and his floating pride and joy.

Some nights he'd wander down from his condo and we'd sit and talk on the stern deck, sharing a drink and our thoughts on how we'd solve the world's problems. But I didn't expect him tonight, or even in the next few weeks with the current state of his injuries. I made a note to check in on him in the next few days, then proceeded to the boat for a quiet night in with Murphy. Quiet turned into wet in short order, the storm unleashing its fury overhead. Aboard *Hank's Midlife Crisis* I was snug and secure, though the boat did its share of rocking in the wind.

Around 8 p.m. the sky cleared. I'd fed Murphy and was finishing cleaning dishes from the dinner of pesto-and-sausage pasta I'd made myself. I was about to pick up the Robert B. Parker novel I was working on and settle in for some reading when my phone buzzed.

Hank Martin's face showed on the caller ID.

"Hi, Hank, what's up?"

"Luke, there are police lights over at the airport. Ambulance maybe. Maddie and I can see them from here. Get over there and see what's going on, will you?"

"Plane crash?" I asked.

"No. Nothing on the runway. They're at the T-hangars. I think it might be Bud's."

"Shit," I muttered. "On my way."

Murphy picked his head up from his paws, but I told him to stay and left him looking out the rear sliding doors of the galley at me as I vaulted to the wooden dock and ran for my Jeep.

I didn't bother to towel my seat off. I just drove, using a keycard on the terminal gate and accelerating across the quiet north ramp and around the blast fence. A squad car blocked the access to Taxiway Charlie when I got there.

Someone had opened the hangar door though, and light shone from the fluorescent overheads. Two uniformed police officers stopped me from getting close as I walked up.

"I'm sorry, sir. You'll need to stay back. This is an active scene."

"That hangar belongs to a friend of mine," I explained. "Is Bud Truman in there?"

"Just keep your distance for now while they're working. We'll have more information soon."

Another pair of officers were talking to Israel Jones, one of the line guys who moonlighted as a plane detailer in the evenings. A manager from the FBO was standing arms crossed at a golf cart nearby, so I headed his way, my eyes on the hangar. A pair of EMTs were conversing quietly near Bud's plane. Then I saw

Bud. He was still in the plane's cockpit, his head slumped forward, face pale.

Madre de Dios.

Eric Feldman managed fuel sales and hangar rentals for the airport and I didn't see him out of his office much, but he was there, shifting his feet and looking nauseated. I walked over and pressed him for what he knew.

"Izzy came over here a bit ago, opened the hangar to do a detail job. Found Bud like that in his plane. Apparently it scared the shit out of him," he explained. "Izzy called me and I called 911."

"He's dead?"

"Looks that way. They didn't try to revive him. Must have been in there a while."

"I just saw him this afternoon."

"That's what Izzy said too."

I swore.

One of the uniformed officers who'd interviewed Izzy eventually made their way around to where Eric and I were standing. When she learned I was a mechanic who knew Bud and worked on his plane, she had a few questions for me.

"Is there any chance he would have run that engine indoors?"

"Never. He would have pulled it out first. Blows things around the hangar otherwise."

Ruling out carbon monoxide poisoning as a cause of death.

"It's also against the rules to start up in a hangar," Eric added.

"And he's in the back," I said, pointing to the seat Bud was slumped in. The plane was a tandem configuration where the pilot sat in front with a passenger directly behind them. A canopy slid over both like a tiny fighter jet. Bud was slumped in the passenger seat. "The engine's controls are in the front."

"You have any idea how hot it gets in these hangars during the day?" the officer asked.

That was a good question. "Very" didn't seem adequate to cover it.

"Poor old guy might have cooked in there," she said.

"What the hell would he be doing just sitting in the back of his plane in the heat?" I asked.

"We'll have to ask the ME when they get here. That might be them now."

A new vehicle had arrived on scene.

Someone had the sense to turn the blue-and-red lights off on the vehicles to prevent a distraction for landing aircraft. But the ensuing darkness wasn't any comfort.

Izzy Jones was still shaking.

And Bud Truman had made his final departure.

TWELVE
SMEARED

IT WAS ten-thirty when the airfield went quiet. Squad car taillights flashed on First Street headed north. They'd taken Bud to the morgue around nine-thirty, the ME tossing his gloves in the trash with an air of finality.

I wasn't a cop, so I didn't get a report, but I got the gist of it from what I overheard.

No evidence of foul play.

Preliminary assessment was natural causes.

Bud Truman had collapsed inside his airplane, possibly due to the heat. It wasn't clear why. The canopy of the aircraft was open. Bud should have been able to exit anytime he wanted. But he hadn't. He'd settled into the rear passenger seat, and never climbed out.

He was seventy-eight.

I was one of the last to leave the scene, staring at the yellow police tape the local PD had strung over the door. They said they'd likely release the hangar in the morning to management, but for now it was off limits.

I drove home.

Hank and Maddie's lights blinked out in their Bayfront condo as I passed the building. I'd filled them in on the situation by phone—shock in their voices at the news. But they were in their mid-eighties. Bud wasn't the first friend they'd lost along the way.

Murphy met me in the galley when I came aboard the catamaran. He stretched, accepted a brief tussling of the fur behind his ears, and then laid back down on his dog bed. I tried to get him to go outside to take a leak, but he just stared at me. Bladder of iron, that dog.

I slunk over to the couch and crashed onto it, hating that the hours continued to roll by with a good man like Bud no longer alive to see them.

Flying in the afternoon. Dead by nightfall.

And the fact that I couldn't shake from my mind was that Bud had been inside that hangar, possibly inside his plane, at the time I'd stopped by after work. If I'd moved my ass and gotten off the golf cart, tried the doorknob, actually gone in and looked, would Bud still be alive right now? Could I have saved him, or changed the course of events in some way?

I'd have to wait for an autopsy report to know Bud's cause of death. If he'd had a cardiac event, it was possible there was nothing I could've done to save him. But if I'd been there to catch it sooner, found him help, or if the cause of his death had been simple heatstroke and incapacitation, might I have been the one who would've made the difference?

Was Bud being dead *my* fault?

The thought rankled me for an hour till I fell asleep.

The news of Bud's death spread slowly at first. I'd been the one to tell my crew when we opened in the morning.

But whispers trickled out from there. Sierra Noble heard and put together a tribute post about Bud set to music and featuring photos of the two of them together after she'd passed her ATP checkride. I didn't see it, but everyone agreed it was tasteful and moving. It made Elsbeth, my bookkeeper, cry.

Then the word was out.

Stories circulated. Friends discussed who'd said what to Bud last. Everyone expressed shock that he was gone. Golf carts circulated around the airport, quiet conversations murmured and repeated. Someone said we should host a memorial at his hangar —an airport sendoff for the community. A few dedicated do-gooders got to work organizing.

Mid-morning, I spotted a squad car pull through the gate and followed it with my golf cart out to Bud's hangar on Taxiway Charlie. Eric Feldman was there in his pickup truck to meet him. The young officer's name was Horowitz. He told us the ME had released the scene. They had forgone an autopsy due to the likelihood that Bud's death had been from natural causes and only did an external exam on the body. The report wasn't finalized, but there'd been no reason to suspect foul play. He didn't know the details about when a report would be available. Said it could take weeks. But the hangar was no longer restricted.

I thanked him.

"You two were close?" he asked me.

"I'll miss him. He was a good man."

He canted his head. "You look familiar. Have we met before?"

"Not that I recall."

He took a moment to admire the view. "Sure was a killer spot he had out here. I can think of worse places to go." He nodded toward the hangar. "Didn't leave all this to one of you by chance?"

"Would be nice," Eric said. "But the T-hangars have a long waiting list. We tell new people calling to expect to wait ten years."

"Holy cow," Horowitz said. "Never knew it was in such high

demand." He adjusted his gun belt higher on his hip. Then he snapped his fingers and pointed at me. "The skydiving video. The one with the old guy almost pancaking in."

"Ah," I said.

"That's our Luke," Eric said slapping me on the shoulder. "A local hero."

"I knew I'd seen you somewhere." The cop sized me up. "Is that the wildest thing you've ever done?"

"At least on video."

He seemed to run out of things to say after that, so he tipped his hat to us, gave his condolences once more, and drove off.

"We'll have to make sure this place stays locked to keep the tool pirates out," Eric said. "Things can walk off after someone dies, especially from a trove like Bud's. I've exchanged emails with his daughter but she's out in Denver. Won't be here till late tonight, and she'll have funeral arrangements and Bud's house to deal with. Might be a while till she gets down here to make sense of this."

"Mind if I have a look around inside? I can take some pictures, make sure we know what to account for."

"Good idea. If you can do that, send me the photos and I'll pass them on to his daughter. That way she knows what she's dealing with when she comes. She might need help recognizing what she's looking at, especially the aircraft-specific tools and equipment."

"We'll help her sort it."

"Thanks, Luke. I'll leave you to it. Just make sure to lock the hangar up when you leave, will you?"

I nodded.

His truck pulled away, then I stepped inside the hangar.

Most days, the first thing I'd do would be to run the hangar door up for better lighting and some airflow, but there was something private about the space now that felt wrong to exhibit.

A museum. The Bud Truman memorial collection. Opening the hangar door also would have invited attention, and that was the last thing I wanted. I needed time alone to think.

When I turned on the timer for the light switch, it set up a low buzz that emanated from the overhead fluorescent lights. Opaque fiberglass panels in the ceiling also acted as skylights during daytime, but the fluorescents helped.

It was still early enough that the temperature inside the space was manageable. The RV-8 sat silent in the center of the space, its paint shiny. The hangar was tidier than mine. Bud was the type of mechanic who custom made foam cut-outs for the drawers of his tool chests so that each tool had a designated indent to occupy. Meticulous. The hangar decor skewed toward vintage. Signs from old airshows. A signature from aerobatic champion Patty Wagstaff on a headset carefully mounted on a stand. As an added element of authenticity, the headset was mounted upside down.

His daughter would have a popular account on Ebay if she decided to sell this stuff.

I made my way around the hangar, my eyes roaming. I remembered my camera duties and began taking pictures. A Matco tool chest. Snap. I opened the top drawer. Snap. The American flag, the drill press, the motorcycle. Snap snap snap. Bud had a bank of file cabinets with dates from prior years on them. I opened one and found reams of files catalogued inside. All the prior applicants he'd tested. Nina hadn't been kidding. If the FAA headquarters ever burnt down, they'd find plenty of backups here. Bud's daughter was going to need to invest in an industrial shredder.

The lawn chair he liked to sit in at night was a worn-in, frayed thing. The one item that looked past its prime. And the last place I'd seen him.

I held my camera up, but I didn't take that picture.

Something about the vacant chair twisted my guts. I looked away, walked around the plane instead.

The canopy was open.

A Vans RV-8 sits low, a hot rod of a kit plane, tandem seats, the pilot up front, and a cramped space behind for a passenger. A modest baggage space sat behind that once you removed a panel and a seat cushion. Many RV-8 kit plane builders left bare metal exposed in the cockpits. Proof of their riveting prowess. Shiny aluminum left them looking industrial and bare. Bud had gone through the extra effort to upholster his interior, cutting individual side panels with adequate pockets for stowing snacks or water bottles, and the assorted bric-a-brac that came with flying. His upholstery was a light gray, stitched with care by a local aircraft upholsterer.

I held up my camera. Snapped a shot of the front seat, along with the instrument panel. But the angle was poor so I climbed up on the wing to get a better shot. But I paused.

There was a dark smear on the upholstery of the seat that I hadn't seen from a standing position outside. A crescent shaped grease spot on the forward left edge of the seat cushion. It was vaguely reminiscent of a ring one might leave with a coffee cup, only larger. Something round. Bud certainly wouldn't want his plane photographed like that. And it wouldn't help his daughter sell the plane, if that's what she'd do with it.

I recalled the one time I'd squeezed myself into the back of Bud's RV for a flight. Bud had been particular that I not leave my dirty mechanic's bootprints on the upholstery. This was no boot print, but I knew it would have bothered Bud to have it there. I touched the curved smear with my finger. It came away gritty. Dirt and what? Motor oil? I sniffed the residue on my fingers. Could be oil. Or possibly hydraulic fluid. It was filthy in any case. If it was left there long it might stain. I went and found a rag and a bottle of cleaner I'd spotted atop Bud's toolbox, came back. I wiped the smear away.

The rest of the plane looked pretty good. The canopy had some fingerprints on it—on the interior side where the back passenger would sit. Possibly from Bud or a passenger opening and closing it from inside before securing it to fly.

I found a clean side to my microfiber rag and sprayed a foamy blob of window cleaner onto it to wipe away the fingerprints. That's when I noticed the outside of the glass already had residue from cleaner on it. The outside glass was clean but the inside wasn't. Was that what Bud was doing when he died? Had he cleaned the outside of the canopy and then climbed inside to have a go at the interior of the glass and never finished? Perhaps the exertion of climbing into the plane had somehow been the trigger. His heart gave out?

I didn't know. I looked down at the spray can of cleaner in my hands and the microfiber rag.

But if Bud had been in the process of cleaning the plane, shouldn't these have been in the plane with him and not over on his toolbox where I'd found them?

I supposed the EMTs could have moved them when the medical examiner authorized them to pull Bud's body out.

"You're not a damned detective," I said to myself aloud. "You're the clean-up crew."

But I didn't clean anything else. I walked back to the toolbox and left the cleaner and rag where I'd found them.

I'd send some photos to Eric. My job would be done.

I'd begun to sweat. A dark spot appeared in the center of my T-shirt.

And the hangar was no longer comfortable. I walked out and locked the door behind me.

Museum closed.

THIRTEEN
INVITE

HANK MARTIN CALLED me at 11 a.m. with a summons.

"We're having a small gathering over here at Bayfront Tower tonight. I want you to come. Apparently you're famous on the internet and Maddie's friends insist on meeting you. And I need to hear what the hell's been going on down there. Bud's dying has everyone riled up. Can you make it?"

I told him I'd be there.

Diana frowned at me when I swung by her office and told her. "Bummer. I was hoping tonight might be the night we get dinner. I'm supposed to be the one with the busy schedule, remember?"

"Come with me," I said. "You can be my plus one."

"I *do* love Maddie. Fine. I guess someone has to make you look good. But it's not the right scene to wear that dress I bought. I'm saving that for a proper date. Plus everyone will probably be feeling down about Bud."

"You want to meet here later? Walk over? Or should I pick you up?"

"Walk? In this heat? You're crazy."

"I could hit the building with a bottle rocket from this window. Otherwise, we'll spend more time finding parking than getting there."

"I'm starting to see why you're still single, darling. It's a good thing you're so handsome. Now get out of here before I start doing things to you that would be unprofessional in a workplace."

Back in my hangar office, I opened my email and found that Rip's drug testing results had come through. I felt a morbid curiosity as I opened the document, but scanning down the page, all was normal. Every test they'd run showed negative.

A relief.

I called Rip to my office to tell him the good news.

"Of course it's clean, man. Told you I'm feeling fine," he said. "And it's a good thing too, because I have a biplane ride scheduled later. Why anybody wants to fly open-cockpit, middle of the day in the dead of summer is beyond me. Gonna fry our faces off. But it'll still be fun."

He trooped back down the stairs with a spring in his step and I fired off a copy of the email to Mike Rodriguez at the FAA.

One less thing to worry about.

Though I still didn't have an answer as to what had caused Rip to pass out on that skydive in the first place.

I pivoted in my swivel chair and looked out the back window of the office toward the long runway and Taxiway Charlie. Had he just been another victim of the heat?

I'd grown up in Florida, lived here most of my life. It was inarguably hotter now. Every year, newscasters posted graphs of the latest record-breaking highs. But deadly? That was something for Texas and Arizona to worry about, wasn't it?

At lunchtime, I watched Rip taxi by in the Stearman. He crossed Runway 7 to the north ramp to pick up his passenger and a while later I heard the rumble of the Continental R-670 radial engine on takeoff.

The old Boeing trainer had been around since 1941 and had been used to initiate cadets headed for the war. Slow and stable, it was like riding a Harley in the sky, but with the benefit of not having dangerous Florida drivers to contend with. Rip would fly his passenger out to the beaches, introduce them to some easy maneuvers like lazy eights, then when they'd expressed they weren't feeling airsick, he'd plunge the Stearman down to 120 MPH, pull back on the stick, and pitch up for a big loop. The passenger would get their first view of the world from upside down. The smiles typically got broader from there. Rip would roll the big biplane around its longitudinal axis, maybe do another loop or a combo of the two and then bring the passenger back jubilant for a warm welcome from their friends and family. They'd take photos by the plane and march off declaring it was the coolest thing they'd ever done. In thirty minutes it would be posted somewhere on social media.

And so it would be today.

I found myself watching the western sky for the Stearman's return and the assurance that Florida sun and heat hadn't claimed any additional victims. Just when I was starting to wonder, the distinctive silhouette of the biplane reappeared in the sky. The plane rumbled down to Runway 7 and rolled out. Within forty minutes the plane was put away and Rip was back on the shop floor, cracking jokes with my father. He'd added some sweat stains to his Archangel Aviation T-shirt but seemed to be every bit as vital and enthusiastic as when he'd left. I was pleased to see he was even rehydrating with Gatorade instead of his frequent energy drinks.

Nothing to report in terms of trouble. Thank goodness.

FOURTEEN
TESTED

IT WAS GETTING LATE in the afternoon when Reese walked
into my office and caught me staring out the window again.

"You want to talk about it?"

"About what?"

"Whatever's eating you up."

I sighed. "It's a sad day. Bud being gone."

She hung her thumbs on her belt loops. "And?"

Damn she was perceptive. It was a useful skill she had, but I
preferred when it wasn't directed at me.

"You don't *have* to tell me."

I frowned.

She sat down on the edge of one of my office chairs, rested
her elbows on her knees, and stared at me. Maybe she just
wanted an excuse to sit in the AC. I told her anyway. About how
I'd been out at Bud's hangar the night before. Not gotten off my
golf cart. Even though he was likely in there at the time and in
trouble.

She nodded. "I'm the last person you need to tell about
survivor's guilt. Not a week goes by I don't feel a gut punch about

our shitstorm in Al-Murad. Specifically what happened to Nuñez and Vang."

The two soldiers in her unit had been taken out by a rocket propelled grenade on their final run for the helicopter. Reese's commanding officer had pulled her kicking and screaming back into the aircraft to prevent her from running back out after them. I'd seen it all happen from the pilot seat of the UH-60 and I got us out of there with Reese barely aboard.

"If you'd've gone back to get them, you'd be dead too. And so would I, because you wouldn't have been onboard to keep me from bleeding out when that ricochet tagged me in the neck coming back to base," I said.

"I know. I've played that day over in my head plenty. Probably more times than you. But it doesn't stop the second-guessing. And it doesn't stop the guilt."

One of the tattoos on her upper arm was of her unit insignia. It was a permanent part of her now.

"Well, I can't help thinking that if I'd been less lazy last night, checked the hangar instead of only calling his name . . ."

"You said he could've got himself out. Canopy was open. Had to be something catastrophic if he passed out in there. It's hot in those hangars that time of day, but not *that* hot."

"Not everyone is as used to the heat as you are."

"Let's go see. Bring a thermometer."

It wasn't the worst idea she'd had. I knew what she was doing. Letting me work through the problem by being active. Sitting around thinking about it was consuming me so she was assigning me chores. Harmless but cathartic.

"Fine. Let's do it."

We took the golf cart. I had a key to Bud's hangar hanging on the inside door of my logbook cabinet so I took that with us. Murphy rode along but opted to linger outside and sniff grass while Reese and I entered.

"It's certainly not cool," I said as we walked in.

"You wouldn't eat your soft serve in here," she agreed. "But let's get a reading. "She'd brought a thermometer that had static temp function and also a laser you could aim at exhaust pipes and cylinders to get engine temps. "You be Bud. Go do whatever you think he was up to."

What had he been up to? Just finished a checkride with Nina. Probably had paperwork to do. Logging the results with the FAA on the laptop maybe. But he also could have done that at home later where it was cooler. No need to do it here with the door closed. He'd either closed his hangar door or never opened it in the first place. He and Nina had flown one of the discount rental planes out on the ramp, not his hot rod RV-8. So why was he climbing into it?

"He was in the back seat when Izzy found him," I explained.

"Couldn't have been messing with any avionics updates. There aren't any instruments in the back," Reese said, peering in. "It's tight. You fit in there?"

"Not in that seat. Bud had to use a slimmer profile cushion for me the one time I flew with him. My head sticks up too high otherwise and the canopy won't close. It was tight anyway."

"I could fit," Reese said. She climbed up on the wing and then stepped over the edge of the cockpit, sliding down into the rear seat. She checked her thermometer. "Was eighty-eight when we walked in. Reading ninety now."

"That's it?"

"It's warm. But I don't see how this would kill him. Plenty of fresh air. Comfy seat. Maybe he fell asleep. That's why he didn't hear you yell."

We waited while the thermometer in Reese's hand crept up to ninety-one degrees but it stabilized there.

I frowned at the plane. It didn't make sense.

With the canopy open and this temp in the hangar, Bud would have been sweaty. But dead?

"Had to be medical, right?" Reese said. "Some condition he had you just didn't know about."

My eyes rested on the latch for the canopy. That was one thing that always bothered me about these planes.

"What if the canopy wasn't open?"

Reese tilted her head. "Huh?"

The latch is in the front. The pilot typically closes it. If someone had you in the back seat and closed the canopy, you think you could get it open from back there?"

Reese considered that and shrugged. "Let's try it."

I took hold of the outside latch of the canopy and slid the whole thing forward on its track until the canopy hit its forward stop. Then I turned the handle and latched it. Reese peered up at me from her spot in the back seat. She leaned forward and stretched an arm around the pilot seat headrest, but it came up shy of where the latch was.

She shifted and tried again, trying to reconfigure herself to reach it. Sweat glistened from her brow.

I tapped on the plexiglass. "What's the temp in there now?"

She showed me. "Hotter." The thermometer now read 93 and her voice was muffled behind the canopy.

"Any chance Bud reaches that latch?"

Reese studied it. I could tell she was working the problem, taking into account Bud's size, age, and flexibility. She leaned forward and was finally able to get a hand on the latch, but it was at the limit of her reach.

"Yeah. He could get a hand on it if he tried hard enough." She unlatched it, then latched it again.

Then a morbid thought occurred to me and I rested my hand on the outside of the latch. Held it. "How about now?"

She met my eye, put her hand back on the latch and tried

again. But with me keeping my hand on it, she had no leverage to fight me. She strained briefly against my grip, the handle pressing into the flesh of my palm.

Finally she gave up. "You don't win that fight from inside."

I nodded. Then I tapped the plexiglass again and pointed to the thermometer. "You think you'd cook eventually?"

Reese checked the thermometer, then leaned back in the seat and looked around. Finally she shook her head. "Still don't see it."

I opened the canopy for her again. She was damp, but barely flushed.

We'd proved that it was possible to effectively trap someone in the back seat if you wanted to. It hadn't taken much effort or arm strength at all on my part. But that in itself wasn't deadly.

"You remember your desert combat training? What did they say the body's core temp needs to get up to for heatstroke?" I asked.

"Fatal? I think you'd need to be above 105. You hit 107-110 on the inside, you're cooked."

I took the thermometer from her hand and aimed the laser light at her temple. I took a reading. She'd barely cracked 99.0.

"You happy, Columbo?" she asked. "Bud obviously had some other factor to his death. Probably cardiac. You coming in and seeing him last night likely wouldn't have mattered." She patted me on the shoulder. "Let yourself off the hook."

The facts were hard to argue with.

"And didn't it storm last night?" Reese added. "That would have brought the temps *down* in here, not up. If Bud was sitting in that cockpit alone for any length of time, we know he wasn't stuck, and it got cooler as it went."

She was right. That was the reality of it.

Murphy barked outside the hangar. I opened the pedestrian door and admitted him. He did a quick sniff-check of both of us and then scampered back outside. We followed. I locked the hangar back up.

Tropic Angel peered at me from the ramp. My beauty of an airplane, hangarless, but adding to the scenery. Jason Brooks' Cirrus sat beside it today, also cooking in the late afternoon sun. On the other side of that was the discount rental Cessna Nina had taken her checkride in.

"Back to work?" Reese suggested. "Almost cleanup time."

I checked my watch.

Reese studied me. "You're not ready to let this go yet, are you?"

"Can you put Murphy in the office for me when you head home for the day? I'll swing back later and grab him."

"Sure. But why? Where are you headed?"

"Don't worry about me. I'm going to visit the pediatrician."

FIFTEEN

WHAT'S UP, DOC?

THE LOBBY of Gabby Turpin's office had plenty of seating, and some of it came in bright primary colors that sat only a foot off the ground.

A toddler with a runny nose stared at me from her mother's arms and then proceeded to stick a wad of her mother's hair in her mouth. Her mother seemed more curious what a grown man was doing sitting there watching Bluey on the television with no child in sight. I waved at the little hair-eater and got a cautious wiggle of the fingers back. Then the mother distracted the girl with a puffy book she could chew on.

It was fifteen minutes till my name was called, a rotund nurse eyeing me skeptically from the doorway to the exam rooms. "Luke Angel?"

"That's me." I climbed out of my chair and she admitted me through to the hallway.

"It says here that you're applying for a second-class medical certificate?"

"But with first-class enthusiasm."

She took my weight and noted that I'd gained two pounds since the last flight physical.

"Has to be muscle," I said.

"Stomach muscles *do* work hard."

I tried to look offended.

She took me to a line of tape on the floor and pointed me toward an eye chart. "Cover one eye, read line ten."

"Ten? Geezus. Okay." I covered my right eye. Were they always this fuzzy? "F T L C uh, Z . . . No, I think that's an E, D O P."

"Now the other eye. Same line backward."

I repeated the process with my other eye, trying hard not to change any of my answers.

She scribbled something.

"Did I pass?"

"You missed one both ways."

"Shit. Is that bad?"

"The 20/20 line is actually up on line 8. I was just giving you a hard time."

I breathed a sigh of relief.

I followed her to an exam room, and she asked a few more questions about my medical history, checked my pulse and blood pressure, and then left me alone.

The door opened ten minutes later and Gabby Turpin arrived wearing a blouse with brightly colored dinosaurs on it. She closed the door and glared at me. Her hair was up in cute side braids with a few loose strands that looked kinda flirty. But her voice wasn't. "Luke Angel. You are under forty. Your current medical doesn't expire for another three years. You're not applying for a higher class. So what the hell are you doing here at thirty minutes till closing time?"

"Good to see you, Gabby. Thanks for squeezing me in. How's the 182 running?"

"Great, if I could ever find time to fly it. Patients keep jumping onto my schedule last minute. The little kids can't help it. They lick germs off handrails for breakfast. What's your excuse?" She swiped something on her tablet. "It looks like you filled in your FAA MedXPress forms about five minutes before you walked in here."

"You heard about Bud Truman?"

"I did. Damned shame."

"What can you tell me?"

She lowered her tablet and studied me. "You came to *me* for answers? You're the one at the airport. You were closer to it than I was."

"But you're his doctor."

She planted a hand on her hip. "His FAA doc, not his primary care physician. You know full well how much you guys tell me versus the other guys. You ask a pilot for their medical history, they tell you they've never been sick in their life. We're not even going to touch the mental health issues."

"Pilots don't get sad," I said. "We're not allowed."

She held up a palm toward me and then let it fall, as if to say "Exactly."

"But you're at least *one* of his doctors," I said. "You've examined him recently. Were you surprised to hear he died?"

"You know I can't reveal details of another patient's medical history." She unwrapped an alcohol swab and used it on the end of her stethoscope.

"I didn't ask you to. I'm just wondering if his dying caught you by surprise."

Gabby considered me. "You know something I don't?"

I shook my head. "Just a gut thing. I saw him the night before he died. I know he liked his cigars, but—"

"Don't I know it," Gabby interjected, shaking her head. "Take your shirt off."

I complied, yanking my T-shirt over my head. "I know he carried some extra weight, but try to tell me Bud didn't still seem healthier than a kale farmer dating a yoga instructor."

"Bud's wife actually was a yoga instructor at one point. You didn't know that?"

"See? This is what I'm talking about."

Gabby sized me up. "I'll admit I was surprised. Given his medical history—that I'm definitely not going to share with you, I *was* caught off-guard."

"And if he'd had a serious cardiac event in the past or bloodwork that suggested he was at risk . . . it would be safe to say that you wouldn't have been so surprised."

"What is it you're fishing for specifically?" She put the earpieces of her stethoscope in her ears, then put the cold steel end of it to my chest. "Deep breath."

I inhaled.

"You ever play a musical instrument?" I asked between breaths.

"Violin. Some piano." She had me pivot on the exam table and switched the stethoscope around to my back. I inhaled deeply again, and she repeated the process several places.

"When you're playing piano, there's a flow to the melody. And when you hit a note that's off, it jumps out at you, right? Almost like it offends your ears."

Gabby dropped her stethoscope back around her neck and reached for the little light thingy on the wall. She put a fresh cap on it and stuck it in my ear. "So Bud's dying is your sour note. Feels off-key to you."

"I'm not a religious guy," I said. "I don't claim to know the ins and outs of who's pulling what strings from anywhere other than here. But if you're alive long enough, and you're paying attention, you see things. A sort of order to the way the world works. What seems natural and what doesn't. If there's a God, He or She has a certain way of doing things. And when something happens that doesn't fit that style, it makes you think it wasn't part of any grand design."

Gabby ejected the used light cap into the trash can. "You're talking to a cradle Catholic who has also seen three-year-olds develop leukemia for no good reason, so I've learned to take a broad view of what can and can't fall inside of a divine plan. But I assume this gut feeling of yours comes with some evidence beyond the other-worldly? Lie back."

I stretched out on the table while she probed my abdomen. "The details are strange. Bud was just sitting there, in the back seat of his RV-8. And whatever killed him couldn't have taken long to do it."

Gabby seemed to think on that. Finally she asked, "Barring medical issues, is there anyone you can think of who might have wanted to do him harm?"

"A few possibilities have started to come to mind."

She looked me in the eye. "Then, I think . . . maybe you should trust your gut and keep asking around. Can't hurt, right?"

I rose to an elbow and met her gaze. "Thanks."

"Don't mention it. Now stand up and drop your pants. We're doing the hernia check next."

"What? When are we, 1985?"

"You wanted a medical exam, you're getting one. You're lucky pediatricians don't stock equipment for colonoscopies. We'd be here all night."

SIXTEEN
SOIRÉE

WHEN I FINALLY BROKE LOOSE FROM Turpin's office, I pulled my Jeep back up to my maintenance hangar and located the hard top for it. I preferred open-air driving, but compromises had to be made for the fairer sex and their hairdos. Once I had the top installed, I loaded up my dog and raced home to the boat and showered, knowing full well I might need another one later. It was that kind of summer.

What Gabby had said ran through my head while the water poured over me. I was confident that if Bud had been at risk of a coronary, Turpin would have been more forthcoming with it. Or at least hinted. But what good that information was going to do me was unclear.

Maybe Hank would know something tonight that I didn't.

Garbed in a clean button-down linen shirt and jeans, I left Murphy with dinner and a fresh chew stick and departed.

Diana had texted her address. I picked her up at a quarter to seven.

She might have been saving the "date dress," but what she had on tonight was no nun's habit. The sweetheart neckline of the black-and-white pencil dress was going to prove hazardous to my vision.

"Diana, you look lovely," I said.

"You make me sound like a flower."

"You smell like one."

"I do not. This is Wood, Sage, and Sea Salt by Jo Malone. But thank you. You like it?" She offered me her neck. I leaned closer for a sniff.

"Of all the salty things in my life, you might be my new favorite."

That got a smile from her.

I helped her into the Jeep and then walked around to my side. "Apologies if you end up with any dog fur on your dress. Murphy mostly sits in the back, but that stuff flies everywhere."

"I'll survive. Are you wearing slip-on boat shoes?"

"Should I not be?" I started the engine and got us rolling.

"Just a bold choice in the company of Veronica Noble."

"Who's that?"

"The host of this soirée tonight."

"I thought the Martins put it together."

"The Martins are the ones who invited *you*. But the party is Veronica Noble's idea. So buckle up."

"Noble. So that's Sierra's . . . ."

"Mother. I'm sure Sierra will be there too. Unless she found a way out of it."

"How do you know all of this?"

"It's my job to know the St. Pete social scene. How do you think a non-profit relief service like Sunshine gets its funding? Veronica Noble is a donor I've been trying to land for years. The Martins are regulars, of course. They donate on a schedule. But getting Veronica on board has been my white whale."

"She's loaded?"

"Her husband was an investment firm CEO who retired

early. Wanted a place he could watch airplanes all day. So they came down here and bought in Bayfront Tower. But he died less than a year after they moved in."

"That's sad. How old was Sierra?"

"She must have still been in college then."

I spotted a guy pulling out of a space on First Avenue South and nabbed it. It would have been cheaper to park at the marina where I had a parking pass, but we'd save ourselves a few steps here.

Bayfront Tower loomed overhead as we walked up. I don't think I'd ever tried looking straight up it from the sidewalk before. It was a sight. There were certainly taller buildings in the city, but something about this place had old-school grandeur.

When we boarded the tower's wood-paneled lobby elevator, Diana put her arm around mine and leaned into me. Then she lifted my fingers with hers interlocked between them. "Do these hands ever come clean?"

I inspected the deep creases in my knuckles that were still vaguely stained from motor oil.

"This is about as clean as I get," I said. "Does it bother you?"

"No, you're my big hero," she said and squeezed my bicep. The elevator doors opened on the twenty-eighth floor. "But up here, you might be the one who needs saving."

SEVENTEEN

HIGH-RISE

I'D ALWAYS LIKED HEIGHTS, especially the way the world looks from the sky. Tiny cars and tiny houses, thousands of little people going intently about their days, eyes level, focused on immediate worries. From up high, the worries never appeared as large. Little problems for little people. A shift in perspective that was gifted by the shift in altitude.

Standing at the balcony on the top floor of the Bayfront Tower gave me a different feeling. The waterfront of Saint Petersburg was fanned out before me: the St. Pete Pier, Demens Landing Marina, The Salvador Dali Museum, and the city's crown jewel —Albert Whitted Airport.

But instead of feeling distant, it all seemed fragile—a diorama of cardboard from a child's science fair. The pieces looked glued down for now, but in danger of being moved. Perhaps this was how the world was viewed by hurricanes—or condo developers.

I located *Tropic Angel* on the ramp of the airport, on the far side of the runway. The sight of my beloved seaplane anchored me. Though it too looked like a child's toy from this distance.

Hank Martin limped with me to the rail. "Figured you'd want to head straight here," he said.

"Plant me by the view and leave me alone," I said. "I'll be a happy party guest."

"This is where I come to see if you're taking good care of my boat."

Hank's Midlife Crisis was in plain view on the end of its dock in the marina. The catamaran's twin hulls rode sleek and shining in the golden evening light.

Diana had peeled away to say hello to Maddie and a group of women in stylish blouses inside near the circular bar.

"You live a charmed life," I said, taking the place in.

Hank flapped his right arm that was still in a sling. "Not so charmed at the moment."

A voice came from behind us. "They catch the guy who did that to you?" A grey-haired friend of Hank's slapped him on the shoulder as he walked up. Hank gave him a broad smile. "Robert. Glad you could make it. Do you know Luke Angel?"

"The hero of the hour. Of course I've heard of him." The man shook my hand. His little bird of a wife bobbed beside him and extended her hand as well.

"I'm Kathy. We're so grateful to you, for saving our dear Hank. What a traumatic experience that must have been, falling so fast and *so* close to the ground."

"It all worked out in the end," I said. "Hank is made of tough stuff."

"I feel like that jump instructor ought to lose his license, don't you? Jumping out of a plane with a faulty parachute like that." Her lips pursed tightly when she finished speaking, little wrinkles fanning out from the corners of her mouth proving that this expression of disapproval wasn't new.

"It wasn't as wild as you all are making it out to be," Hank said. "I was about to pull that chute myself any moment."

"Still ought to go after that guy," Robert agreed with his wife. "You could sue him for negligence."

"That instructor I jumped with is actually a close friend of Luke's," Hank explained. "Been on the airport a long time."

"Rip's an experienced jump instructor," I said. "But he had a bad day, that's for sure."

"I'd say. Almost killed the lot of you," Robert said. "I'd still sue someone if I was you, Hank. I'd sue the whole damned jump company."

I sighed, but kept my mouth shut.

We were mercifully interrupted by the arrival of the other women. Diana beamed at me from beside an imposing lady in a long emerald dress. She'd had some obvious work done on her features, but had been gifted plenty of natural poise and beauty as well. She appraised me from over a perfectly straight, thin nose.

Maddie, Hank's wife, extended a palm toward me. "Ronnie, I want you to meet our good friend Luke Angel. Luke, this is Veronica Noble. She's been eager to meet you."

"The mechanic," Veronica Noble said. "You have received a lot of attention this week."

"Partly thanks to your lovely daughter," I said. "She has quite the following online."

"Yes. My internet starlet, obsessed with airplanes like her father. You airplane folk have a club going."

"Airplanes make the world a better place," Hank said. "Just look at young Diana here, all the good she does with her relief services." Diana gave him an appreciative nod.

"Her services and *your* money, you mean," Veronica said. "Don't forget that piece of the puzzle."

"It's a gift to be able to give back," Maddie said. "We won't see the future we want for our grandchildren unless we invest in it."

"Hmm," was all Veronica conceded. "My Jonathan was in your camp, always talking about this plane and that. Insisted on pointing every single one out to me. Do you own your own plane, Luke Angel?"

"I do. You can actually see it from here." I pointed to the Taxiway Charlie ramp. "The big twin-engine Grumman seaplane pointing away from us."

"Is that a jet aircraft or does it have those little propellers?"

"Propellers."

"Ah." She turned to peer through the glass toward the bar. Jason Brooks had arrived and apparently he'd brought a new puppy. Sierra was there too, immediately smitten with the fuzzy little cockapoo in Brooks's arms. "Now look at that handsome devil," Veronica said. "You know his father was quite the rogue as well. A titan in New York. Begged me to have an affair with him once. Now here is his son, another Brooks who can't stay away from us Noble girls. And he brought us a dog. I must go say hello."

Veronica peeled away and left us.

Once she was gone, I caught Diana's eye. "I see what you're saying. Why she's your white whale."

"She has entrenched beliefs about who is worth associating with. Girls from Philly like me are lowbrow."

"Then I can imagine how she feels about sons of drug smugglers."

"You are both as high-class as they come," Maddie objected. "Pay no attention to Ronnie. She'll come around. I'll keep working on her."

"At least Brooks makes the grade." I gestured to how Veronica was smiling at Brooks and the puppy.

"Brooks had a head start with her," Maddie said. "Jason Brooks Sr. is well entrenched in the New York social scene. He's a shrewd businessman."

"Richer than sin, you mean," Hank said. "Generational money."

"Not everyone is lucky enough to be self-made like you, my dear," Maddie said. "Or to marry into money."

"I married you for your looks! Just got lucky that you had brains and money."

Maddie patted him on the arm. "Then it's a good thing you were charming and had excellent taste."

"I prefer a self-made man too." Diana slid over to my side and put her arm around mine and gave me a squeeze. "With muscles."

Hank gave me a wink, and he and Maddie moved off to give us some time alone. Diana and I lingered at the corner of the balcony.

"The airport looks so small from up here, doesn't it?" Diana said.

"Might be my favorite place on earth though," I said. "Any size you make it."

"You're cute," Diana said. "What's a girl have to do to get you to look at her the way you look at airplanes?"

"I don't know, I find you easy to look at too." I pulled her closer and brushed a thumb along her jaw, letting my hand glide around to cup the soft nape of her neck. Her long hair ran between my fingers. Her lips parted slightly as I leaned forward and kissed her. Her mouth was warm and tasted lightly of champagne.

Her breath caught as I pressed her chest against mine. My fingers traced the long curve of her spine until my hand rested at the small of her back.

When our lips separated, Diana's eyes opened, and she gave me a warm smile. "Okay, now we're talking."

A faux sneeze cut the stillness—the sneeze seemed to say, "Getaroom!"

I looked up to find Sierra and Brooks had made their way out to the balcony to enjoy the view as well.

"Gesundheit," I said.

Brooks grinned. Sierra was now holding the dog.

"You two found yourselves a quiet spot," Brooks said.

"Might be the best view in the city outside of a flight deck," I said.

"I don't know, scenery just blasts right by when I look out the window," Brooks said. "You piston guys are the ones stuck enjoying the slo-mo."

"That why Mrs. Noble likes your ride?" I asked. "Comes in jet?"

"Ronnie? She loves me anyway. Flew her and her friends to Bimini one time. She made me apply all of her sunscreen. Or maybe she wanted to apply mine. I can't remember."

"Eww, gross." Sierra slapped at his arm.

"What? She's *your* mother." He lifted his cocktail glass. "You try any of Papa Noble's bourbon collection yet? You should see what her old man had down there. This is one of those aged twenty-four years batches they send on ships all over the ocean to get the barrel flavors just right." He gave a chef's kiss gesture. "Guy knew how to spend his money."

Sierra frowned. Then she looked to me. "Brooks makes him sound like an alcoholic. He did have a bourbon nearly every night, but he didn't get drunk. He just liked to treat himself."

"Smart man. I'm treating myself too," Brooks said and took another sip.

"And who's this little guy?" Diana asked, putting her arms out for the puppy.

"One of Brooks's latest friends. Doesn't have a name yet, apparently." Sierra handed the dog over.

"I'm thinking of calling him 'piss stain,' from what the little bugger did in my car on the way over here," Brooks said. "Gonna have to get it detailed tomorrow."

"Oh no. This little angel couldn't do a thing like that," Diana said. "You just need a little love don't you?" The puppy licked at her face with the rapidity of a machine gun.

While the women cooed over the puppy, Brooks joined me at the railing and pointed at the airport. "Let's see. They need to knock that down, and that down, and that down." His finger tapped at old hangars. "And make that runway two thousand feet longer."

"Small aircraft are what give Albert Whitted its charm," I said.

"Yep. And turbine engine owners buy more fuel. Which one do you think the city wants more of?" He gave me a knowing look. "Charm is great, but half those hangars are filled with home-builts and 172s that barely burn eight gallons an hour. And half of those are probably running Mogas."

"You're talking to the guy who makes a living wrenching on Cessnas and Pipers."

Brooks shrugged. "You know I cut my teeth as an instructor here too. It's got its appeal, but it's never going to be the kind of place that the high rollers in these new condo developments can really use, because there's no space."

"The newspaper complains the airport is a playground for the rich, now you claim we're too poor. Which one is it?"

Brooks peered down at the terminal building. "I told Eric that he needs to start curating the lease-holders by who can afford higher hangar rents. Clear out some of the undergrowth and clean this place up. But he sticks to his waitlist."

"I admire a man with principles," I said.

"Sure. But his principles cost the city a lot of money. Your Mallard out there on the ramp. It's antique, but in good flying shape it's still probably worth over a million dollars, wouldn't you think?"

"I don't know. I don't plan on selling it."

"But it has to pain you seeing it sit through every thunderstorm on the ramp. It pains me. That Cirrus I'm flying is worth just as much."

"You planning on taking it someplace else?"

"I have a hangar lined up over at St. Pete Clearwater soon. But I'd prefer to be closer to home. Don't you?" His eyes passed over the marina and the boat slips and *Hank's Midlife Crisis.* "We all like to keep our toys where we can see them. Look at Hank."

I put my hands in my pockets and shrugged. "They'll build us more hangars eventually."

"Sure. Probably. Let's hope." He clapped me on the back and went back to the women, scooping up the puppy and tussling its fur.

I enjoyed watching the laughter and smiles from Diana and Sierra as Brooks joked with them, but when I turned around to look back to the airport—to find *Tropic Angel,* and ground myself once more in the landscape—the diorama of the airport seemed fragile again. Like all it would take to come tumbling down was one big gust of wind, or a stomp from a schoolyard bully.

And part of what bothered me was that Brooks wasn't wrong. Growth was necessary. Essential even, if we planned to survive.

But growing things need strong roots too. And Albert Whitted Airport had those—a history that went back generations. Brooks was right that change was coming. An unknown future. But our history wouldn't be erased as long as there were people still around who remembered.

I was there. I remembered. And I planned to stay.

"WHAT HAPPENED TO BUD TRUMAN?"

Hank Martin settled onto his couch and asked me point blank.

The party had wound down. Most of Maddie and Hank's friends had faded back to their condos or departed the building. The contingent we had left consisted of Diana and me, Sierra Noble and her mother, and the Martins. Brooks had left with the puppy, citing an early morning flight.

Hank and Maddie's view from the 27th floor looked south and east, the airport and marina still in view out the living room windows. The beach-themed room decor existed in a pristine condition only possible when children and grandchildren have grown and ceased fumbling with glassware and staining the upholstery. Even at my age, I was wary to sit down, lest I elbow a crystal dolphin or knock a vase of shells to the floor. The couch cushions were pure white. A terror. So I stayed standing.

"I talked to Gabby Turpin today at her office. She told me she thought Bud to be in good health," I said.

"We'll miss that man," Maddie said. "Such a terrible loss." She was holding her dog, a bedraggled rat terrier/chihuahua mix that I'd rarely seen awake. It had to be fifteen years old and looked every bit of twenty. Its tongue hung out even while sleeping.

Veronica Noble held a freshly refilled champagne flute and she had begun to list as the party wore on. She was still standing, however, regarding us all with half-lidded eyes. "It was his time. We're taken when we're taken. Nothing we can do to change it. Look what happened to my Jonathan."

"That was another hard loss," Maddie agreed. "Far too young."

"And from what I heard, Bud Truman was a crusty old villain who liked to fail the students to make himself feel important," Veronica said.

"The poor man just died, mother," Sierra objected. "Can you show a little respect?"

"Oh, you don't complain, because he *couldn't* fail you. You'd've unleashed your minions on him."

"I don't have minions. I have followers."

"Tomato, tom-ah-to." She took another sip of champagne and inadvertently dribbled some out of her mouth.

Sierra rolled her eyes. "Veronica Noble, champion of the underdog. Who did you even hear this from?"

"I hear plenty of things," Veronica replied, dabbing her chin with a serviette. "You aren't the only one with friends."

"Bud Truman was a good man," Hank said, as if to settle the matter. "People can gripe about his ways as an examiner if they like, but he did his job."

"I've been meaning to ask how Nina faired the other day," I said. "Haven't caught up with her since."

"She hasn't been in," Diana replied. "Took a few days off

from the flight school or might have called in sick. No one's seen her."

"Doesn't sound positive," I said. I turned to Sierra. "Have you flown with her? You've had your instructor's certificate for a while now, yeah?"

"My daughter doesn't give flying lessons anymore," Veronica interjected. "Since the incident with the boob grabber."

"Mom!" Sierra chided. "Stop."

"Well, it's true, isn't it? One of your minions became over-zealous. I dealt with the same thing at your age, every woman has. But then again, I wasn't putting my breasts all over the internet for the world to covet. It's no wonder you get these stalkers."

Sierra sighed. "I think it's time we called it a night."

"I think your content is all very tasteful," Diana said. "I actually wish you'd post more about where you get your tops."

"Thanks, Diana. I'll send you some links." Sierra picked up her clutch and phone and moved toward the door. "Are you coming, Mother?"

"I live here," Veronica declared. "You don't need to chaperone me around my own building."

"Then I'll go," Sierra said.

"We probably should too," I added, reading the room. Hank and Maddie had too much class to kick us out themselves, but the party was clearly over.

We said our goodbyes and joined Sierra in the hall for the walk to the elevator.

"You'll have to forgive my mother," she said. "Three or four glasses in, the real Veronica starts to show."

"I've made my fair share of champagne decisions," Diana replied. "No apologies necessary." She stifled a yawn as she said it. "I'm toast myself. But this was a really enjoyable night."

"Do you need a ride home?" Sierra offered. "I'm going your way."

"Good question." Diana turned to me. "Do you want to save yourself the drive, hot stuff? I'd be ditching you on my doorstep anyway. It's a weeknight, and I'm not good for much else at this hour."

"Your call," I said. "Happy to deliver you if need be. Though I do still have a dog to walk." I checked my watch.

We halted on the sidewalk, across from where I parked my Jeep. Sierra's vehicle was nearby.

"Go home to your sweet dog," Diana said. "I'll use this excuse to catch up on girl talk. But I'm plotting our next outing."

"We should get a group together this weekend," Sierra suggested. "Maybe Saturday night. Have you been up to Sparrow?"

"I *love* that place," Diana gushed. "We should definitely get together." Diana turned back to me. "Next date. I'll wear the dress. Look forward to it."

"The suspense is killing me," I said.

Diana smiled, then rose up on her tiptoes and planted a quick kiss on my lips. "To hold you over. Keep thinking dirty thoughts about me. I know you have been."

Then she spun on her heel and marched off. Sierra gave me a wave and the two women cruised up the sidewalk arm-in-arm, awash in the warm glow of the streetlights. I turned around. It was a short walk to the marina so I left my Jeep there and would claim it in the morning before the parking enforcement could enact their vengeance.

As I walked around the south side of the Bayfront Tower, I encountered Maddie Coleman-Martin and her little rat terrier on the fringes of Pioneer Park. The ancient dog had evidently trundled its way across the road to the grass, but no farther, taking its time sniffing the dandelions before selecting a spot for its business.

"I liked the sight of that," Maddie said. "You and Diana. You two look good together." She was wearing one of her husband's jackets over her dress.

"Spying on us, were you?"

"Be careful with her. You know she's delicate."

"Delicate's not a word I would've chosen. Have you seen her triceps?"

"I'm talking about her heart, you foolish boy. That no-goodnik she was married to before did a real number on her."

"Heard something about that. Ran around behind her back?"

"Had a whole other life she didn't know about. Online and then later in person."

"Was he a pilot?"

"Some airline out west. Commuted a lot."

"I know how that can be."

"You must. How will Cassidy feel about you and Diana?"

"She was supportive. Encouraged it."

"Did she? But then I suppose she would."

"What does that mean?"

"She has her hang-ups, same as we all do. Life is long, Luke, but it goes by fast. It's nice if you can find someone to spend it with. I hope Cassidy figures that out before life passes her by."

The little dog finally found a spot to go. Maddie unrolled a bag.

"Want me to grab that for you?"

She shook her head. "The day you stop bending is the day you start to break."

She gathered up her dog's business and nudged the terrier back across the street. "Have a good night, Luke. I'm proud of you."

"Thanks for having us tonight." I watched her go, then wended my way back to the boat.

When I was hooking Murphy up to his leash, I looked back up to Bayfront Tower and saw Hank and Maddie's lights had gone out. But high up on the balcony on the twenty-eighth floor, a lone figure was leaning against the railing. I couldn't be sure at this distance, but I had a distinct feeling she was watching me.

Veronica Noble. Three sheets to the wind, but still looking down on the world.

NINA YEE WAS MISSING from the front counter of the flight school for the second day in a row.

The two substitute counter girls were making guesses in a game of Wordle.

"What the heck word starts with an A and ends with EW?"

"You're gonna lose," the second girl predicted.

"Do you know when Nina will be in next?" I asked.

"Supposed to be today but she called in sick. Maybe tomorrow. She usually works Saturdays."

The second girl looked me over while blowing a bubble with her gum.

"She have any flights booked on the schedule?" I asked.

"No." The girl didn't look up from her phone.

"What about Chase? Her instructor. Is he flying this morning?"

"I think he's on the north ramp, actually," the second girl said, chomping her gum back into shape. "Pretty sure I saw him preflighting the Pilatus for Brooks this morning."

"Okay. Thanks. You should try 'askew.'"

"Ass-what?" the girl with the phone asked.

I spelled it for her.

"Holy shit. That's it!" she declared after typing it in.

"What the eff is an askew?" the other girl asked. "This game is so hard."

I considered defining it for them, but decided not to bother. They had phones, they could look it up.

I took my golf cart around the blast fence for Runway 7 and cruised onto the north ramp. The Friday morning breakfast crowd upstairs looked healthy. One young mom was pleading with a pair of boys to stop climbing the railings. I stopped the golf cart to pick up a balsa wood glider with the Hangar Restaurant kids menu printed on it that one boy had accidentally or deliberately launched over the railing.

"You need a clearance from the control tower before takeoff," I shouted up to the boy, waving the glider at him.

"I'm the copilot," the boy shouted back. "He did it!"

The brother he'd ratted out smacked his shoulder.

"If you come downstairs, I'll give it back to you."

"The server already brought us another one," the mother called down. "But thanks."

I walked into the lobby of the terminal and found Chase Dempsey chatting up the girl at the FBO counter. He gave me a nod as I walked up.

"Just the guy I've been looking for," I said.

"If you need a flight review or something, I'm kinda booked this weekend."

"No. I wanted to ask you about Nina. See how things went with Bud the other day."

"What a mess, huh? Told her I wasn't sure what happens when you fail a checkride but the examiner croaks. You think they'll still process the paperwork?"

"She didn't make it then."

"Never does. That old dude has it out for her. Or had, I guess."

"Why haven't you sent her to another examiner? There are others."

"We will now. Have to. But Bud was close by. Nina doesn't have the cash to be flying all over Florida looking for examiners."

"It's more expensive when you fail."

"Tell me about it."

"You have a review flight set up with her yet to go over what she missed?"

He leaned against the counter. "We will. At some point. Gotta fly today, though. Heading up to Asheville and back with Brooks. He's putting in a good word for me with the company, and I help him fly the deadhead legs."

"Logging some right-seat time?"

"Gotta get those turbine hours somehow."

"Getting paid for it yet?"

"Not yet." He sighed. "But it beats the hell out of instructing, right?"

"I don't know, I've always liked instructing."

"Glad someone does."

"Did you talk to Bud the day he died?" I asked.

"Me? Uh, yeah. Sure. Before the checkride. Just real quick. Nina's been through that drill before, you know?" He shifted his weight.

"How'd he seem? When you saw him?"

"Bud? I don't know. Old. Grouchy. Same as always. But apparently not too good, huh? Musta had something going on. Who knows what though."

"Did Nina say anything about how he was during the checkride? Like if he seemed ill?"

"We didn't really talk about that. Just, you know, that he died."

"Was she surprised?"

"What? I mean, sure. Why wouldn't she be?"

"Just curious."

Chase gave me a long look, then picked up his iPad with his flight plan that he'd left on the counter. "I gotta go, man. Brooks is here."

Out the window, Brooks was in the process of leaving his Land Rover keys with Izzy, the line guy. Maybe Izzy was going to wash it for him while he was gone.

I observed the scene as Chase joined Brooks and the two headed for the boarding steps of the PC-24.

I walked out to watch the departure from the line guys' picnic table. Brooks gave me a wave from the flight deck before Chase closed the boarding door. A minute later they had the jet running, the scent of turbine exhaust wafting over the ramp.

Izzy finished marshaling the plane out, then repositioned the safety cones in a stack near me as the plane taxied away.

"That's a nice one," he commented to me.

"You waxed it?"

"Looks good, right? Took me eight hours."

"Who even needs strobe lights when the paint shines that bright."

He grinned at me.

"Hey, have you talked to Nina lately?" I asked.

"Nina? Nah. Not really. Though I did see her the other night over at the wash rack. We bump into each other sometimes in the evenings."

"How come?"

"Oh, you know. 'Cause she likes to make those videos. Her washing a plane in a bikini at sunset, checking the gas, pre-flight, stuff like that. Like all those videos you see about plane girls tryna look cute."

"Nina makes influencer videos?"

"You didn't know that? I guess it's 'cause she's not that popular yet. Not like the really big ones. Not a Sierra Noble. But you gotta give her props for trying, right? But I think maybe she's kinda going the wrong way with the swimsuit stuff. Those sponsors don't always be about that. They like it all covered up, but not *too* covered up, you know? You gotta match their brand."

"You know a lot about influencer content."

"Well, I got my channel too. I see all kindsa stuff, And I'm hoping to get some sponsorships too. I almost had one from Prist, the window cleaner. You haven't seen my videos? We gotta get you on the socials, man. I'll send you a link, show you this sweet-looking Citation I waxed last month." He got his phone out and started scrolling, then texted me. I felt my phone buzz in my pocket.

His radio cracked on his belt, the FBO counter girl calling in a fuel order. Izzy responded back that he heard it.

"Okay. I gotta run. Give me a follow though. You'll like it." He jogged off toward the Avgas truck.

I settled back onto my golf cart and pulled out my phone. I tapped the link he'd sent me, and it navigated me to his page. The video thumbnails were mostly Izzy's smiling face in front of various aircraft on the wash rack. I didn't even know plane-washing videos were a thing. Maybe it *was* time I joined the internet aviation community.

I tapped the main logo, and it took me to the app store to create an account. A few minutes later I was browsing what the internet thought I wanted to see. Or what it wanted to show me, in any case. When I got back to my office in Hangar 4, I settled into my chair and discovered that most of the people I knew around the airport had accounts of some kind or another. Elsbeth. Tyson. Even Rip.

It didn't take me long to find Nina Yee's. And there she was, lathered up in a bikini washing the wing of a colorful Mooney.

The skin-baring wasn't gratuitous, but neither was it subtle. The camera angles were certainly strategized to benefit a male gaze. Comments on the videos showed it. Lots of fire emojis and a few crude comments about what other things commenters imagined she was good at rubbing.

I frowned.

The girl certainly wanted attention. And she was getting it. But was it going to get her where she wanted to go?

Diana Longoria had an account for the non-profit and a personal page. It was mostly pics of drinks and food, but she offered one intriguing shot of her long legs stretched toward a beach sunset. Cassidy had an account too. She hadn't posted in a while, but *Tropic Angel* had made the cut, my vintage airplane running on the taxiway, my stunner of an ex-wife at the controls. Seemed like everyone had at least something they were showing off.

My own new account page sat empty. No content.

I tapped the camera button on the app and pointed my phone at my cat, who was perched on a nearby box of exhaust parts. Blackjack gave me a slow blink. Click. Post.

There we go.

Luke Angel. Internet influencer.

My cat rolled over and settled into an inverted position for a nap. Her fuzzy paws bobbed above her, curled sweetly.

Dang it. That would have made an even better picture. I could see how this could eat up your whole day. But I put my phone aside and scratched the cat under her chin instead. Blackjack purred. Some things were always going to be better in person.

TWENTY
TANKED

MIKE GONZALEZ CALLED my cell phone in the afternoon while I was adjusting the magneto timing on Sierra Noble's Bonanza. The indistinct murmur of traffic in the background told me he was driving. He said he was checking in, and that he had a question for me. I worried it was going to be about Rip, but it wasn't.

"You know Jason Brooks? Flies charter and some corporate work on your field."

"Sure."

"What's your assessment of him?"

"He's a sharp guy. Good pilot. Been around awhile."

"Solid reputation?"

"I assume so. Why?"

"Bud Truman dying has left a hole in our examiner pool, and it's creating a backlog of applicants. Brooks has been on our list for a while as a possible next pilot examiner."

"Oh yeah? Makes sense. He's certainly got the flight hours."

"Flying time is important, but we rate ethics higher. A good relationship with the public and the FAA. For a pilot examiner, we need a resource we can depend on."

"He might be your guy, then. Does a lot of charity flights with a local pet rescue. Seems to be generous with his time. He's been helping other pilots get right seat time in the PC-24 too. I don't recommend his protégé, Chase. That guy needs a recurrent class on professionalism, but maybe Brooks can straighten him out."

"I heard a rumor about that. Bud said something about wanting a word regarding a local flight instructor next time we talked, but we never met back up. Shame about that."

"We're all going to miss him."

"You'd make a good examiner too," Mike said. "Have you thought about applying?"

"I have enough on my plate."

"But you've been at the airport a long time. People know you. You've got the requisite ratings. Running a charter service with a big twin like your Mallard would look good on an application."

"I'm not sure I'm the quality of pilot that could fill Bud's shoes."

"Few are. But someone needs to. His schedule was booked out for months with applicants seeking ratings. We'll sort them out with the other examiners in the area for now, but having a reliable resource at Albert Whitted in the near future would make my life easier. You should consider it."

"Examiner. That's a role I never figured you'd want me for."

A pickup truck pulled up out front of my hangar with Holden, one of the Bayside mechanics in it. He climbed out and headed my way.

"You've got a stellar reputation on your airfield," Mike continued in my ear. "Especially after those skydiving heroics with Hank. That really put you on the map with the community. You put in an application, I'd be happy to champion you to the FSDO manager."

"I'll give it some thought. But hey, let me go. I've got a two-hundred-pound big ugly problem walking up to my toolbox right now."

"All right. We'll talk later."

I hung up with Mike and threw out a fist bump to Holden.

"Who you calling ugly?" Holden objected. "I'll have you know I was a semi-finalist for the country's cutest baby contest on Oprah when I was a kid."

"Oprah, huh? So you peaked in year one?"

Holden grinned. "Basically." He hitched his belt a little higher. "Hey, you mind if I borrow your nitrogen bottle for a bit? We're somehow out." He gestured to the back of his pickup truck, where two nitrogen tanks were riding around. "We usually keep the spare for when we need to run the big tank up for a refill, but when I went to use it today, the little one was already empty. Someone must have used it up and not told anybody. Right in the middle of a job we're trying to get out the door today, too."

"It's no problem," I said and fetched the nitrogen cart we rolled around to service various landing gear components.

"Thanks. I'll BRB with it, ASAP."

"No rush. I don't think we have any struts to fill this afternoon."

"I'll have to run up to the welding supply later to get ours swapped out. If you're not in a rush to get yours back, you want me to refill it while I'm up there and give it back to you full on Monday?"

I checked the tank pressure. "You know what? Yeah. That would be handy. Save me a trip soon. Thanks."

"You got it, brother." He lowered the tailgate, and I helped him unbuckle the tank from our cart and hoist it into the truck bed. Then we closed up the tailgate and he was on his way. I rolled our now-empty hand truck back over to the wall where we kept it. As I spun it around and nudged it flush against the wall with the toe of my boot, my eye caught on the wear spot the cylinder had made on the flat horizontal surface of the cart. The orange paint was worn off to reveal a gray half-crescent that ended at the edge of the dolly.

I stared at the shape, trying to recall why it mattered. I'd just seen that same-sized crescent shape, hadn't I? Only it had been in the form of a grease stain.

A grease stain I'd wiped off the seat upholstery of Bud Truman's RV-8.

The imprint of a gas cylinder?

I looked west toward Bayside Maintenance, my mind working, trying to catch up to itself.

A lot of things could have that same shape. But how many at the airport?

I called out to Reese. "Hey, I'll be right back. I want to check something."

I jogged to the golf cart and climbed aboard. Murphy spotted me and darted over to ride along.

"Hang on, buddy," I said, grasping his collar as he sat, and depressing the accelerator. We shot out of the hangar and across the hot ramp as fast as the little cart could go. I raced all the way around the far side of the Bayside Maintenance hangar and skidded to a stop near Holden's truck. He was still unloading the cylinder he'd borrowed. One of the other guys on his crew was there to help.

"Hey, Luke. You didn't have to ride over," Holden said. "We've got enough hands to manage."

"I actually had a different question for you."

"Shoot."

"Can I see the spot you usually keep these nitrogen tanks?"

"Uh, sure. We keep them in the back shop. On the far side of the tire changing table. You need me to show you?"

"No. You mind if I take a quick look?"

Holden shrugged. "Help yourself."

I walked past a Cessna 310 they had on jacks and ducked under its wing to make my way to the back shop. Murphy followed close on my heels, though his intentions were likely more focused on sniffing out Bayside's hangar cat, Lucy, to antagonize her.

A couple of other mechanics were working in the back shop. One kid was busy at the sandblaster, another was cleaning bearings in a parts washer. I gave them both a nod and made my way past the tire changing table to where Holden had indicated. The space next to the workbench was just large enough to hold two hand trucks very similar to the one I used in my shop. One large, one small. Both carts were empty—as the cylinders were currently in the back of Holden's truck—but the area where they'd sat was clearly marked by their absence. The centers of the hand truck bases were relatively clean—covered up most of the time by the cylinders—but the crescent-shaped perimeters of their outlines were well-defined by a layer of hangar dirt and errant bearing grease from the tire changing table.

I stooped low and wiped a finger through the dirt for good measure, then rubbed the residue between my fingertips. It was black and gritty. I borrowed a shop rag from a nearby table and took another swipe of the grease on the dolly, then tucked the rag into my pocket.

Gunk from the bottom of nitrogen tanks.

I rose back to my full height and stared down at the empty carts.

Same grease. Same shape. What were the odds of that being a coincidence?

Nitrogen was a harmless gas we breathed all the time in the open air. Seventy-eight percent of our atmosphere is made of nitrogen. It's impossible not to breathe it. But always in the correct concentration. In a confined space, like a closed room, or a closed cockpit? There, an increase in nitrogen would displace the oxygen in the environment—dilute it to dangerous levels. And nitrogen is odorless. Tasteless too. Totally undetectable to the senses. If it was leaked into a small confined space, like from a hose, or just from the open end of that twenty-seven inch servicing cylinder?

"Are you okay, man?" The young mechanic at the parts washer gave me a wary look. "You need help with something?"

But there wasn't anything he could do for me. I needed help, that much was true. But I'd need to call the police to get it. Because at that moment, I was facing a new realization.

Bud Truman hadn't died from the heat.

And he hadn't died alone.

Bud Truman had been murdered. And I'd just found the murder weapon.

I KNEW one homicide detective in my city, but she wasn't on duty when I called the Saint Pete police non-emergency number. What I got was a dispatcher who routed me to a shift supervisor named Sergeant Zimmerman. The good sergeant dutifully listened to my theory, but was unimpressed.

"We don't have an open homicide case related to the death of Mr. Truman," he explained. "The ME already filed it as a death by natural causes. If you want to add a comment, I can list it in a supplemental and attach that to the incident report."

"Will that reopen the case?" I asked.

"No, sir. Without additional evidence, we have no cause to open a homicide investigation at this time."

"I just told you why you should."

"And I noted what you told me. That you found a stain on the upholstery of the deceased's plane that matched what you believe to be the shape of a nitrogen tank. And there was an empty tank in a nearby hangar, but the stain on the aircraft upholstery has subsequently been wiped away. You *suspect* it's possible that Mr. Truman could have died from an overabundance of nitrogen in the cockpit, assuming the cockpit canopy was closed. Even though that is not the state the canopy was found at the time the body was discovered."

As he read his notes back to me, it made me realize how unactionable my report was. All I had was a wild theory. I'd wiped away the only evidence, and even that had been thin. None of it warranted further investigation from their point of view, and I couldn't blame them.

"If you want me to post a note and have a homicide detective make a follow-up call when they get a chance, I can do that. But that's the best I can do. And honestly, they're going to say the same thing I did."

I gave him my phone number anyway and hung up frustrated.

Shit.

Where was I supposed to get *more* evidence?

I'd told my discovery to Reese before I'd made the call, and as I tromped back down from my office, she was waiting at the bottom of the stairs.

"What'd they say?"

"It's not gonna fly," I said. "Not enough to open a homicide case."

She bobbed her head. "I was worried about that."

"Do *you* think I'm onto something?" I asked.

"I think if someone put an open bottle of nitrogen in the cockpit with Bud and closed the canopy, it would certainly explain why he died. But you don't have anyone at the scene who would do such a thing. And what the hell would be their motive? I've watched enough crime shows to know you're missing several pieces of the puzzle."

"Motive," I said.

"And opportunity," she added.

I crossed my arms and frowned. "I need to talk to Nina Yee. She was the last person to see Bud alive."

"She's not here today."

"Then I'm gonna come in and talk to her tomorrow."

"Don't scare the shit out of her."

"Why would I?"

"Because you have that look in your eye that you get when you aren't going to leave something alone."

"Bud Truman was murdered."

"You *think*. Maybe."

"Right."

"Just know not everyone is going to share your enthusiasm for this problem. Most people didn't know Bud as well as you, and the ones that did are still grieving his loss. Getting everyone riled up about the possibility that he was murdered might be . . ."

"Indelicate?" I offered. "Poor taste?"

"Just be careful."

I started for the golf cart again. "I will."

"And Luke?"

"Yeah."

"If someone *did* kill Bud, there's a good chance it could be someone we know. Maybe even someone here on the airport."

That gave me pause. I nodded but didn't say anything else.

I made sure Murphy was aboard again and took off for Bud's hangar.

Here on the airport. At Albert Whitted?

That felt wrong. This wasn't a place bad actors hung out. It was place of business. A place of leisure for weekend warriors to enjoy their airplanes. A training ground for eager students. Airports weren't dangerous.

Not to say it never happened. The terrorists who flew the planes into the World Trade Center had quietly trained on the Gulf Coast of Florida. In a post 9/11 world, there was always cause for vigilance. But terrorists didn't take out seventy-eight-year-old pilot examiners in their home-built RV-8s. Though somehow that was easier to wrap my brain around than the idea that it was someone I knew.

9/11 had happened on a blue-sky Tuesday.

No one suspected we had anything to worry about that day either.

Inside Bud's hangar, I walked around the RV-8 to the toolbox where I'd left the rag I'd used to clean Bud's seat cushion. It was still there. I unfolded it, located the smear of grease on the blue micro-fiber cloth and then reached into my pocket and pulled out the shop rag I'd taken from Bayside Maintenance. I unfolded that next to it and located the second smear I'd taken as a sample.

They looked the same.

I wasn't in a laboratory. The chain of evidence at this scene was destroyed. There was no way the police were going to put any weight behind my findings. But I was looking at evidence of my own. Drawing my own conclusions. It was all I had to go on.

My gut told me I was heading in the right direction.

But I was also old enough to know that the right direction isn't often synonymous with the easy direction. To get to the bottom of this, things might get harder before they got easier.

And I had no idea how far down this rabbit hole I'd have to go to find answers.

Or who would be waiting at the other end.

When I walked out of the hangar again, a truck was pulling up. Eric Feldman rolled down his window as I walked around to the cab.

"Saw your cart. Glad I could catch you," he said. "Bud's daughter is coming to see this place on Monday. Any chance you'll be around then? She's coming around ten."

"I can make a point to be."

"Thanks for the photos by the way. Those were helpful. But

she and I won't know where to start on some of these tools and gizmos he's got in there. The son-in-law is going to trailer the bike. They'll probably sell the plane. Though I figure they'll probably leave it in there till after the memorial. I told them that some of the airport people are planning something. It'll have to be soon though. I've got to turn this place over at the end of the month."

"Big rush?"

"You know how this place is. Anybody gets a whiff of a hangar freeing up and all the airplane owners circle like vultures."

"I'll bet. Hot commodity. You been offered any bribes yet?"

"Some have been more relentless than others. But I'm sticking to the list. It'll piss off somebody anyway I do it, but I'll piss off fewer by playing it straight. And fair is fair."

"Who's the lucky winner?"

"I'm not supposed to say, but I guess it will get out soon enough anyway. It's Chase Dempsey. A flight instructor over at the school."

"Chase? Does he even own an airplane?"

"He's been on the hangar waiting list for five years. Must have put his name in when he first started flying here. So he's the one who gets it. Evidently he's going to partner with someone on an airplane or buy something. Plenty of guys out here would be happy to go in on a plane with an instructor, especially if the deal comes with primo hangar space."

"Lucky guy."

"Yep. He gets to join the fancy few out here on Skyline Boulevard. Just him and the sunset watchers. And of course, the biplane rides guys." He nodded to the hangar next door. "They do actual business. Though that hangar still technically has Hank Martin's name on the lease."

"I forgot he was involved in that."

"Sure. He was one of the first ones to get them on the field. The biplane guys wouldn't be in business at all if they hadn't teamed up with Hank. Not like you can keep an old plane like that outside."

"Chalk another one up for the old man."

"Don't I know it. This place has a lot of history. Some days even I can't keep it all straight." He shifted the truck back into gear. "See you Monday?"

"See you Monday."

He rolled away and I was left pondering the view.

I took Murphy out to the Gulf after work, and I swam the buoys at St. Pete Beach for an hour. I finished before sunset, dripping my way back to my towel and watching the sun settle toward the horizon.

Cassidy said not everyone wanted this. Maybe she was right. Though I couldn't see why not. Beauty was right in front of me.

But as much as the watery sunset imagery was arresting, my mind kept wandering back to the airport and the view from Bud Truman's hangar on Skyline Boulevard.

It was another rare scene. Privileged.

And it made me wonder what Chase might have been willing to do to earn it.

I OPENED the door to the flight school early the next morning and let Murphy in ahead of me. He was always the most welcome anyway.

"Murphy!" Nina shouted as I followed the dog in. Murphy vanished around the back of the sales counter with his tail wagging, and when I walked up to the counter and peered over, I found him happily getting his chest scratched by Nina's fingernails.

"One dog, as promised," I said.

Nina looked up and smiled. "Always makes the day better when we get the dogs in."

A few weekend students chatted in the hallway to the classrooms, and more were out preflighting airplanes on the ramp.

I filled myself a cup of coffee and admired the lineup of clipboards with Hobbs hour meter sheets stacked near Nina's computer. "Busy flying day."

"Seems like everyone wants to go up this morning," she said. "And we finally have an afternoon forecast without thunderstorms."

"It's been a soggy mess of a week," I said. "How have you been? Heard you were out a couple of days."

"Yeah, just personal stuff. And I was in a funk."

"It happens. Checkride blues?"

"You heard?"

I shrugged. "Sorry you didn't make it. I know you were studying hard."

"And now my examiner is *dead*," she said.

"You'll be able to find another examiner."

"Yeah, eventually. Though I think I might take a break from trying for a while. I don't want to go and use just anyone. It's *so* stressful going with someone you don't know. Bud was hard, but at least I knew him. Maybe it will be easier with the next one."

"Could be. My local FAA guy actually asked me yesterday if I wanted the job."

Nina's eyes widened. "Really? You?"

"What? You don't think I'd be a good examiner? I'd have to shower more often, I'll grant you that. But look at me in my festive weekend wear." I gestured to the Hawaiian shirt I currently had on. "Doesn't this scream professional pilot?"

"I didn't know you might be applying. Figured it would be . . ." She shrugged. "I don't know, someone else."

"Neither did I, till yesterday. But hey, you mind if I ask you a quick question about Bud?"

"Not if it's about my being such a terrible student that it killed him. That's what Chase said."

"I know it wasn't that. But you're the last person I know that actually saw Bud alive. Do you remember what he was like that night? Did anything seem off about him to you?"

"Off how? Like he was about to die?"

"I don't know. Was he agitated? Was he talking to anyone on

the phone? Was anyone else around when you were wrapping up the checkride?"

Nina gave me a wary look. "I mean, I guess he was pretty annoyed that I failed again."

"Annoyed with you?"

"Not exactly. He was going off about Chase. How mad he was that Chase didn't prep me right. Said he was going to give him a good talking to. Said he was even going to call the FAA and let them know. That part made me worried."

"Worried the FAA would come down on you?"

"I don't know. I just have a really hard time with this material. I don't want them to tell me I can't test again."

"That's not how it works."

"Well, it still wouldn't be good. It's certainly not going to look great on my applications if I ever want to get hired with an airline. They care about that stuff now. Chase says it's super competitive. And he's worried it's going to make him look bad now too and lower *his* chances of getting in. If Bud reported him to the FAA and he got written up, it could tank the interviews for the jobs he wants."

I mused on that. "Thanks. Was Chase around after you finished the checkride?"

"I texted him when I landed. Let him know I failed."

"Did he know Bud was mad?"

"Maybe? I don't really know. I think I should probably just give the whole testing thing some space, you know? Try again later." She shifted in her seat and gave Murphy a rub on the head. My dog was sniffing around the cabinets. Probably hoping to discover the treats.

"Did you know anything about Chase going in with someone on buying an airplane?" I asked.

"He might have talked about it. I think he'd like to be

independent. He could instruct without the school if he had his own plane. Keep more of the money."

"He told me he hated instructing."

"That's probably true." She said it like it might be her fault. But she didn't dwell on it. "Are you going to Bud's memorial at his hangar when they have it?"

"Probably. You?"

She shrugged. "I don't know yet. It feels strange now. Like it changed the way things are around here. One guy dying can't kill the whole vibe of an airport, can it?"

"Let's hope not."

Murphy came back around to my side of the counter with his tail wagging. Ready for the next stop.

"You know if Chase is flying today?" I asked.

"He's not on the schedule this morning."

"Okay. Thanks. I'll catch up with him later. If you do see him, can you tell him I'm looking for him?"

"Sure."

I walked out of the flight school with Murphy. The conversation with Nina had given me my next goal.

Find out everything I could about Chase Dempsey.

But getting close to him might prove difficult. It wasn't like we hung out outside of work.

I took my phone out and tried his social media accounts. He wasn't hard to locate. His posts were often of the airport. Flights in the Pilatus. One shot of him working out at a gym, several at bars. A few of him zipping along North Shore Park on a One Wheel scooter. It struck me as pretty typical single-guy stuff to post.

He followed a number of other accounts from the airport. Plus Sierra Noble. Despite his snarky comments on the plane, he'd liked a number of her posts and videos. It was easy to see why. Her content was as well put-together as she was. Her jumping from planes, her landing seaplanes, her heli-skiing down mountains. It was no wonder her followers were so enthralled. The more I watched, the more she looked like an A-list celebrity.

I thumbed over to my phone contacts and dialed Sierra's number. She picked up on the third ring.

"Hey, Luke. Don't tell me it's bad news about my baby."

"I never deliver bad news on the weekend if I can help it," I said. "Come Monday it's fair game though."

"That's not going to make for a relaxing weekend."

"I'm kidding. Your plane's doing fine. I was actually calling about tonight."

"Yeah, I hope I wasn't horning in on your date with Diana. If you two want to go out alone, I totally get it. I was just coming out with Enrique anyway, and we figured we could say hi for a bit, but we don't mean to intrude."

"It's no intrusion. I was actually going to ask if you'd mind inviting a few more people out."

"Oh, really? Who were you thinking?"

"Chase Dempsey."

She gave a long pause. "Chase. Is he a good friend of yours or something?"

"Not exactly."

"I was wondering. He wasn't especially nice to me at the seaplane shoot. I'm not sure Enrique is a fan of him either. Why do you want to invite him out with us?"

"It's a long story, but I need a way to talk to him in a social setting. Maybe get him off guard a bit. And you might be someone he'd be willing to come out and see. Maybe if we got the whole group together again, it would make it less obvious."

She was quiet while she thought that over. "We don't all have to stay together the whole night, do we?"

"We can make an excuse to break things off if the evening doesn't trend that way naturally."

"Have you talked to Diana about this?"

"Not yet. But I'll fill her in if you think you can get him out."

"I'll see and call you back. Why is it so important to talk to him? Is this something serious?"

"I'd rather not worry anyone about it just yet, but it might be."

"All right. I'll see what I can do."

"Tell Enrique that the first round's on me for the trouble."

"His taste in drinks is expensive. You might regret that."

"See you tonight."

I hung up with her and climbed back aboard my golf cart with Murphy.

The Saturday morning flying crowd was lined up three planes deep on Taxiway Alpha waiting for departure. Capitalizing on good weather while we had it.

But this was the Florida Gulf Coast. Even with a good forecast, you never knew when a storm might brew.

"MY EYES ARE GOING to catch fire," I said when Diana Longoria welcomed me at the doorway of her townhouse that evening. The dress had made its appearance.

It was as red as red gets. Wowzers.

Diana gave it a twirl. "You like?"

"How do you feel about guys who stare? Because I don't think I'll be able to help myself."

"When it's you, I don't mind. If you're good, you might even get to touch."

I folded my hands in front of me like a choir boy. "Hallelujah."

I guided her to the Jeep and we made our way downtown. Parking on a Saturday night was a function of luck and persistence, but we got lucky early and scored a spot right in front of the Central Avenue Police Station.

Our short walk past Ferg's Sports Bar drew a few wolf whistles and hoots of approval from the locals that Diana pretended to ignore. One guy threw up a high-five for me as I walked by. I ignored it. Then he booed me. It was going to be one of those nights.

The bar we were headed for was on the rooftop level of the Moxy Hotel and a guy at the bottom of the elevator gave us a once over before admitting us into a car with a few other patrons also dressed up and perfumed. But when the doors opened on the floor marked R, the strongest scent I caught was of chlorine and pool water. A few towel-toting hotel guests in bathing suits dripped patiently in the hall, on their way in from the neighboring rooftop pool.

Our destination lay in another direction, through double doors into an elegant space with expansive views. The white marble-topped bar stretched for miles and the view might have competed with Bayfront Tower had it faced the airport. But this view faced North, overlooking the Grand Central bar district and out towards the high point of the peninsula. It did offer a possible view of the final approach for the Clearwater/St. Petersburg Airport, so I made a mental note to look that way for airplanes later.

Sierra had made us a reservation, and we found her and Enrique already seated at a lounge area at the far end of the bar. Enrique rose and stretched his arms wide for Diana, reuniting like old friends. Cheeks were kissed, outfits swooned over. I fetched drinks for Diana and myself and we camped out on the comfortable seats feeling good about the arrangements.

When Chase Dempsey arrived, I was surprised to find he'd brought along Nina Yee. She'd done up her hair and make-up and looked almost another person from her typical mousy self. I was reminded of those 90s high school movies where a director would take a gorgeous actress, stick her in oversized glasses the first half of the film, pretend she was homely, only to have her undergo a makeover at the sixty percent mark so she could wow everyone with what a stunner she was all along.

Chase, by comparison, looked his usual self, if not more so. He was still in work clothes. A charter service polo and khakis that could use an ironing.

Their arrival caused a notable shift in Enrique. No one's cheeks got kissed this time around, though Nina got plenty of compliments on her outfit, which only seemed to turn her face red.

"She has till midnight to bring it back," Chase said. "Then poof! Pumpkin."

Diana and I ordered appetizers. Bang Bang shrimp tacos for me and a tuna tartare something or other for Diana. Enrique and Sierra went the sushi route while Chase and Nina stuck with drinks. I tried to think of ways to engage Chase in a conversation about Bud, but finding a way to start was difficult.

"You getting back to flying this week?" I asked Nina.

She'd already told me that morning that she wasn't, but I hoped the question might get Chase talking.

"Nina's taking a break," he said, not biting.

I tried to understand their dynamic. Were they dating? Were they fighting? There was some tension there I didn't understand.

Conversation swirled around the virality of Sierra's skydiving video. The follow-up she'd done of *Tropic Angel* and our group at Egmont Key had also seen a lot of views. It turned out that she'd tagged all of our individual accounts in it, and it had led her followers to click through to our pages as well. I checked my account, and sure enough, even my one photo of Blackjack had received dozens of likes from people I'd never heard of.

Nina had plentiful questions regarding how Sierra had gained her following, courted sponsors, etc. It was Greek to me, but the rest of the group seemed to follow along. When the food came, Diana and I ate eagerly, though Nina and Chase not having meals stood out.

"Chase loves the wings down at Ferg's," Nina said by way of explanation. "We're going to get something down there later."

"And catch some of the game," Chase added.

Sierra nodded along but Diana gave me a look. When Chase and Nina had gone to the bar for their next drink, Diana turned to me. "I think this place might be a little pricy for them."

I got that. Cocktails were running close to twenty dollars with a tip, and even the burger at this place was twenty-four bucks. It wasn't absurd, but also not the prime pick for a twenty-something student pilot and a flight instructor on a budget.

"Should we all relocate?" Sierra asked.

"To a sports bar?" Enrique's tone of revulsion needed no translation.

"We invited them to join us," Sierra explained. "It would be polite."

"Mister Mechanic over here is the one who insisted," Enrique said.

"This was your idea?" Diana asked me.

I realized I'd forgotten to mention that to her. I tried to think of way to explain why I needed Chase there, but then Nina and Chase were back. We chitchatted through our remaining drinks and Sierra surprised us by picking up the entire tab.

"It's my treat," she said. "For you guys chipping in to help my channel."

She brushed off our attempts to pay for some of it. "You can get a round at the next place."

So we trooped downstairs. The two margaritas I'd enjoyed were starting to make their effects known, and I was feeling good. The bar crowd at Ferg's must have been feeling good too because they were even rowdier than when we'd first passed. Cheers erupted as the Rays scored another run in their current bid for a playoff spot.

Ferg's was mostly a covered outdoor patio bar, cramped and

busy, but the staff kept the drinks and food flowing at an admirable speed despite the crowds. Enrique was the one out of his element, his elbows squeezed tightly against his sides, fists balled, doing his best not to touch anything. We snagged a four-top as a group was leaving, and I helped buss the table clear so the women had somewhere to sit. We had a round of drinks ordered with the exception of Sierra who opted for water this go around. All seemed well, despite the rise in temperature from being back outdoors. But then Sierra got recognized. A girl came up to her, asked for a selfie. Sierra accepted graciously, throwing up her characteristic peace sign and smiling brightly with the young woman.

"We're out with a celebrity," Diana said. "How cool."

But the attention hadn't gone unnoticed.

"How about me? I'm ready for my selfie," a guy nearby declared. The stack of empties on his table and the mustard on his shirt were clues he'd been there awhile.

"Not right now. Thanks so much though," Sierra replied.

"What, she gets one and I don't?" the guy objected.

We ignored him, hoping he'd settle down. And he did, for a while. But stares continued from nearby tables. Around the time Chase and Nina's wings came out, the guy was back, trying to edge into our circle, scoping out the women and making snide comments.

"Back off, buddy," I said. "We're trying to have a private conversation."

"I know who that is," the guy replied, pointing a fat finger at Sierra. "We looked her up. You too, flyboy. How much for you to teach me to fly an airplane?"

"Gonna be well over ten dollars," I said. "Better get to saving."

He grinned at me and leered at Diana. "How much did you

pay for this one? She's older, but she still looks good." He made a move to squeeze her ass.

I planted a hand on his chest and shoved, tipping him off balance just enough that he missed his grab at Diana's rear. But that just made him mad.

"You put your hands on me, son?" he boomed.

The bar was loud enough that the shout only penetrated to the nearest tables, but they turned to look.

"Time for you to go," I said.

Diana put her hand on my arm. "Luke, don't. It's not necessary."

But after a couple of drinks, some people don't listen. I might be one of them.

The guy came at me with a swing he thought he'd camouflaged, but I saw it coming so far in advance I was able to step around it and deliver a right uppercut into his midsection to take the wind out of him. But the guy twisted at the last moment and I got more ribs and side than abdomen. And then he was in close, surprising me by going for a bear hug attack. He was shorter than me, but stockier and heavier. I'd guess a former wrestler the way he was trying to sweep my legs and throw me to the ground. I scrambled to keep my feet. He'd failed to pin one of my arms, however, and I brought a short right hook into the side of his head. But damned if the bull-headed son of a bitch didn't just shake it off. He was squeezing the air out of me and trying to hurl me down by brute force. I spread my stance wide for stability, wedged my arm under his chin and used all my strength to push my elbow into his windpipe, prying his head back. That's when Chase stepped up and clocked him from the side. The guy's head snapped back and he went limp long enough for me to break out of his grip. He staggered back a step and I popped him hard in the nose with a left jab. He went over backwards.

The guy had buddies. For a moment I thought we might be in

trouble. Chase and I stood back to back, ready to take on all comers, but they thought twice and did the responsible thing and simply picked up their friend from his spread-eagled position on the dirty floor and carted him outside. When they tilted him upright, his nose bled onto his shirt.

Bar security showed up then. And a police officer. It was another ten minutes till the adrenaline began to ebb. I was threatened with handcuffs at one point until enough bystanders voiced their support and put the blame squarely on the obnoxious guy.

But the look Diana gave me when we finally regrouped on the sidewalk let me know I hadn't escaped all consequences. Her arms were crossed and her jaw set.

I'd been married long enough to know nearly the full alphabet of a woman's non-verbal cues. I was plenty fluent in this one. Disappointment.

"You okay?" I asked.

"I think I've had enough fun for one night."

"I'll get the Jeep."

"I already called an Uber. You've had too much to drink."

Some mental math of the drinks I'd consumed verified her claim. I'd anticipated more time to sober up before being asked to drive.

Sierra and Enrique, and Chase and Nina huddled quietly on the sidewalk. Something about Diana's posture made me think the ride wasn't meant for both of us. My suspicion was confirmed when it rolled up. Diana didn't go for a kiss goodnight. I got a brief nod and an "I'll call you tomorrow." Then she and her red dress were locked away out of reach behind the slam of a car door.

It moved off into the flow of Central Avenue traffic.

I'd forgotten how to hallelujah.

But I remembered plenty of swear words.

TWENTY-FOUR
THE IRISH

IT'S an awkward feeling losing your date in the middle of a night out. Doing it around people you know makes it even more embarrassing.

Standing on the sidewalk out front of Ferg's sports bar, I was suddenly conscious of my age. A man in his mid-thirties hanging out with a bunch of twenty-somethings and now looking a fool in front of them. Diana had been my connecting link to the group. Youthful in appearance and attitude but closer to me in age and life experience, she'd easily bridged the gap between me and this younger crowd. Now I felt her absence.

"Want to head to another spot?" Sierra asked. "Plenty of options around here." Her smile was still there, if slightly dimmed.

Enrique eyed me cautiously. As if after my recent violence, I might still be a hazard. We still had Chase and Nina in tow as well.

Chase had come in handy. He'd stepped up in the fight.

"Thanks for having my back in there," I said.

He shrugged. "How often do you get a chance to lay some dude out? Gotta take your shots when you can."

Nina gave a disapproving frown.

But I knew what he meant. Fights were almost universally a bad idea. Hardly anyone ever "won" a fight. You just bruised your knuckles and frightened people. Got yourself thrown out of wherever you were. Maybe even arrested. But there was an undeniable camaraderie that came from it among men. I'd seen it plenty in the Army. Even the guys who were the ones fighting would leave with a grudging respect for one another after a fight. Something primal. Even necessary. I doubted sporting competitions would have ever existed otherwise. We all needed to prove something. Especially young men.

But I wasn't that young anymore, and I wasn't sure what I'd proved tonight.

"My Jeep's still parked here," I said. "I'll probably just sober up and take it home."

"Why don't I drive it?" Sierra offered. "I'm fine to drive. We can even drop it off for you and Uber back. Don't you want to stay out a little longer?" There was a look in her eyes. A question inside the question. I realized she was talking about Chase. My request of her to get him out, get him talking.

She was right, of course. I hadn't had much of a chance to get anything out of Chase, and this was the best opportunity I was going to get.

"We could always go to the Irish bar," Nina offered. "Right by your marina. I think Brooks is there tonight. Maybe we'll meet up with him."

Chase frowned at that but said nothing.

The Irish pub was right in the base of Bayfront Tower, a stone's throw from the marina entrance.

"Fine by me," Sierra said.

"You can invite your mother down," Enrique joked.

"Let's not," Sierra said. "Unless we *all* want our night ruined." She put her hand out to me. "Keys?"

I handed them over. The group split, Nina and Chase heading for their own ride. Enrique came with us.

As I walked around the passenger side of my Jeep and helped Enrique into the back, it occurred to me that the manual transmission might be a hurdle, but Sierra didn't balk at it, and by the time I was in and buckled, she had the vehicle in gear and moving.

"Please don't kill us all," Enrique said looking around the back seat. "This thing looks like it was built last century."

"The best things were," I said.

"I like it," Sierra said. "I drove Jeeps out west one time in a canyon tour near Sedona, but those we got to take bouldering."

"I stayed at the spa that day if you remember," Enrique said. "For good reason."

"Probably why it was so fun," Sierra joked.

Enrique glared at her. "You did *not* just say that."

"I'm kidding. You know I love you. But not everything has to fit the channel."

"We do what's on brand," Enrique said. "Which is why I'm so glad we're leaving this place. Sports bars? Ew. Not our scene."

Sierra glanced over at me. "You'll have to excuse him. He has limiting standards."

"I limit the amount of *weird* we attract," Enrique sang back. "Like drunk lurkers playing grab ass."

"It was actually Luke who saved us from that tonight," Sierra explained.

"I had my pepper spray," Enrique said. "That guy was lucky."

Sierra looked to me. "Did it feel good, punching that jerk?"

"Not especially." I flexed my knuckles. "Diana certainly wasn't a fan."

"Well, you can't really blame her. With the husband she had?"

"I keep hearing about this guy. Was he violent?"

"Yeah. Apparently made for an angry drunk. Picked fights. Made him verbally abusive with Diana. That's the story I heard."

"Damn it," I muttered. "And here I went playing the part."

Sierra cringed. "A little bit. My dad used to have this saying. 'The strongest man never needs to fight.'"

"He was a more mature man than me, then. I've been in fights all my life."

"But at least you did it for a good reason? I'd bet Diana will forgive you."

"Let's hope."

"If I was her, I'd be jealous. I'd love to be able to haul back and slug some guy who was bothering me. Guys have all the advantages. Though I'd bet Diana could hit pretty hard too."

"You would not win that fight," Enrique agreed.

"Obviously," Sierra said gesturing to herself. "Look at me. That's what I'm saying. It would be nice to be the one that's intimidating for once."

She seemed pretty fit to me, but I knew what she was saying. Despite what Hollywood movies liked to tell us, the bigger guy almost always wins the fight.

But I wasn't feeling especially proud of my victory. It had cost me what could have been a promising rest of the night. Now I was fighting to salvage what was left.

The Irish Bar was a short walk from the Demens Landing parking area. Since we were so close to the marina, I took the time to retrieve Murphy from the boat.

"Now this is a vibe I'm okay with," Enrique said when he got a look at the catamaran. "When I find a sugar daddy."

"We'll take it out sailing with Hank sometime," I suggested. "Add it to your filming calendar."

The lights of the Irish bar glowed brightly as we walked through Pioneer Park and across Beach Drive. Chase and Nina had arrived ahead of us, and true to Nina's prediction, they'd found Jason Brooks sitting at one of the outside tables with some friends and their dogs.

Murphy was quick to make their acquaintance. Dog butts were sniffed. Tails wagged.

I tapped Chase on the shoulder. "What are you drinking? First one's on me."

He followed me to the bar where I ordered a round for him and one for Nina and myself. Nina lingered outside with Brooks and the dogs. Sierra and Enrique were still studying the menu, talking about ordering more food.

While the bartender poured our drinks, I tried another angle with Chase. "So I heard through the grapevine that you'll be getting some hangar space soon."

He eyed me skeptically. "That didn't take long to get out."

"Small airports."

"Tell me about it."

"Prime real estate. You must have big plans for it."

He eyed the group out the window, watching Nina. She was petting Brook's dog and laughing. "Not really," he said. "Not everyone needs to be about hanging out in their hangars all day like a hobo."

"Bud seemed to like it." I studied his face. Seeing if the mention of the name drew any response.

But it didn't. "Thanks for the beer," Chase said, reaching across me and taking his pint from the bar top. He vanished back outside, not bothering to bring Nina's drink with him. I delivered it to her myself and she gave me a weak smile.

I'd ordered a Woodford on the rocks and sipped that while I contemplated my next moves.

I was striking out tonight on multiple fronts. But what did I expect? That Chase was going to spontaneously fess up to murder while out at a bar? I had nothing to provoke him with. Just a suspicion. A vague hint of a motive. And no evidence.

"Hey there, prizefighter," Brooks said. "You going to knock anyone else out tonight?"

That story had circulated fast too.

"Wasn't much of a fight," I said.

"Only matters if you win," he said. "You weren't the one knocked on your ass. So that's a W."

"There's that." I took a longer swig of my bourbon.

Sierra and Enrique had started a game of darts indoors. Enrique missed the board entirely with his first two throws. Sierra hit twenties with all three of hers.

Guys at the bar all stared in her direction when their girlfriends weren't looking.

Online or off, she garnered attention.

I realized I was staring too. When I turned around, I caught the smirk on Brooks' face. "Nice view, huh?"

I grunted.

"Little old for needing a babysitter, though, don't you think?"

"What do you mean?"

"Enrique. Her flam-boyfriend," Brooks explained. "He's on Mama Noble's payroll. Has been for years."

"What for?"

"To rein in her unruly daughter. Keep her civilized."

"Sierra seems to have plenty of self-control on her own."

"The good girls are always the ones that surprise you. I hear she used to be pretty wild. Tell me you wouldn't mind seeing that one go a little crazy though."

Inside, Sierra was doing a victory dance after hitting a bullseye. Reminded me of the dance moves she'd used at my hangar.

"Are you saying you like wild girls?" Nina asked.

Brooks smiled. "All women have a little wild in them somewhere. And I think Luke here probably digs it. Maybe it matches his crazy. I know it does mine. What do you think, Prizefighter?"

Nina eyed me curiously.

"I've got other things to think about," I said. I gulped the rest of my bourbon down, and slid the empty glass onto the table. "I'm going to go walk my dog."

"Every party has a pooper," Brooks said.

I had a feeling I was watched as I went. And if conversations were had about my departure, I wasn't sure they'd be flattering. That's if anyone cared at all.

But once the alcohol did its job, I wouldn't care much anymore either.

So much for my night out.

TWENTY-FIVE
NIGHT OWLS

I WOKE to the sound of a single bark from Murphy. I'd fallen asleep on the salon couch, several of the interior lights still on in the galley. *Hank's Midlife Crisis* rocked in gentle waves and nudged the dock. My shirt lay in a ball on the coffee table, but that was evidently as far as I'd gotten in the process of making it to bed.

"What's the matter, Murph? You have a bad dream?"

But my dog didn't look like he'd been asleep. He got to his feet and padded to the sliding door to the rear deck, claws clicking on the floor. He canted his head and listened, his tail still, ears perked. Could have been a dolphin feeding nearby. Murphy occasionally barked when they cleared their blowholes too close to the boat.

I pushed myself off the couch and stood, picked up my shirt and carried it to the galley. I needed to relocate myself downstairs to bed anyway. I filled a glass of water first and chugged it. I was still buzzed from the bourbon so I couldn't have been asleep very long. The clock on the oven read twenty past two.

Then something clattered amidships. Like it was on the roof of the cabin. A thud.

Murphy turned to face the bow and growled.

"What the hell?" I muttered. I set my glass and shirt down and opened the sliding door to the stern, then stepped out into the humid night air.

"Stay," I said to Murphy, and he begrudgingly obeyed.

I took a right, climbed up through the helm station. All was as it should be. Then I walked forward along the port rail, in search of the source of the commotion. It didn't take long.

Sierra Noble was righting herself on the forward lounge cushions of the bow.

She turned and faced me as I walked up.

"I slipped," she said. "It's slantier than it looks on this boat." She got to her feet but wobbled.

"Whoa there," I said and took her elbow, stabilizing her.

"I saw your lights were still on," she said. "We thought you might be awake. But then I saw you through the window, sleeping."

"We who?"

Sierra looked around, seemed momentarily confused by the lack of anyone else around, but then shook it off. "We, me." She gave me a crooked smile. "Aren't you happy to see me?"

"Is this what it feels like to have a stalker?" I asked.

"I'm more fun," she said. She waved her free arm, seeming a little steadier on her feet. "This is soooo nice. Can't believe you get to live here."

"Looks like you had some fun too after I left. Where's Enrique?"

"I told him I'd stay with my mom upstairs tonight, so he could leave." She leaned in closer and whispered loudly to me. "He met a cute boy."

"Glad someone found romance tonight," I said.

"Right?" she agreed. "Good for him." Her head bobbed, then she refocused on me. "Have I told you how jealous of you I am?"

"Of me? Of what?"

"Of this. The life you have. Nobody telling you what to do. You go to work, dance all day to the radio. Fly cool planes, pet all the dogs, and come home to this killer boat where nobody ever bothers you."

"You might be oversimplifying the work scene. I'd classify the dancing as 'occasional.'"

"It's the best. I'm so jealous. I like, want to *be* you. Can I be you? How do you get this life?"

"I can point you to some good A&P programs. How do you feel about airplane maintenance?"

Sierra smiled. "Could you imagine?" She turned around and faced the skyline and Bayfront Tower. "Did you hear that? I'm going to be a mechanic! I'm going to get all sweaty and dirty and smell like airplane engines *all* day. What do you think of that, MOTHER?" When no reply came from the skyline, Sierra turned back around to face me. "She would die. Absolutely die."

"Let's hope not."

"Look at you," Sierra said, studying my bare chest. "You don't even have to wear clothes. I have people telling me what to wear *all* the time. Be sexy, Sierra. But not too sexy." She deepened her voice in mock seriousness. "You need to be classy, Sierra. But don't be such a prude." It went back up again. "Guys have to find you attractive, Sierra, but don't act like you like it or they'll think you're a slut." She rolled her eyes. "What I'd give to be a guy. You have it sooo easy. When was the last time someone called you a skank, but then also called you a tease?"

"Can't say it's ever happened."

"See? I got called a tease *today,* in my comments section. And it was a video about people who forget to put their landing gear down in Bonanzas. Explain how that can possibly be a turn-on to anyone."

"Gear up landings are never sexy."

"Exactly." She gave me an appreciative nod. "Want to know who it was who called me a skank though?"

"Someone not worth your time."

She let out a long sigh. "Right. I know." She turned around and walked to the port rail, facing the skyline again. "How about this, Mother?" she said. She slowly peeled one spaghetti strap of her top from her shoulder, then the other. She slid her arms free from the straps and raised them high, letting her dress fall to the deck, leaving her bare-breasted in the moonlight. "I'm going to live on a boat, like Luke Angel! And NEVER wear clothes. And I'll be a *mechanic*. And I'll be as skanky as I want and be goddamn happy!"

I gave a quick glance around the docks. I was at the far end, and few of the people I knew with live-aboards in this marina were likely to be awake at this hour. But Sierra wasn't exactly being quiet.

I approached her from behind. "Now that we've got that cleared up. I do have neighbors."

She turned around. She was wearing panties, thankfully, but her dress was around her ankles. No need to wear a bra. The perks of being under thirty, with a toned body and nothing yet in need of lifting. She'd done a 180 but was still standing inside the circle of her fallen dress. I crouched to the deck, pivoted the dress around her feet for her, and rose again, raising it as far as her bare hips.

She stood relaxed and compliant. "What? You don't like this look for me? Boys get to go topless anytime they want. At least I'm not being a prude, right?"

"I'm not complaining," I said. "But you've had too much to drink."

She slung her arms around my neck, rested them there. "I don't get drunk. It's not on brand."

"Hmm," I replied.

Then she rose up on her tiptoes, her fingertips grasping my neck, and kissed me.

She didn't taste like alcohol. She tasted like summer. Salt and heat. Her warm lips parted and I felt the soft pressure of her tongue between my lips. Fervent and eager.

She cupped my face, pressing her body to mine. Hungry for more.

I pulled away. Looked her in the eyes. She stared back, eyes half-lidded, and so young.

I peeled one of her arms from around my neck, slid it though the spaghetti strap of her dress, then repeated the process with the other arm, tugging the dress back up to cover her chest, then I repositioned the spaghetti straps on her shoulders until they were even.

"You should go home," I said. "I can walk you back to your mom's."

She took my hand then, and pulled me over to the lounge and sank onto it. When I didn't make any move to join her, she tipped over to lie horizontally. "I can't go home," she said. "I can't find my phone. I think maybe Enrique has it."

I frowned. I dropped her hand.

"Your mother can let you in."

"The elevator keycard. Is on. My phone."

"Won't the concierge downstairs know you? They can let you up."

"Wake Veronica? At three a.m? I'd. Rather. Die."

Her eyes were closing.

"Hey, don't fall asleep here. Not the place for it."

"But it's sooo nice," she muttered. "I want a boat."

I looked up at the stars and blew the air out of my cheeks.

When I looked down again, she was no longer moving.

Damn it. I rested my hands on my hips. But there was nothing else for it.

I scooped Sierra up into my arms and stood, then carried her back along the starboard rail to the stern, pushing the door to the salon open with my elbow and then a foot. Murphy was there to greet me, tail wagging. He stood on his hind legs momentarily, getting a good sniff of Sierra in my arms.

"We have an unexpected guest," I said. "Make some room." I managed to get the door closed behind me. At the stairs to the guest berths, I paused and tried to rouse my slumbering cargo. But she only murmured some gibberish and failed to wake. I swore, then propped her momentarily on her feet so I could hoist her up over my shoulder in a fireman's carry. Then I backed down the steps to the guest berths with her, mindful not to bang her head on any corners. There was a full-sized bed at both ends of this hull. I chose the forward berth for Sierra and flopped her down on the bed. Her shoes must have still been up on deck because they were no longer with us. I rummaged through various drawers until I found a comfortable spare T-shirt, this one from a long-forgotten fishing tournament in the Keys. Then I stood at the edge of the bed and debated. "Do I put her in a shirt?" I asked Murphy. "I've already seen her topless. Or is that weird?"

Murphy tilted his head and gave me a curious look.

"You're right. Might be weird," I said. I tossed the shirt back on top of the chest of drawers and simply pulled the covers down on the bed. I slid my guest's legs securely beneath them, then pulled the covers up around her chin. "Sleep tight," I said.

Sierra contracted herself into a fetal position, tucking her chin as she found a softer place on the pillow.

I left a light on for her in the head.

Then I finally called it a night.

I guess my night out hadn't been all bad after all.

TWENTY-SIX

REVERSAL

I MAKE a habit of watching the sunrise, most days viewed with a cup of coffee from a folding chair on the bow. Today I missed it by a solid hour. In addition to my coffee, I had my phone out and was on my third attempt to word an apology to Diana in a text message. "Sorry for punching that guy last night" lacked the nuanced emotion I needed. I was trying to come up with something more refined, but was interrupted by an annoying notification banner. I'd swiped it away three times, but it kept reappearing. Finally I tapped it and it took me to my newly created social media profile. The little notification flags glared at me and then told me I had numerous comments on a photo.

The comments were on my image of Blackjack, the only content I'd created thus far, but there were a lot of them.

"Sketchy AF. I hope your cat bites you in the face."

"You're a walking red flag. Bet your cat knows it."

Some of the comments had nothing remotely to do with the cat. Like, "You should be ashamed of yourself. Someone should delete your existence with your account."

I frowned. All of the comments had been left this morning.

Was this the Sunday ritual on the internet these days? Roast random newbies?

I didn't know any of the commenters. Strange. I didn't need this nonsense. Neither did my cat. I closed the app.

But when I tried to go back to my inadequate text apology, I noticed a new text from a number I didn't recognize.

<<< Is she still there with you?

Then a few seconds later, <<< This is Enrique. Where is Sierra? Text me back ASAP.

Enrique.

I texted back.

>>> She's here. Sleeping.

The little dots appeared immediately and he texted back.

<<< I need to talk to her. Right NOW. Wake her up.

Pushy. But it was probably time I woke my guest anyway. I stopped by the coffeepot and filled an extra mug. I didn't know how she took it, so I gave it a splash of half and half as a best guess and took that with me down to the guest cabin. I knocked before I descended.

"Sierra? You awake?"

Hearing nothing, I headed down. But she stirred when I got close to her bed.

"Good morning, sunshine," I said. "How are we feeling?"

Sierra's eyes blinked open, and she rolled over. Then she saw me and sat bolt upright. "Wait, what the hell? Where am I?" She looked around. Then her hand went to her head.

"*Hank's Midlife Crisis* is a home for all. Especially the inebriated."

"Oh God." She looked down at the rumpled dress she still had on, then to me. "How did . . ."

"Your guy Enrique is texting up a storm wanting to talk to you," I said, dodging the potential question. "Coffee?"

She blinked a few times and nodded. "Yeah. In a minute. I

feel like my head is IFR right now." She looked around, her confusion evident. "Have you seen my phone?"

"You didn't have it on you last night that I saw."

She frowned. "Ugh. I really need to pee."

"The head's this way."

She teetered in the direction I'd pointed, gradually finding her balance.

My phone vibrated in my hand. Still Enrique, this time calling.

Persistent this morning. I picked up.

"Yeah, man, good morning."

"Is she there?" Enrique asked.

"In the bathroom. She'll be out momentarily."

"Give her the phone," he said.

"She's peeing."

"Tell her to pee later, this is important."

"What's the big crisis?"

"You of all people should not ask me that right now. Do you have any idea what you've done? You might think this is some fun conquest for you, but posting it? That's next-level stupid."

"I don't have any idea what you're talking about."

Sierra opened the door to the head and blinked at me. "Who are you talking to?"

I handed her my phone. "See if you can decipher this."

She took my phone and put it to her ear. "Yeah. I'm here. What's going on?" Her brow furrowed. "What? When?" Her eyes went to me. "Who did? When was this?" She looked around. "I don't even have my phone. How could I?"

Enrique's explanation of whatever was going on caused her face to blanch. "No. I swear I didn't," she protested. "At least I don't think so. I don't remember any of this. Oh my God. How bad is it? Like actual nudity? Send it to me. No, just send it to *this* phone. I want to see it." She was glaring at me now. "I can't believe this." She pressed her hand to her forehead. "What the actual fuck. Yes. I'm here. On Hank's boat. Come fast."

She pulled the phone from her ear and stood glaring at me. "I thought *so* much better of you than this. I don't believe this is happening."

"What?" I asked. "Tell me what's going on."

"Last night. Whatever *this* was." She waved a hand between us. "You *posted* it?"

"No. Of course not."

"Then who? You're trying to tell me *I* posted it?"

"What are we even talking about?"

"Why can't I remember anything?" She put her hand to her head, squeezed her temples, then pulled the phone back up. Tapped something. "He just texted it."

I edged around her, trying to see. It was a video from Sierra's social media account. Shot at night, the bow of the boat. It was set to low, melancholy music. It showed a view of the bow that captured me standing, hands on my hips. Light coming from a distant dock light.

Then I had Sierra's hand as she lay on the lounge cushions. I pulled her upright, got her to her feet. Then I was peeling the straps of her dress from her shoulders, exposing her bare chest. The angle showed the action from Sierra's back, but Sierra gasped. "Oh my God."

"Wait, hang on," I muttered.

Then video version of me put Sierra's arms around my neck, kissed her.

Then I pulled her dress the rest of the way off her hips to the floor. Sierra turned around. Someone had darkened the area of her chest, but it was obvious she stood bare-breasted on display to the skyline while I loomed behind her.

"Are you fucking kidding me?" Sierra said.

She didn't wait for the rest. She wheeled around and swung

at me. Not a slap. A fist. And she caught me right in the cheek below my eye. I reeled backward in surprise.

"Ow," I muttered and put a hand to my face.

"Ow," she echoed. "Damnit." Cringing and clenching her sore fingers. But then she turned tail and flew up the stairs to the galley.

"Sierra, wait!" I shouted. "That's not what happened!"

By the time I caught up to her, she was storming around the boat searching for belongings. She'd found her clutch, rifled through it. Swore. Then flew around the salon some more. "Where are my goddamn shoes. Where is my phone?"

"That video isn't real," I said. "That's not what happened last night."

"Nice try, dickhead. AI is good, but that *wasn't* AI."

"I didn't say AI. I just know what happened, and that wasn't it."

"What's unreal is that I trusted you. I thought you were cool. And you're supposed to be dating Diana. God, you're such a sleaze. How did I not see it?" She looked around for more belongings. "How did I even get here?"

Murphy cowered on his dog bed, pretending not to exist.

"Look at the video again," I said. "It has to be tampered with."

"*I'm* the one who's been tampered with!" Her voice cracked. Tears had sprung to her eyes and dripped down her flushed cheeks. "I don't even remember what you did to me, goddamnit." She wiped away a tear. "Where are my shoes?" Then she stormed out the back door without them, fleeing.

I pursued her. But when she cleared the gangplank and made the dock, she broke into a run.

There were other marina residents out. People on their boats with morning coffee, a small family shepherded children along one dock toward their cabin cruiser for a Sunday morning pleasure cruise.

Sierra sailed past at a dead sprint.

I slowed. Aware that pursuing a barefoot girl in her going-out dress from the night before was hardly a good look.

I gave one of my neighbors a sheepish shrug as I walked by. New meaning to the term "walk of shame."

A resident I'd known for years slowly shook her head at me.

In the parking lot, a white Ford truck screeched to a halt outside the fence. Enrique climbed out the passenger side while a big dude with a beard stayed behind the wheel.

Sierra flew into Enrique's arms, and he did his best to console her. As I approached, Enrique pointed a finger at me. "You stay the fuck away or I swear to God, Greg is gonna kick your ass."

Greg was evidently the guy in the truck. Our eyes met, but he looked about as confused as I was. "Hey, I'm just the driver here," he explained.

"The hell you are," Enrique said. "What if someday we got married and had a daughter and some asshole did what he just did to her? Would you sit there and do nothing? You're supposed to back me up."

Greg raised his palms from the wheel and got out of the truck, not looking excited about a confrontation.

"You guys just meet last night?" I asked him.

"We're not talking about me," Greg said. "What did you do to the girl?"

He *was* a big dude. But I doubted he'd hit me.

"Nothing. I gave her a place to sleep." I turned to Sierra. "That video's wrong. I don't care what it shows."

"It wasn't faked," Sierra spat back. "That was you."

"Doesn't matter if it's fake or not," Enrique interjected. "It's up and we need to get it down." He tuned to Sierra. "Hurry up and get on your phone and take it down already."

Sierra looked at the phone in her hand and realized she was still holding mine.

"She was hoping you had hers," I explained.

Enrique swore and swapped phones with Sierra. "Log into your account on mine." He tossed my phone into the weeds.

"Hey," I muttered.

Big Guy Greg and I stared at each other while Sierra tried to log into her social media account. She swore. Tried again. "My password's not working."

Enrique glared at me. "What did you do to her account?"

"Me? You're joking," I said. I walked over and picked up my phone.

But while I did that, Enrique bundled Sierra into the truck and followed her, giving more advice she didn't need about resetting her password. Greg climbed back into the truck too, and then I was watching them drive off through the marina lot.

When I got back to the boat, Murphy met me, tail giving a cautious wag.

"I know, buddy. I'm as confused as you are. But we'll figure it out. Everything is fixable."

My phone buzzed in my pocket again. I read the notification. Maddie Coleman-Martin.

The text was only one line.

<<< I'm so disappointed.

"IT'S BACKWARDS. You can tell if you look hard enough," I said.

Reese and I were on her back porch watching Murphy tear around the back yard with her newly acquired rescue dog, Oreo. Oreo was an energetic breed, some kind of terrier mixed with an electrical capacitor. She had two discernible speeds: lightning fast and recharge, and so far I'd mostly witnessed the former. Murphy was panting hard trying to keep up.

"There are a few spots that give it away," Reese said, rewatching the video. "But I have to admit they did a good job. It's been spliced to cut out any parts that would look obvious, like walking."

"Who the hell would do this?" I asked. "And why?"

I'd taken a screen recording of the video, assuming Sierra would get the original down from her page soon, though that must have proven difficult because for now it was still up. I could tell because I kept getting notifications from people bombing my cat photo with mean comments. My direct messages inbox was even worse. Reese showed me how to disable it.

"I'm trying to figure out the angle too," I said. "It had to be filmed from the next slip over. It's close."

"Weird question," Reese said. "But is there any chance Sierra set this up herself ahead of time while she was drunk?"

"I heard her banging around on deck beforehand, but she never left my sight afterward. I put her to bed downstairs, and she was stone-cold out."

"Right. Seems unlikely she'd wake back up, go outside and post a racy video of herself on the internet. Uh oh," Reese said. "You might want to handle this one." She handed me the phone back. The text was from Diana.

<<< I see you didn't take long to trade me for the younger woman.

I swore. In the fallout with Sierra and Enrique and my subsequent drive to Reese's place in Kenwood, my half-written apology text had gone unsent. Now I was in far deeper.

I dialed Diana's number.

Two rings and then sent to voicemail. I left a message, telling Diana I owed her a thorough explanation and an apology and to please call me back.

Reese's girlfriend, Nora, appeared on the back porch with croissants. She waited till I hung up and gave me a sympathetic nod. "You're having quite the morning."

"I think I'll be needing a lot more coffee," I said.

Reese met me back at the boat an hour later, and we browsed the neighboring slips around *Hank's Midlife Crisis*.

The only plausible place to have shot the incriminating video the night before was from a neighbor's thirty-foot Tartan sailboat.

The owner was a friendly guy named Clark. He lived here part of the year and the rest of the time in the Carolinas. But he'd been gone since May, and I knew he wouldn't mind me walking around on his boat. What he *would* mind is that someone had jimmied the latch on his companionway and left the hatch ajar.

The drop boards had been closed unevenly, and a gap was visible where the hatch ought to align. Someone had left it in a hurry.

I opened the companionway again and slid the hatch open far enough to see inside. The boat wasn't fancy. Not a true live-aboard either, though it was comfortable enough for sailing around the bay. I'd been aboard once or twice with Clark when he'd asked me to look at things. Being known as a mechanic had its hazards as well as its uses. I didn't need to enter the companionway. Right where I was made a perfect place to view Hank's catamaran while remaining out of sight. Especially in the dark.

"Stand over there on the bow, will you!" I shouted to Reese. She was aboard *Hank's Midlife Crisis* as my point of reference.

"Here?" she shouted back.

"Yeah, that's it. Pretty sure this was the spot."

"Hey, Luke. Come over here," she shouted back.

"Why?"

"I found a phone!"

When Enrique showed back up in the parking lot, there was no sign of his guy Greg, or of Sierra. He stayed in his car with the engine running while I walked the phone out. It felt like a do-over of the morning with half the cast.

Enrique eyed me suspiciously as I walked up, but he rolled his window down.

"You get the video taken down?" I asked.

"No help to whoever changed her passwords. Took an hour online with the useless tech support bot. Not that it matters. The video's popped up a dozen more places now where we can't get to it."

"I'm sorry to hear that." I handed him Sierra's phone. "Found this wedged in the cushions up on the bow."

"Convenient."

"Not for me. You do know that video was backwards, don't you?"

He didn't deny it.

"Are you planning to put it back up to show it that way?" he asked. He seemed resigned. Much calmer than our last meeting, but still simmering with anger.

"No. Though it would clear up a few things."

He put Sierra's phone on his passenger seat and sighed. Then he gripped his steering wheel with both hands. "You know it's my job to keep her safe. To prevent things like this from happening. And I failed."

"She's a grown woman. Maybe you should let her make her own choices, and she wouldn't have so many repressed emotions to get out."

"Oh, it's that easy? That's a very man-splainy thing to say."

"She got drunk. Made some poor choices. Should anyone crucify her for that? What's so wrong with letting her fail every once in a while? We've all been there."

"Except she didn't *get* drunk," Enrique snapped. "She got taken advantage of."

"You were the one buying her drinks at Sparrow last night. What were those cocktails you were ladling into her? Flaming Disco Balls?"

"A 'Disco Ball on Fire' is a non-alcoholic mocktail," Enrique said. "Sierra hasn't touched an alcoholic drink since her dad died. And if you knew her like I do, you'd have known that. But thanks for telling me how to do my job. Now I'm headed to get my friend a blood test and see what really happened to her last night. If it turns out she was roofied, don't be surprised if I'm back with the police."

He shifted the car into drive and pulled away. For the second time in the same day, I watched his taillights vanish back toward downtown. And for the second time today, I was left feeling like the fall guy.

My life was spinning out of control. And I didn't like it.

TWENTY-EIGHT
DEFENSE

FRANK ANGEL STEPPED aboard *Hank's Midlife Crisis* around 3 p.m. carrying a foldable chessboard and a six-pack of Modelo. It was a Sunday afternoon ritual we'd recently developed since his return from prison. When the weather was favorable, we'd swim the buoys out at the beach together instead, often having a beer out there afterward. But when thunderstorms loomed, it was chess. Activities that kept us busy had proven useful, a way to bridge the conversational gap of his nearly twenty-year absence.

"I texted Rip earlier," I said. "Told him to pass on the message that I wasn't feeling up for chess today."

"Must have slipped his mind," my father replied, pulling a pair of beers from the six-pack and sticking the rest in the fridge.

"When are you going to get a phone? Our relay system clearly isn't working."

"Why should I?" my father replied. "Everyone else I know has a phone I can use. When I was a kid, if I wanted to reach my father, I had to leave a message with a guy at the corner bar. We all turned out fine."

"You call *your* life 'turning out fine?'"

"It is now. Look at you. That phone making you happy?"

I set my phone down. It hadn't been making me happy. Quite the opposite. I'd fallen down a rabbit hole of comments people had left on Sierra's latest social media reel. She'd offered an apology for the previous content being posted, stated that it hadn't been her that posted it, and that her privacy had been invaded. Most comments were supportive of her, and plenty had painted me as the villain.

But another contingent had inexplicably labeled Sierra as the problem, as if she'd brought this all on herself. The vitriol astounded me. As many comments as I'd found blaming me for taking advantage of her in the video, there seemed to be an equal number condemning her for being in the situation to begin with. One commenter had already assigned her a place in Hell with Jezebel and an additional cast of whorish sinners they'd insisted would be sharing her fate.

Whatever benefits Sierra was reaping from internet stardom, it was certainly exacting a toll as well.

"Rip drove up to Zephyrhills this morning," my father said. "Probably why he couldn't relay the message."

His comment brought my attention back to the situation with the Feds. "Have they made any determination about his expired AAD?"

"He seems to think they'll slap him with a reprimand. But it's not illegal to jump with an expired battery at his age, so what are they really going to do?"

"He has a parachute rigger license. And he was jumping tandem. They'll expect better of him."

"Rip will be a good boy and get his rigs fixed and play by the rules for a while and it will all blow over. He just needs to smooth things out with his jump school buddies."

"And we still don't know why he blacked out in the first place."

"Well, he's laying off the caffeine. Drinking a shit ton of water. Guy spends half the day taking leaks now. He'll be all right." He laid out the chessboard on the table and began arranging the pieces.

I sighed and slid into a seat opposite him. He cracked the second beer and handed it to me. "How are you doing?"

"In what capacity?"

"Heard you got yourself some unwanted eyeballs last night."

"Has everyone heard about that? You don't even have a phone. How is it *you* know already?"

"Rip showed me the video before he left this morning. He's worried about you." He opened with a king's pawn. I opened with a knight.

"So that's why you're here. I forgot Rip was a rabid Sierra Noble fan. Can't imagine what Tyson is going to say tomorrow."

"You could take a couple of days off. Lie low. Let everything cool down."

"I have a business to run. Sierra's Bonanza is still sitting in my hangar midway through an inspection. I have a charter flight coming up soon. And there's Bud's memorial this week."

"Skip it."

"I can't skip it. I've known the guy for years."

"So what? It's a memorial. He won't be going to yours." He developed a pawn in the middle of the board. I got a bishop out to free myself to castle.

We traded moves in silence for a few minutes.

"Your problem is you play too much defense," he said. He attacked into my territory with a knight, threatening a fork to my king and rook on the next move. I castled preemptively to avoid it. "When you're always on defense, you let other people dictate the course of the game."

"A good defense can save your ass," I said, threatening his knight with a pawn.

"Not when you're too predictable," he said. He ignored my attack on his knight and brought a bishop out, threatening both my queen and the rook that was now ill-positioned behind it.

"Damn it," I muttered. I moved my queen. He took my rook, winning the trade. I knocked his bishop off the board with a little more vehemence than usual.

"Your head's not in the game." He casually moved his knight out of danger again. "You figure out who posted the video yet?"

"Someone out to do damage. I assume it was someone targeting Sierra. Enrique seems to think she was roofied."

"Nobody uses Rohypnol anymore. They changed it."

"Do I want to know how you would know this?" I began an attack up the side of the board to get at Frank's un-castled king.

"A guy I knew inside got busted for trying to spike girls' drinks at bars. He didn't realize the drug company had changed the recipe. Made it all fizzy and color-changing. Must not have tested it first. He wasn't the sharpest tool in the shed to begin with. The smart date rapers use ketamine now. Makes you all chilled out and relaxed. Plus it wipes your memory."

"'Smart date-rapers' is an oxymoron. But that would match what happened to Sierra. She didn't seem to remember anything."

My father shrugged. "Not surprised. Could have been any dirtbag at the bar. It's a regular party drug. Shit gets around."

"Enrique told me not to be surprised if the cops show up. So I have that to look forward to."

"That's bad form. In Union he'd get blackballed. One thing I can say about the guys in stir, we handled our own problems. You drag in the guards, that's a sign of weakness. The strongest tribe is strong from within. That's a law of nature. It's your move by the way."

But I wasn't thinking about the chess game anymore. I was still thinking about what he'd said about a party drug getting around.

I picked up my phone and looked through my email, then fired off one of my own. "How long do you think labs keep blood samples from drug tests around?" I asked.

"I don't know. A week? Why?"

"Because before you decided to expound on the benefits of prison values, you made me wonder if Sierra was the only one who could have ingested a party drug this week. And I'd like to find out."

TWENTY-NINE

COPIES

MONDAY WAS ROUGH.

I opened early and called a meeting first thing to address the proverbial elephant in the hangar.

Nearly every member of my crew had seen the original video posted to Sierra's account, with the exception of Elsbeth, whose algorithm evidently preferred to serve her videos of doctors popping pimples and extracting severe blockages of ear wax. But even she'd seen the subsequent video that Sierra had posted with the explanation.

The fact that the original video had been reversed wasn't common knowledge, though it did buy me some credit with my crew. Everyone except Tyson, who looked at me like I'd defiled a family member when he walked in. His expression had changed little with my explanation.

"Don't matter which way you play the damn video, it's still sus," he said. "People be sayin' I'm working for Rapers 'R Us up in here."

"I didn't assault Sierra," I said. "It's the truth, no matter what some internet mob says."

"You expect us to believe that part where your mouth was all over hers was really the back of yo head?" Tyson asked. "It's still susser than sus, bruh."

"Why not post the other version of the video online, and clear your name?" Rip asked.

"Because it reflects even worse on Sierra than the original did," I explained. "I'm not trying to sink her boat to float mine."

"You're getting the shit end of this stick," my father said. "Especially if all you did was put that girl's clothes back on."

"I'm confident that the issue will blow over," I said. "How long can this last? In the meantime, we have plenty of work to do."

"For *now* we do," Tyson said. "Till we're all cancelled."

The rest of my crew looked skeptical as well but did their best to buckle down.

It was a good idea in theory, but harder to implement. An hour later I made the mistake of looking up the mentions my business had online and found a slew of new social media comments, reposted videos, and even detailed information about where my business was located. Some irate busybody had gone through the effort of finding places where Archangel could be reviewed on Google and other sites and posted examples of what he suggested they write. And sure enough, my page now had a crop of fresh one-star reviews. The latest of which was titled, "Predator Pilot puts your safety last."

I scowled at the headline and closed the page.

They say if assholes could fly, the internet would be an airport.

But I had enough trouble at the actual airport.

The one person I hadn't heard from was Diana. She hadn't returned any of my calls or text messages, and I wasn't about to invade her office uninvited, so that conflict remained unresolved.

Even if she somehow figured out that the video of me and

Sierra had been posted in reverse, it didn't get me off the hook. Tyson was right. Sierra had still kissed me, and I didn't look like I hated it either direction you played it.

But I had another obligation to worry about for now. I took Murphy along on the golf cart and cruised out to Bud's hangar to meet Eric Feldman, and Bud's daughter, Amelia.

Despite sharing the famed aviatrix's name, Amelia brushed her short black hair behind her ear and confessed she knew next to nothing about airplanes.

"Dad tried to get me interested when I was younger, but I didn't have the right stomach for it. I get sick if I even read in the car. I wasn't much good in an airplane that goes upside down and twirls around."

"He was proud of you just the same," I said. "He talked about you all the time."

Amelia stared at the mass of Bud's belongings in the hangar and sighed. "My husband said he wants to do something with the motorcycle. Sell it, if I have anything to say about it. And maybe the toolboxes? But I don't know what to do with most of this stuff. Is it valuable?"

She seemed to be addressing me.

Eric was frowning. "It doesn't have to be Luke," he said. "There will be other folks happy to help too."

Amelia's eyes crinkled when she squinted. "Your email said Luke was the guy I wanted. What was it you called him? Most trustworthy guy on the airport?"

"Yeah. I guess I did say that," Eric murmured. "But honestly, everyone around here is nice. Luke's pretty busy and I don't want to take up a bunch of his time."

"I don't mind," I said. "Bud was a good friend."

It was evident Eric's opinion of me had diminished over the weekend.

"A woman called about that memorial they're planning here

for my dad. Something for the airport people and his local friends. As soon as that's done, I'll bring a truck. I know you said you have other tenants waiting."

"But no rush," Eric said. "Take all the time you need."

Staring at the the RV-8's open canopy had my mind turning again.

"Amelia, did you get to talk to your father in the days before he died?"

"Mostly texts unfortunately. We hadn't actually spoken on the phone lately and I wish we had. Life's just been so busy. He was planning to come up for a visit next month. Said he wanted to get out of the heat."

"He didn't mention he was having trouble with anyone at the airport, did he?"

"Not that I remember. But I have a hard time keeping all his airport friends straight."

"We're going to miss him," Eric said.

Amelia nodded. "There was one more thing I wanted to ask you though. Maybe you can help me." She pulled Bud's old leather satchel from her car. "This old flight bag was in his truck when they brought it to me. I wasn't sure if any of these papers were something important that belonged to anyone? For the government?" Several applicant files were inside.

"Most of the paperwork is filed online," I explained. "There's a good chance it's all just his backups. Bud tended to like to keep the hard copies."

"That sounds like him," she said. "You should see the newspaper articles he's got saved at home." She sighed.

"I can forward them by our local FAA inspector if you like. Just to be sure," I offered.

"Would you?" Amelia brightened. "That would be one less thing on my plate." She offered me the old satchel.

"You want to keep his flight bag?" I asked. "It's got a lot of character."

Amelia nodded, but gave a rueful smile. "I know it was sentimental to him, but I've got a whole houseful of his things to go through as it is. If you like it, keep it. Dad would be happy to see it go to someone who would use it."

"Thanks," I said. "That's kind."

"I appreciate you guys," Amelia said. "You've both been such a big help. This has all been overwhelming."

"Anything we can do," Eric said with a tight-lipped smile.

Amelia thanked him and left in her father's vehicle.

Eric waited with me after she was gone. His eyes lingered on Bud's flight bag.

"I appreciate you coming over here like we talked about," he said. "But I don't think you necessarily have to be the one to handle this. I'll get some of the line guys to come by and catalog the rest of Bud's things, make sure they're taken care of. I'm having the city guys change the lock later this morning. You won't need to get in anymore."

"Have you been spending a lot of time on social media lately, Eric?"

"I'm the FBO manager. Someone has to look out for this airport and its tenants. Because not everyone around here seems to know how to do it. Even the people you thought would know better."

And with that final jab, he walked to his crew car and drove off.

I was left standing in the heat with Murphy and my thoughts. Luckily, Murphy hadn't abandoned me yet. Because I was starting to think I was running out of friends.

THIRTY

POPPED

"WHAT'S ALL THIS?" Reese asked.

It was Tuesday morning. Day two of my airport life as pariah. But I was getting used to it. I'd barely come out of my office. The hangar was quieter today anyway. Fewer airplanes lined up outside. We were nearly finished with Sierra's Bonanza too, but I'd had no word from her. Just as well because I was caught up in my own thoughts. Right now I was focused on some copies of logbook entries I'd unstapled and had scattered around my desk.

"You look tired," Reese said. "Did you sleep here last night?"

"Stayed late, came in early. A lot on my mind."

"Do I need to get you a new scanner? What are we doing here?"

I patted the battered leather flight bag. "This all came out of here. Bud's last week of work. I'm the relay service to the feds just in case Bud didn't get any of this logged before he died."

Reese picked up a loose 8710 form. "Sierra Noble has a lot of flying hours."

"You're not kidding. Hey, did you ever find it weird that Nina flies Six Two Delta instead of the Bayside planes?"

"That app-based rental plane out on Charlie? Not really. It's cheaper, right?"

"But Nina works at Bayside. She gets an employee discount on their rentals. Why not use their aircraft?"

"Maybe they're always booked. They fly the pants off those planes."

"True. But what if there was another reason?"

"Okay. I'm interested. What've you got?"

I turned a loose-leaf page around so she could view it. It was one of the logbook copies that Bud had marked up. "I think she might have flown Six Two Delta because no one at Bayside would bother to know its schedule. Before Bud died, he requested photocopies of the entries in Nina's logbook so he could review her checkride prep and qualifications. He was kind of old school that way."

"That tracks. What are all the highlights?"

"I was wondering that too. At first it looks pretty normal. Just basic flight lessons. All stuff you'd expect to see in a student pilot's logbook."

Reese read. "Instrument approaches, night landings, a night cross-country flight to Punta Gorda. A Pilatus flight? That's fancy for a private pilot."

"Yeah. Looks like she scored a ride with Brooks the other day. But it's a pretty average training log until you look at all the lessons Bud noted. What do you see?"

Reese picked up another of the pages from my desk and compared it to the first. "The ones he's highlighted all happened in the same airplane. Six Two Delta."

"Exactly."

"So she flew a lot of her flights in a discounted app plane. I still don't see a smoking gun."

"I didn't either at first. But then I looked at the dates. Specifically, this one." I pointed.

"Cross-country flight to Crystal River on May 30th," Reese read. "Okay. What am I missing?"

"Nothing. Unless you also happen to have this." I reached into my desk drawer and pulled out a work order with a copy of an annual inspection log entry sticker attached to it.

"You signed off an annual inspection on Six Two Delta on June 1st?"

I flipped the entry up and showed the work order beneath. "I signed it off on the morning of the first, but we did the work starting on May 28th."

Reese read through the work order. "I remember this. One of the exhaust stacks was cracked, and we had to replace it." She looked at me. "So Nina couldn't have flown the plane to Crystal River on May 30th because it was here in the maintenance shop."

"Bingo. And her flight wasn't solo. Look who signed off her flight log as 'Dual given.' They even logged some of the flight in 'actual instrument' conditions." I pointed. The instructor's scribbled signature in Nina's logbook matched most of the others.

"Well, shit. That's falsification of records."

"An offense you can get your certificate revoked for if the feds catch wind of it."

"Chase Dempsey was helping Nina falsify her flight log? How many flights?"

"Hard to say. But you know who had a great view of the Taxiway Charlie ramp where Six Two Delta ties down?"

She thought for a moment. "Bud Truman."

"What if Bud had his own reason to suspect that plane wasn't flying on a date or time Nina said it was in her logbook? Maybe he was out sitting in his hangar one day when she claimed the plane was gone and he knew it wasn't. Or who knows? Maybe Chase and Nina accidentally wrote up a day when another student was having a checkride in it with Bud."

"Once might be written off as a mistake," Reese said. "But not a dozen flights."

"Nina told me Bud was angry with Chase for his poor instruction. But I think that was only a half-truth. I think Nina has been failing her checkrides because she doesn't have anywhere close to the hours she says she does. She could fudge all the numbers, but she couldn't fake the lack of skill."

"Wow. That's ballsy. Why would Chase help her lie? Why risk his license like that?"

"I'm curious about that too. Maybe he felt sorry for her. Or he knew she didn't have the money and still wanted her to succeed. Or they might actually be dating. They came out together Saturday night. Like they were a couple."

"Maybe she makes a convincing argument then," Reese mused.

"What's that supposed to mean?"

Reese shrugged. "Just rumors in the rumor mill. Apparently Chase boasted to Tyson and implied something a while back about him getting BJs from a girl while flying. Never said anything about it being Nina, but he never said it wasn't her either."

"B-J, ew gross. Why was Chase telling Tyson this? And how did you hear about it?"

"Tyson tells me all kinds of things. Especially if it's about girls."

"Where was I for this conversation?"

"It's not all about you, man. And you're the boss. Ty's not gonna tell you that stuff. You gotta let the rest of the crew bond in our own ways."

"Okay. Fair. But still unprofessional of Chase to bring it up."

"Are you mad because no one ever offered you a BJ while flying or because they have and you don't want to talk about it?"

I shifted in my seat. "Maybe we should all mind our own business."

Reese shrugged, but she had a smirk on her face.

"In any event, I want to have an in-depth discussion with Chase when I see him," I said. "I'll add this to my list of gripes about his conduct."

"Even if Chase found out that Bud knew any of this, you really think that could have been motive for murder?"

"Some pilots are over a hundred K in debt by the time they land their first right seat gig in a commuter airliner. It's the captain's chair or bust. Literally. If someone came along and threatened to pull your plug right before you landed your first commercial gig? How desperate would that make you?"

"You know if you confront him with this, he can just lie," Reese said.

"We'll see." I swiveled my chair around to face my computer. "Bud was suspicious enough that he planned for this to go to Mike Gonzalez at the FSDO. So I'm going to pass it along, see if they have something to say about—."

My office phone rang, cutting me off. I was tempted to let it go to voicemail until I saw the caller ID name. "Hang on. I gotta grab this." I picked up.

A woman's voice spoke in my ear. "Hello, this is Doctor Patel, medical review officer from LabStar Medical. May I speak with a Mr. Luke Angel?"

"Speaking."

"Mr. Angel, we received your request for an extended panel on Mr. Thomas Wilson, and the test came back with a positive result. I've just emailed your employer portal with details if you'd like to discuss it."

"Okay, wow. Hang tight."

I verified I had a new email in my inbox with a subject line that read: Confidential Under 49 CFR Part 40. I clicked on the email and was directed to log in to my employer health portal, where a message was waiting for me.

The subject read: Employer Copy. Confidential: Verified positive result for extended panel for Tom Wilson.

"Are you all right?" Reese asked. "You just went kinda pale."

"Uh, yeah." I covered the microphone on the phone. "I just need a minute. I'll fill you in later on what happens with . . . that other stuff."

"Right." Reese's eyes lingered on me a moment longer as she slid toward to the door. "You sure you're all good?"

"Totally."

She nodded and walked out of the office.

Only I wasn't all good. Because according to the email, Rip's extended drug panel had just tested positive for ketamine.

RIP HAD a smile on his face when he came up to my office. That made it worse when I delivered the news.

"This is bullshit, man! I already passed that drug test."

"The first time they didn't test for ketamine. This one did."

"You know I don't do any drugs. Just ask your dad."

Relying on Frank Angel for anything wasn't a strong defense. But it didn't matter whether I believed him.

"I have to suspend you indefinitely from maintenance duties," I explained. "And you'll be grounded from flying biplane rides too, unfortunately. Any duties that are drug-test limited."

"Are you kidding me? I've got flights booked all week. Nelson's kid ran him over with their jet ski trailer and his foot's in a boot. I'm the only pilot we've got!"

"You're not suspended from work entirely. You'll still get a paycheck. We can put you on non-maintenance duties for the time being until we sort this out."

"What? Scrubbing the toilets? This is absolute horseshit, man. I didn't jump out of an airplane on goddamn ketamine!" He slammed the office door so hard on his way out that Blackjack jolted from where she'd been sleeping on my credenza and scattered a stack of AOPA magazines during her frenzied sprint up the bookshelf. When she'd looked around from the top shelf and her fur settled back into place, she switched quickly to cleaning herself, pretending nothing had happened.

I stared at the door Rip had nearly knocked from its hinges and sighed.

The situation didn't get any better when I got the call from Mike Gonzalez. I'd been mandated to report the drug violation immediately, and he called back to verify that I'd pulled Rip from maintenance duties. The conversation took up so much focus that I didn't have a chance to broach the subject of Bud and the logbook copies.

He sounded like he had enough on his plate. Some of it new.

"Do you know how many calls we've had from people yesterday about you?" Mike asked. "I fielded three myself. Not counting anyone else in the office who had to bother with it."

"All from that Sierra Noble boat video? People called the FSDO?"

"I don't know what your relationship is with the Noble girl, but you really stepped in it with her fans. And a lot of them are pilots. They'd like to see your certificates revoked. Not that it works that way. But still."

"I didn't take advantage of that girl, Mike. The video was edited to play in reverse."

"It's none of my business. And I believe you. But not everyone in the office knows you like I do. Your reputation is currently in the shitter."

"What happened to me being the local airport hero? That faded fast. Am I still on your wish list for an examiner slot?"

"That ship has probably sailed."

Damn.

I thought about bringing up Nina's pilot logbook then as a

way to change the subject. But my father's words rang in my ears. "The strongest tribe is strong from within." Albert Whitted Airport had held off its myriad foes for a hundred years. If that wasn't a sign of a powerful tribe, what was? I'd look into the Nina thing on my own and not bother Mike with it just yet.

I let him go and hung up the phone.

The examiner thing rattled me though. Was one internet video all it took to ruin a person's reputation?

Then again, Sierra Noble was probably wondering the same thing. I considered calling her. Asking how she was doing. But that was probably a bad idea.

Either way, I was tired of hiding in my office waiting for the storm to blow over. I stood and gathered my keys and sunglasses. It was time to get out of here.

I slipped down the stairs and out to my golf cart.

Humidity sat on the field like a wet blanket, thick and muggy. The air resisted movement. No breeze. Even my hangar fans strained to move it.

My brain felt just as muggy and muddled. Murphy lay unmoving on the concrete near the break area. Even the promise of a golf cart ride couldn't roust him today. But I forged out into the baking sunlight anyway.

My chest beaded sweat by the time I reached the flight school. Nina Yee sat barricaded behind the office counter. Our eyes met as I walked into the welcome blast of A/C and she held my gaze till I reached her.

I laid the stapled copies of her logbook entries on the counter, slid them toward her.

"Seems these are yours," I said. "At least some of them."

Nina's eyes rested on the stapled sheets for a moment, but then she refocused on me. "Thanks," she replied. "But I have the originals in my logbook." She dragged the copies off the counter and shoved them directly into the trash.

"You've done some interesting flights. How's Six Two Delta been treating you?"

"Fine."

"You run into any trouble with vapor lock with that engine out in the heat? Because of the fuel injection?"

"Um. No?"

"That's good. Probably because you do most of your flights after work when it's cooler?"

Her brow furrowed. "Wait, I thought it had a carburetor. Not fuel injection."

I snapped my fingers. "You're right. Glad you've been studying. I'm getting it mixed up with a different plane. I do that all the time." I smacked a palm off my forehead. "And I should know better. I just did the annual on Six Two Delta at the end of May. Right after Memorial Day."

"Right. Well, anyway. You need anything else?"

"Chase around?"

"He's not in."

"Pity. For a flight instructor, he doesn't seem to do that much actual instruction anymore, does he?"

Her eyes narrowed. "He flies a lot at night too. Because of the heat."

"Makes sense. You two have that in common. According to your logbook."

She opened her mouth to say something, but shut it again.

"Tell him I'm looking for him. When you see him."

"He's pretty busy," she said.

"Tell him it's important," I said. "You might even say 'life and death.' Depending on how you interpret that sort of thing."

She didn't respond. She just stared at me.

"I'll leave you to it," I said. "I've got work to do too. These planes aren't going to magically fix themselves, are they?" I gave her a smile. "Though it would be nice, huh?" I waved an imaginary wand and pretended to sign my name in the air and punctuate it. "Poof. Done. Signed off." I walked to the door and pushed it open. "You have a good day now."

Nina hadn't moved. But by the time I was back on my golf cart and headed toward the Terminal, I was confident she'd be on her phone.

And that was just what I wanted.

THIRTY-TWO
COOLER

CHASE WASN'T at the terminal when I looked for him. And his old truck never showed in the flight school parking lot that afternoon. By closing time, Sierra Noble's annual inspection on her Bonanza was complete. I needed to call her and let her know, but put off the call till everyone else had gone home. Finally, I mustered the willpower and dialed. Thankfully, it went to voicemail. I gave her the total for the bill, a brief rundown of issues we'd addressed, and told her to come by and settle up whenever she had time. Before I hung up, I had a temptation to bring up the night on the boat. Some sort of apology? But I kept it professional instead and just hung up.

Coward.

But I was less angry at myself than I was at whoever had gotten us into this mess.

Without much thought, I found myself picking up my cell phone and automatically opening the app for my social media profile. Ending up there was like flying on auto-pilot lately. The warm glow of people living their best lives. The fervor had slowed down on my page. I guess there were only so many nasty comments you could make on one cat photo.

But I'd been mentioned numerous times on Sierra's profile. I clicked the notification and found myself in the comments section of the video she'd posted of me saving Hank and Rip during the skydive. It had already been viral before, but a new crop of frenzied comments had sent views into the stratosphere.

Most of the original comments praising my heroics had survived but were now gathering their own subthreads of comments regarding the deleted boat video. Rabid Sierra fans lashed out at anyone who made positive comments about the skydive save, spilling the proverbial "tea" in the subthreads about what a nefarious scumbag I was. A few guys had stuck up for me, but not in ways I wanted. Their comments tore down Sierra and blamed the entire situation on her, labeling her an attention-seeking fraud and worse names. I was reminded of Sierra's comments on the boat. "When was the last time someone called you a skank, but then also called you a tease?"

There was even a theory being floated that I'd deliberately sabotaged Rip and Hank's chute to make myself look like a hero. Several people had latched onto that as fact.

Views were in the hundreds of thousands. Good Lord.

My head began to spiral, my mood in a nosedive with it.

Finally, I got out of the comments section and just watched the video again. The group of us climbing aboard. The cheers celebrating Hank, the jump and free fall, then the dramatic moment when I pulled Rip's chute. Rip and Hank on the ground, shaky but alive.

It was good to remind myself of the truth. I'd saved the lives of two friends that day, no matter what the internet thought.

The video automatically replayed. Climb aboard. Cheers. Jump. Fall. Save.

Cheers. Jump. Fall.

Cheers.

I paused the video there. My finger on the screen. The bright red of Rip's energy drink standing out among the others.

Had someone used the energy drink to drug Rip with ketamine? But how did they know it would end up being him that drank it and not someone else?

I recalled how Chase had opened the cooler. Offered it to Hank and Rip first. The birthday boy and his jump instructor.

I stood up and walked downstairs, Murphy at my heels, and headed for the break area. I pulled open the door to the refrigerator. The shelves were packed with all manner of treats like brownies and cinnamon rolls plus a few maintenance items that required refrigeration. In the door sat a row of red energy drinks. A line of blue painter's tape along the shelf was labeled in faded Sharpie. "Rip's stuff. Don't touch."

And unlike many energy drinks, Rip's preferred brand came in a plastic bottle with a twist-off cap. It had a tamper evident seal. But at altitude, with the engine noise and vibration to account for, was it likely he would have noticed that the cap had been previously opened? Someone may have banked on not.

We all knew Rip preferred those drinks. And anyone who opened the hangar fridge would know too. But that still narrowed things down, didn't it?

My mind rewound. Chase Dempsey lugging the cooler to the plane.

"You must be thirsty," I'd said.

I locked up the hangar and hoisted Murphy into my Jeep. We left the parking lot and drove out to Fourth Street and south.

Chase Dempsey rented in Old Southeast. I'd never been invited to his home, but I'd been past it, tucked away behind a revered Old Florida restaurant called The Chattaway. I parked in The Chattaway's lot and the flip-flops I'd changed into crunched coquina shells as I walked out to the road. His place was fenced in. A rundown bungalow survivor, not yet razed in the rampant gentrification of the neighborhood. The sparse lawn showcased more weeds than grass. Those had proliferated with the summer rains.

The rusty chain-link gate squealed as I swung it open. A sticky-sweet smell of pot hung in the air, wafting from a neighboring porch. The neighbor gave a lethargic nod. I rapped on the battered screen door of the bungalow. The inner door was open, allowing a view into a cluttered living area. From somewhere inside, a wall unit A/C rattled, straining to fend off the oppressive heat. Harder with the front door hanging open. I waited.

After thirty seconds, I knocked again. Nothing stirred. There was background noise coming from somewhere. A low musical melody I didn't recognize, but it repeated itself after a short while. Reminded me of the intro menu on a DVD. Did anyone still watch those? Maybe it was a video game.

I pounded on the doorframe one last time. "Chase? You in there?" Murphy whined.

"I think he went out!"

The pot-smoking neighbor had yelled from next door.

"He ain't there," the guy added.

"Thanks!" I gave the guy a wave. "You know where he went?"

All I got was a shrug in reply.

There was a ball of crumpled up paper resting on the porch beside a potted plant that had also recently been used as an ashtray. It looked like someone had tossed the wad of paper at the planter and missed. I stepped over and picked it up in case it was some kind of note. But the City of St. Petersburg's seal on top gave away the origin.

It was an eviction notice. Didn't appear to be the first.

I read the notice, then crumpled it again and dropped it back where I'd found it.

No wonder Chase wanted to move on to the next gig so badly. His crash pad was getting bulldozed. Likely making room for another millionaire New Yorker who'd build a monstrosity on the lot and let the place sit vacant half the year.

The screen door wasn't latched. I could walk in and make sure he wasn't there. But I held myself in check, especially with a neighbor watching and Murphy in tow. I walked over to The Chattaway instead, biding my time. I could watch the front of Chase's place from there, if someone came or went. With the door hanging open, I figured he wouldn't be long. Ran to a corner store, perhaps?

Murphy sniffed the vintage pink bathtub planters the restaurant had scattered around the property as decoration. The place was about as Old Florida as Old Florida got. Outdoor, cash only, and steaming hot. Only the most seasoned locals dared the summer off-season here. And they did it with damp shirts and parked in front of a fan. But the food was decent and the beer was cold. A determined young guitar player was even setting up to battle the evening's mosquitoes via song. So I headed for the bar and ordered a Corona and a basket of jalapeño poppers.

I regretted sitting down almost immediately because no sooner had I settled onto a stool when a man on the far side of the bar stood up and stormed his way over.

Nelson Vargas could move quickly even with a limp. Rip hadn't been lying about the boot. It was a clunky thing that Nelson dragged around the corner of the bar. Murphy backed away and gave the man room.

"What the hell are you doing to Rip with this drug test, man?" Nelson said, uncomfortably loud. He held a beer in his hand that I guessed wasn't his first. "You trying to put us out of business?"

"You come in hot, don't you?" I asked. "How are you, Nelson?"

People around the bar had turned to watch.

"I've got a business to run!" Nelson spouted. "How do you expect me to pay my hangar rent if you take my best pilot out of commission for some bullshit drug bust?"

"You know the drug test rules the same as I do, Nelson."

"He already passed that drug test, man. What the hell are you doing sending it back for more? What kind of asshole move is that? You trying to ruin the man? Lord knows he's got enough on his plate taking in your jailbird dad."

I sighed.

"Rip's my best friend. I've known him twenty years," Nelson continued. "If you think I'm letting you kick him around like this, you've got another thing coming."

"We'll get it sorted out," I said.

"*You're* gonna get it sorted out. And you're gonna make my business right in the meantime."

"I know it's a hassle to have to cancel rides for customers. We'll get Rip back in the air as soon as we can."

"Cancel? What the hell are you talking about? I'm not cancelling shit. You're gonna fly 'em."

I frowned. "I've got my own business to run, Nelson."

"And you're the only pilot left on my company drug program," Nelson said. "I'm not going to tell the customers that our mechanic is the one flying them around, but what other option do I have? You're it. If you want to keep doing our maintenance, you'd better keep our business in the air. You hear me?"

I opened my mouth to object, but then closed it again. He was right. Of the mechanics in my shop listed on his drug program, I was the only pilot with the tailwheel hours needed to satisfy his insurance requirements. The odds of finding another qualified pilot on short notice and also getting them on the drug program were next to nil.

"I can fill in for a few days," I said. "Just until you find another pilot or get your foot out of that boot. But don't book any more flights than you already have on the schedule."

"I'll book what I have to," Nelson retorted. "Because someone around here has to have a level head for business. You sure as hell don't."

He stormed back to his side of the bar, muttering a litany of gripes on the way.

My jalapeño poppers showed up flaming hot, and even the beer didn't help to cool me down much after the confrontation.

Looked like I'd be flying part of the coming week upside down. That seemed to fit. The rest of my life was upside down anyway. And I was losing sight of where I was even headed.

I sipped my beer and mulled that ominous thought.

Failure to keep your bearings in flight never boded well for a pilot's longevity.

Usually, it was the fastest way to the scene of the crash.

CHASE DEMPSEY never showed back up at his house. The Chattaway regulars had been good company, but my surveillance had been a bust. The screen door was still open at Chase's place when I drove by, but no Chase. I noted his truck in the terminal parking lot the next day, however.

"I think he might be flying in the Pilatus?" the girl behind the fueling desk told me. "Brooks was here this morning. They fly together a lot these days."

"Any idea where they flew to?"

She shook her head. "You could look it up though."

And I did. When I entered the plane's registration number into FlightAware, the route showed they'd gone up to Asheville again. Already landed.

Work at Hangar 4 was light today, and while my crew didn't look especially thrilled about the implications of the slowdown, I was okay not being needed. The looks I was getting from Tyson and Rip were icy. Especially when it became known that I was headed to the Stearman hangar to fill in for Rip on the flights he was scheduled to be flying today.

"You're straight-up frontstabbing our boy," Tyson said. "That's some cold-ass work."

"It's temporary," I said. "Helping them out."

"Band-aids don't fix bullet holes, man."

I paused. "Are you quoting Taylor Swift lyrics? Is that what you've been listening to with those headphones on?"

"What? Girl writes some deep tracks."

"I'm going to go fly. Reese is in charge till I'm back."

"Aight. I guess even a sinking ship needs a captain."

And with that cheery thought, I rode out to Skyline Boulevard and opened up the Stearman hangar. The preflight inspection didn't take long. I ran the prop through by hand a few times to check for hydraulic lock on the cylinders, sumped the fuel, and checked the oil. In a matter of minutes, I had the plane pulled out and was priming for start. Despite being old and large, the plane was simple in its design—a flying machine built in an era of no frills—with a cockpit you could theoretically bail out of if things went south. But there were scant few issues that would get me out of the airplane unless the wings were on fire. And even then, I'd have my reservations about jumping. I'd had enough of skydiving lately.

At the prompting of the starter, the Stearman's R-670 Continental engine awoke with an irritated grumble, but then evened out to a measured purr. The seven cylinders set up a pleasing cadence as I released the brakes and got rolling. One flaw in the design of the early Boeing aircraft was visibility. Manning the controls from the rear cockpit of the old trainer meant you couldn't see much of anything ahead of the aircraft. The solution was taxiing in a fishtail motion, weaving down the taxiways like a drunk sailor on a boardwalk.

I contacted ground control and crossed to the north side of Runway 7 to the terminal ramp. There I revved the engine momentarily to clear the spark plugs and shut down. My first eager passenger of the day was waiting for me inside. His name was Lenny and his wife had bought him the ride for his birthday. Lenny had just turned sixty and was a vintage car guy usually but loved the sight of airplanes flying overhead. I shepherded him to the aircraft with a giddy smile on his face. His wife, Donna, followed behind with a camera and the bundle of worries she was trying hard not to let show. I reassured her, touting the aircraft's safety record and mentioning it was going to be a guaranteed hit of a gift.

I wasn't wrong. Getting Lenny in the plane was a flexibility test for the big guy, but once he was in, he got settled okay. They'd decided to forgo aerobatics for this ride. "His tummy isn't the strongest," Donna whispered. And since we weren't wearing chutes I got to skip the briefing on what to do in the unlikely event we'd have to bail out. Plus, I knew the only way I'd get Lenny's bulk out of that cockpit midair would have been to roll the plane upside down and shake him.

A problem we weren't going to encounter today.

The flight was a leisurely half hour, over the Skyway bridge, out to the beach for a wave at the sunbathers, then up to altitude for some gentle turns and a chance for Lenny to try his hand at flying. He did a fair job at the controls and, with a little praise from me, was eager to fly us all the way back to the airport. He did so until I took the controls for the landing. When Lenny heaved himself out of the plane back on the ramp, he was positively beaming. Donna glowed too, elated to have her husband safely back on the ground and soaking up the affection when he gave her a big squeeze and a sloppy kiss. They were so pleased they barely registered the pain of paying for the ride, and Donna listened patiently as Lenny regaled her with the story of his aeronautical prowess.

My next ride was already there, a couple from Ottawa, lingering nervously nearby. I greeted them and was about to start the entire process over again when my vision snagged on the figure of Sierra Noble blowing through the terminal doors. She strode right up to me and fixed me with her sharp blue eyes. "We need to talk." Her gaze took in Lenny, Donna, and the couple from Ottawa, and added, "We'll do it in the plane."

I'd been standing there with a parachute draped over each arm, but she snatched one from me and marched out to the ramp with it.

I turned to the couple from Ottawa and apologized. "Sorry. Forgot I had one more quick one ahead of you guys. I promise it won't take long."

"Oh, no problem at all!" the woman said, sounding relieved. "We'll just wait right here. You take your time, dear."

God bless the Canadians.

Sierra suffered none of Lenny's agility issues. Neither did she need a briefing on how to use a parachute. By the time I made it outside, she had clipped in and settled into the front cockpit. I cruised by the front of the plane and gave the engine another quick shot of fuel for the primer, then climbed up onto the wing beside Sierra.

"I doubt anyone can hear us out here."

She glanced over at the terminal building and up to the railing of the Hangar Restaurant with its array of breakfast patrons. "We'll talk in the air." She scanned the wings. "Are there any cameras on this plane?"

"Not today."

"Good."

So I took her up. I flew due west this time, direct to the beach and up to altitude. The steady throbbing of the radial engine and the wind whipping past the flying wires made for a soothing background noise, but I had a feeling what was coming wasn't going to be easy listening. Still, the division of the seating gave us greater physical separation than in most aircraft, Sierra with her back to me, her face invisible other than a reflection in a small mirror on the upper wing. A cockpit confessional. Though I couldn't tell which of us might be dealing out absolution.

At twenty-five hundred feet, I did a couple of Cuban eights, still waiting for Sierra to speak. Then I pitched down, gaining speed, hit 120 MPH and pitched up, stick all the way in my lap and we went up, up, and over, the world going inverted, sky replacing sea, sea for sky. Sierra's hair lofted in the breeze at the top as we went momentarily weightless. We were both facing up, but up was down—watching the planet slide beneath us. Then gravity reclaimed us and we continued our arc, straight down, then arrested our descent, my hand pulling back on the throttle to keep the engine from redlining. We bottomed out in a smooth finish, the g-forces easy to manage in this old bird.

As I leveled the wings on the horizon again, Sierra finally reached for the intercom button, stabbing it with a finger.

"Mind if I take it for a few?"

"Your airplane."

She repeated my process, gaining speed in a dive, full throttle, then up. Up and over. Weightless. Then speeding earthward again. But this time at the bottom of the loop she kept the velocity going, pitching up above the horizon again as she threw the stick left. I flipped the smoke on and it shot out the right side of the plane in our slipstream. We rolled. Once again the world slipped out from under us, aircraft inverted, like we could unload whatever tension rested between us if we just spent enough time upside down.

Sierra completed the roll, gained speed in another dive and pitched upward again, climbing, climbing, looping once more, the smoke trail painting a giant circle in the sky behind us. We roared back down from the heights.

Finally she leveled the wings again. I flipped the smoke switch off.

I caught a flicker of a smile on her face as she turned to note the trail we'd painted in the sky behind us. Maybe we'd managed to burn off some of the tension with it.

Sierra reached for the intercom.

"I saw the whole video from that night. Played in the proper direction. Whoever edited it, deleted the original, but they didn't delete it from the trash on my phone."

I waited for the rest.

"So I know you didn't instigate whatever happened. And I'm sorry I implied you did."

It was hard to tell with the wind noise and the sliver of her reflection that I could see in the mirror, but it seemed like her voice had shaken some while speaking.

I keyed the intercom switch on the control stick. "Nothing else happened that night. You weren't . . . tampered with."

"I know."

She leaned her head back and stared skyward, then pressed the intercom again. "So I guess what we need to know now. . . is whether whoever made that video that night was doing it to hurt me, or you. Because as much as this might sound strange to say, if it was to hurt me, they could have done a lot worse."

I tried to imagine what she'd been through in the last couple of days. The embarrassment, the humiliation. The indignity of deciphering what had been done to her. Piecing together physical signs and wondering if she'd been violated in ways she couldn't recall. It wasn't lost on me how much it had taken her to be here, to be having this conversation.

I keyed the intercom again. "The only reason I'm flying today is because Rip Wilson failed a drug panel for ketamine."

Her eyes found mine in the mirror. "That's an awfully big coincidence," she said. "Because my tox screening came back with the same thing."

I wasn't shocked.

I keyed the mic once more. "When we get back on the ground, I think we might have a lot more to talk about."

THIRTY-FOUR

TEAM UP

ONE BELATED flight with Canadians later, I put the Stearman back in its hangar.

I picked up Murphy at Hangar 4 and golf-carted my way to The Tavern at Bayboro, a wood-decked restaurant tucked into the neighboring University of Florida's St. Pete campus, and a common haunt for airport employees.

Sierra Noble's youthful appearance blended in well among the student population. If any of the other patrons recognized her as an internet celebrity, it didn't show. The ones not actively in conversation were too busy scrolling their phones to look up and notice us anyway.

I ordered myself an iced tea and a grouper sandwich and met Sierra on the outside deck to talk while I waited for it.

"Enrique still doesn't want me talking to you," she said. "My mother either. But I'm feeling pretty over having my life dictated to me. If there's one silver lining to this whole thing, it's that I don't have to worry about wrecking my brand anymore. The worst has already happened."

"I've seen the online backlash," I said. "It's harsh. I underestimated what you were trying to avoid there."

She brushed a few crumbs from someone else's lunch off our table. "I've already lost two channel sponsorships. They were very polite about it. No one directly came out and called me names. But our brands are evidently 'no longer aligned.'"

"I'm sorry to hear that."

"It's okay. At least they don't come repo the equipment from my plane. *That*, I would cry about."

"I'm sure you'll find new sponsors."

"Maybe. It's fine. It's liberating in a lot of ways. Playing a role all the time is exhausting. Keeping up an image that won't offend anyone is nearly impossible to maintain forever. You end up a mannequin. It took this happening to make me realize just how much it's been limiting me."

"So from here you're headed straight for the nudist colony?"

She laughed. "I don't know what I'm doing. I just know it won't be directed by Veronica Noble anymore. You know what her biggest concern was?"

I waited.

"She worried it was going to make me undesirable to quality men. As if that should be my main concern."

"She's old-fashioned."

"That's a kinder word than I'd use. She's been trying to set me up with Jason Brooks lately. She thinks I've ruined my chances now."

"Have you two dated?"

"No. Not really. He's known my mother awhile. He asked me to dinner that day we flew to Jacksonville together. But I don't know. He's definitely a good-looking guy. I love that he volunteers and does charity work. He's super smart. His plane is *gorgeous*. And my viewers all swooned over him in the seaplane video. They've already shipped us together."

"A long list of pros. I can see why your mom likes him."

"Ugh. She liked his dad. He was this bigshot up in New York that always fawned over her. Dad loathed him, though. I think he might have had a few words to say about me dating Brooks."

"We aren't all doomed to become our parents," I said.

Sierra nodded. "Right. Let's hope not." She sized me up. "I bet my dad would have loved meeting you, though. You remind me of him in some ways."

"Equally obsessed with airplanes?" I offered.

"You attract good people," she said. "Dad used to have this saying. He had a lot of sayings, actually, but one was, 'You never judge a man by the balance in his bank account. You judge him by the quality of his friends.'"

"Wise words."

"Especially from a hedge fund manager," she said.

"Sounds like I would have liked your dad."

"Yeah. Anyway. The whole flight back from Jacksonville, I was thinking how Brooks had just been out with whatsherface that morning. Katerina?"

"Katya."

"Right. What ever happened to her?"

I shrugged.

"I don't think I want to be the next Katya. I made Brooks drop me back in Clearwater at my car and haven't committed to anything. That was the afternoon after the video shoot."

"I remember. It was the same day Bud died."

She gave a somber nod at that. "I'm sad about Bud. He seemed so healthy during our checkride. I can't believe he only had a couple of days left."

I sipped my iced tea and set it back down. "About that. I have a theory. And I've only told a couple of people so far. Reese and the Saint Pete police."

Sierra leaned forward. "About Bud?"

Our lunch arrived midway through my explanation, and I had to pause briefly, but I got out all of what I'd found regarding the nitrogen cylinder and the fact that Chase Dempsey had doctored Nina's logbook for her checkrides.

"That's insane," Sierra replied, her mouth open in disbelief. "Holy shit. You think Chase could have killed Bud to keep it quiet?"

"It sounds wild when I hear it out loud," I replied. "But it's a possibility."

"What did the police say?"

I recounted my ordeal with explaining the evidence to the local sergeant. "They said they'd have someone from the detective bureau follow up, but I'm still waiting. Unless I come up with more proof, Bud's case is staying closed."

"Do you think Nina knows?"

"Whether Chase killed Bud? I'm not sure."

Sierra dug a fork into her blackened chicken salad and dangled a chunk of lettuce over her plate. "He seemed off lately. Chase. Not that I knew him well to begin with. But that morning aboard *Tropic Angel*, he seemed on edge." She took a bite and chewed. "But if he was covering up something Bud knew about the logbooks, what would that have to do with the skydive we did for Hank's birthday? You said Rip tested positive for ketamine too. You think it's related?"

"That I don't know. I know Chase carried a cooler full of drinks onto that plane. But I can't think of one good reason why anyone would want to hurt Rip."

"Or Hank?" she asked.

"Or you," I added.

"Or you," she said in reply.

If it was all tied together, I still couldn't see the knot at the center that connected it. I focused on my sandwich instead.

"What are you going to do?" she asked. "Confront Chase?"

"That's proving harder than I expected." I wiped a dab of tartar sauce from my lips with the back of my knuckle. "I think he's dodging me."

"He came out for me," she mused between bites of salad. "When I invited him out Saturday night. You predicted that he'd show, and he did. Maybe he'd do it again."

"Another night out?"

"I don't know. But I'll think of something. And I'll call Diana too, by the way. Help you clear things up between you two. She should know what really happened that night. It was my fault and she should know it."

"Not yet," I said.

"What? Why?"

"Because whoever set us up went to a lot of effort to get us mad at each other. And as far as they know, it worked. It certainly looks that way online."

"But I can post another video of us together as friends. It'll fix that."

"I don't want you to. Because this works better if whoever set us up still thinks we're enemies."

"A fake-out?"

"Right. A ruse. If we can get them to think what they did is still working, their guard won't be up. If anything, we'll elevate the situation and make it worse. Stir up more drama online."

"Jesus. Really?"

"You said it yourself, the worst has already happened, right?"

"You might make me rethink that." She brushed a strand of hair behind her ear. But her eyes were bright—eager. "What do you want me to do? Not gonna lie, I'm a pretty good actress. You want drama, I can make it."

"We want Chase to talk, right? I haven't been able to nail him down in person, but we know he watches your social media posts. He evidently knows he needs to dodge me, but he doesn't know what you know. So you'll post something he can't ignore. A reason he has to reach out."

"What on earth can I say that will force him to talk to me?"

I shrugged. "You're the social media expert. What do you do when you want to hook a viewer so well they've got no choice but to watch? You have that trick down yet?"

Sierra thought for just a moment, then the corners of her mouth curved up into a smile. "Actually. I know just the thing. And if I'm right, it's going to be my most viewed video yet."

TYSON WALKED over to me at the end of the day with his phone in his hand. "Uh, Bossman? You might want to see this."

He showed me a social media post with a timer ticking down. Sierra Noble was going live tonight. A tell-all. The description on the video read: "Secrets and Lies. The Truth about Me. And Him. And it's not who you think."

It already sported hundreds of "Wow" emojis.

The photo slideshow that accompanied the post was the most significant. A still shot of the cheers from the Skydive, a photo of Sierra with Bud Truman after her checkride, and another still shot from the now-deleted boat video that showed Sierra and me in profile in the darkness. The fourth and final image, however, was of the *Tropic Angel* seaplane video. The entire group of us standing atop the wings in bathing suits. It was slightly off-center. The focus of the shot seemed to be moved to the right. Tyson hadn't made it in the shot at all. Only his left arm was still visible. And in the new center of the shot was Chase Dempsey and Nina Yee.

How the photos were connected was left vague, as was who the "Him" was she was referencing. But I smiled when I saw it.

"This a good thing or a bad thing for you?" Tyson asked.

"We'll find out. I'm hoping good."

"Then how come I got deleted from the picture, bruh?"

"Protecting the innocent."

"Aw, man. Innocent? That's the worst rep I can get, dude. This shit's unfair."

Sierra had set the timer on her social media post for 9pm. But I got a call at quarter till seven. Sierra on the phone.

"I've got a bite."

"Chase?"

"Brooks called me, told me Chase called him and is freaking out. Wants to talk. Evidently, he wants to see me in person."

"Where is he?"

"Saint Augustine."

"Fly there in your Bonanza?"

"Brooks says we can take his company Pilatus. He has a passenger to pick up at Jacksonville Exec tomorrow morning anyway."

"He's hoping you'll spend the night?"

"I don't know. Probably. But I was thinking you could follow in my plane and pick me up."

"That'll be tough because I'm coming with you. There's no way I'm letting you meet Chase alone."

"Chase won't try to hurt me with Brooks there."

"I'll ride along anyway. We won't tell anyone I'm coming. If we get what we want, I'll have someone from my crew fly up and get us."

She sounded skeptical, but she agreed. "We should get going. The Pilatus is at PIE."

"I'll meet you there."

I hung up the phone and gathered my keys from the hook in

the galley, but took another detour. I unlocked the top drawer of the boat's navigation console and extracted my Sig-Sauer P365. I checked the load, pocketed a spare mag, and clipped the appendix holster inside the waist of my pants.

The St. Pete–Clearwater International Airport wasn't a far drive. Close enough that I was doubtful even taking a plane could get me there faster. So I took the Jeep for a windy ride up I-275 to Roosevelt and then the long loop of Fairchild Drive around the far side of the airport to the Sheltair Aviation Building. The ramp here was far enough from the main terminal for privacy and the preferred location for the jet-setter crowd.

Sierra met me in the parking lot of the FBO and we walked to the corporate hangars together. Brooks was finishing a preflight on a PC-12 when we found him.

"Ah. I wondered if you might bring someone else along," he said to Sierra. "But this is a surprise." He held out a hand to me. "Luke. You've been all over my newsfeed lately. Can't say it's been flattering."

I took his offered hand and shook it. "Shouldn't believe everything you see on the internet."

"Well, you know me. I'm only on there to post dog videos."

"Prince of Puppies."

"The girls do love 'em. You should try it sometime. Though you might need to post a hell of a lot of puppy videos to turn your rep around. You doing okay? Heard business was slowing down. I can bring this Pilatus fleet by for their compressor washes if it helps."

"Thanks, but we'll manage."

"All aboard then," he said, and gestured to the boarding stairs.

We climbed into the PC-12 and Brooks latched the cabin door behind us.

"No jet tonight?" I asked as I took a seat.

"Sometimes even I have to make do," he replied, and stooped

as he showed us the amenities. "You guys want sodas or beers or anything, help yourselves to the cooler. The company won't miss them. But I'd try not to drink too much. The lav on this thing is super cramped. I try not to use it."

"We'll be fine," I said. "What else have you heard from Chase?"

"He's dying to talk to Sierra. I know that much." He turned to her. "That video countdown you posted has him freaking out. What are you planning to say tonight?"

"You'll have to find out at nine," Sierra replied.

Brooks checked his watch. "All right, clock's ticking then. Make yourselves comfortable. I'll have you over there in no time."

Brooks slid up to the flight deck and began his starting checklist. Sierra took the sleekly upholstered seat next to mine, and soon enough we were moving. We watched out the window as the illuminated lights of the taxiway glided past.

In a matter of minutes we were airborne, blasting off from Runway 18. Brooks took the PC-12 up through Tampa's airspace and turned us northeast. We were perhaps twenty minutes into the flight when Sierra nudged my arm.

"Should we run through how this is going to go when we get there?"

"I'll hang back so as not to scare him off. You tell him the jig is up and we know what he did. Maybe don't specify how straightaway. Make him feel like you're going to spill the whole thing live on the internet."

"What if he gets violent?"

"I'll handle that. All we need to do is get him to admit what he did."

"I brought an extra camera that will help. My Insta360 Go that clips to whatever. It's low profile and you don't have to aim it. So I thought I could dangle it from my purse strap and just leave it recording." She removed the camera from her bag and demonstrated. It was only the size of a pack of Biscoff cookies, if that. She hung it from one end of the bag's shoulder strap. "See? I keep the little front light covered so it's not obvious when it's on."

"That's handy. If we get a recording to the Saint Pete Police, that should be enough for them to reopen Bud's case."

Sierra let out a yawn. "Gosh. Sorry. I guess this day is catching up to me."

Her yawn made me yawn. It was too short of a flight for a nap, but I could see the appeal. My forearms were starting to tingle. Despite the tension of the situation, I felt relaxed. Calm.

Sierra checked her watch. "We've got a little time to kill." She gave me a smirk. "I guess we could make out."

I fixed her with a stare.

She winked. "I'm joking."

We were reasonably high up now. I was guessing above fifteen thousand feet judging by the view out the window. Maybe eighteen? The service ceiling of a PC-12 was around thirty-thousand feet, but there was no need to go that high on a short flight from Tampa Bay to Saint Augustine.

Sierra was still smiling. Her expression relaxed. I found myself focused on her pert lips. She stared back, curious. I felt a little lightheaded, like I'd had a couple of glasses of wine. But we had yet to touch the mini-fridge.

"You keep staring at me like that," Sierra said, "And I'm gonna start thinking you liked my joke a little too much." She gave me a slow blink, like a cat. "Though I do kind of regret that the only time you kissed me, I can't remember it. You seem like you might be a good kisser."

"It wasn't my worst memory. But I think we've got other things we should worry about at the moment."

Somehow we'd gotten a little closer though across the space dividing us. Our faces not so far apart now.

"Maybe if things don't work out with you and Diana. You could . . . let me know."

"Your lips," I said. "Are kind of . . . blue."

Somewhere in the back of my mind, an alarm was ringing.

I lifted my tingling hands, stared at my fingertips. "I wonder . . . what Brooks has the cabin pressure . . . set to?" I said aloud. "Maybe he should . . . dial it down."

My eyes found their way around the cabin. In a seat near the entryway to the flight deck was a cloth bag. It had a medical tag hanging from the side of it. The label read "Sky Bridge Animal Rescue."

Puppy Pilot. But he didn't fly puppies in this company Pilatus, did he? What would he need his dog meds bag for on this flight?

I was out of my seat though now and headed forward. Walking was harder than it should have been. We were in level flight. Cruising altitude. If there had been a seat belt sign on this plane, the captain would certainly have turned it off. Walk straight, Luke.

I reached the entryway to the flight deck and leaned a shoulder into it.

From the pilot seat, Brooks looked up and smiled. At least his eyes smiled. It was hard to see his mouth because he was wearing an oxygen mask.

"Luke. I was hoping you'd stay awake for the good part." Brooks double-checked the parameters on the auto-pilot settings and climbed out of his seat. He seemed huge in this cockpit, especially standing. He was wearing a portable oxygen bottle on a strap slung over his chest. After he removed the aircraft's onboard oxygen system mask from his face, he stuck a cannula into his nostrils and turned the portable bottle on. One of the cabin pressure switches in the flight deck was set on dump. A warning light blinked in silence. A few more things seemed odd about this situation, but I couldn't quite put my finger on them.

What I knew was wrong was the way Brooks smiled while he cocked a fist back, and the way my arms failed to come up fast enough when I tried to raise them. Brook's fist connected with my eye socket, and I flew backwards down the aisle in a sprawl onto my side.

My vision was stars.

The alarm in my head screamed now. But it was getting quieter. And if I didn't do something soon, everything was going to fade to black.

THIRTY-SIX
WARNING LIGHTS

"CHRIST, THAT HURTS," Brooks muttered, shaking his hand out. "This is why I don't go in for the bar fights like you."

He was looming over me. Still stooped to accommodate his height in the small cabin. But he seemed to fill the whole space, standing near the entryway door and blocking my path to the flight deck.

"This about how it felt the other night? Knocking that guy down?"

I slowly rose to a sitting position, shaking my head to clear it. Then I braced myself on a seat and stood. Brooks let me. He pointed to where Sierra sat slumped behind me in her seat, eyes closed.

"Look at that little passenger princess. Already having a nap." His eyes ran over her prone figure. "Pity there isn't more time on this flight. I'd like to have some fun with that body." His eyes returned to me. "But at least I have you." He gripped the seats next to him for leverage and kicked me. The bottom of his custom Cole Haan hit me in the abdomen. He'd misjudged the distance though, and I was able to back away enough to stay on my feet this time. But there was nowhere to go. Just another set of seats and the rear cargo door.

I came back at him, swinging. But he dodged my clumsy punch and slammed one of his own into my midsection. I absorbed the hit and tried to close on him, wrap him up, but he shoved me back.

"Whoo!" Brooks shouted. "This is fun!"

Even in these tight quarters, I should have been able to take him apart. He was tall but so was I, and I'd fought bigger. The problem was everything about his movements seemed sped up, while mine were sluggish. Even my punch had been weak. I gasped for breath after his strike to my abdomen. The effects of the hypoxia were making themselves obvious. I should've seen them coming on sooner, but the depressurization of the cabin had been gradual, not explosive. The subtle loss of pressure crept up on us. Brooks was still grinning.

"You're the one who drugged Rip," I said, my breath coming fast and ragged. "The ketamine. In the energy drink."

"Never happened," he said. "You saw who gave him that drink in the video. Good ol' Chase."

"Why?" I stammered, ignoring his ploy. "What did Rip . . . ever do to you?"

"Nothing." Brooks laughed. "Though he was dumb enough to tell me that his AAD was expired. And then he strapped himself to Hank Martin. Some combos are just too tempting."

Maybe it was the hypoxia, but I still wasn't connecting the dots.

"Hank was your friend. Your mentor. He got you started in this business."

"A *long* time ago. And he still hasn't let go. I told you. These old timers never know when to hang it up and make room for the next generation."

"There's plenty of room for everyone . . . at Whitted."

"Will be now," Brooks grinned. "Bud's generously donated his hangar."

"Chase," I muttered. "His partner in the airplane. It's you."

"Sorry the Cirrus won't be slumming it outside in the rain with your bird anymore. I told you. Million dollar planes don't belong outdoors."

"So you killed Bud . . . for hangar space?"

"Bud died of natural causes. Didn't you hear? But it looks like I'll land his examiner job too. Talk about a bonus! You're looking at the airport's new top dog."

"You can't . . . expect . . . to keep this quiet."

"Keep what quiet? I was never here. Chase Dempsey took this plane out tonight. He's on a flight to Saint Augustine with Sierra Noble and I guess you must've tagged along. Tragic about the pressurization failure. But I heard his girlfriend just dumped him. He was super depressed. Maybe he lost his will to live. Who's to say? The FAA really needs to work on their mental health reform."

"You. Killed. Chase?"

"No! Well, I don't think so yet. Chase is actually here. He's in the rear cargo hold. Have a look."

The back of the PC-12 had a baggage space partitioned off by a sort of tarp. The divider was held up by clips. I detached one with a sense of dread and let it fall. Part of me didn't want to believe any of this was happening. That perhaps Brooks was playing some elaborate joke. But there was Chase Dempsey. His unconscious body had been crammed into the cargo space. His shaggy head was slumped on his chest. I couldn't tell if he was still breathing.

"Not the first time he's fallen asleep during a flight," Brooks said. He unzipped the duffel bag beside him. He removed the parachute rig I'd seen him in at Zephyrhills. He slid it onto his back and started clipping himself in. "He was a decent co-pilot though. Gonna miss him."

"Turn the pressurization back on, Brooks," I commanded. I fumbled for a passenger oxygen mask near the rearmost seat.

"Sorry, buddy. Those are turned off."

I dropped the mask. My hand worked its way around to my back. Then I drew my Sig Sauer. Aimed it.

"Turn. The oxygen. On."

Brooks gave another of his smug grins, stepped to the side, then back to the other side. I followed with the pistol, but my movements were sluggish—delayed. By the time I had the pistol on him he had moved. It was obvious. Shit.

He'd pulled his helmet from the duffel, and then it was in the air. The helmet smashed off my forehead before I could move, then he was on me, fast. Before I could get a shot off, the gun was gone, yanked from my hand and sent skittering under a seat. He punched me. In the body. Then the head. Again and again. Were my hands even up? I tried to protect my face but now I was on the floor. I'd ducked? Or maybe I'd fallen. My vision was nothing but stars.

Brooks stepped over me, and I lacked the energy to even grab at his ankles.

"I always liked you, Luke," Brooks said. "When the planning committee gets around to organizing a memorial for you four, I'm gonna say really nice things about all of you. I promise. Maybe I'll even tell someone how close you came to figuring things out someday." He picked a glove from the floor where it had fallen, then extracted another from inside his helmet, and donned them. He then retrieved my pistol from beneath the neighboring seat. He tucked it into the waistband of his pants.

"You know, you almost caught me that night you showed up in your golf cart. I heard your shout. Bud never did, of course. He was too busy suffocating inside his RV-8. But I thought, how ironic would it be if you'd managed to stop me twice in the same week. I have no idea what I'd have done if you'd walked in."

"You . . . son of a . . ." But the rest of my words wouldn't come. I didn't have the air.

"He looked a lot like you do now, come to think of it," Brooks said. "*That's* definitely ironic. Good thing you're overrated as a rescuer." He peered down at me. "Can't even save yourself, now. Pity the internet will never see that."

An alarm went off on his watch. He silenced it. "I'd love to stick around and chat longer, but it looks like we've reached my exit. I've got another plane to catch."

With my face a half-inch from the floor, I watched as he pried open the rear cargo/jump door. The wind was deafening. Ice-cold air rushed into the cabin as the warm air fled. Brooks pulled the strap of the oxygen tank from over his head and tugged the cannula from his nose. He dangled the oxygen bottle. "I'll drop this here for you." He had to shout over the wind. He held the bottle out momentarily, but then flung it sideways out the jump door. "Oops. I missed."

I groaned.

He stared out after it. "Now the FAA's gonna be after me. Dropping objects without taking 'reasonable precautions for the safety of people and objects on the ground.' You won't tell though, will you? I'm betting you won't. Considering you'll be headed on an Atlantic deep sea vacation." He grinned that Crest commercial smile at me one more time.

I wanted to shout at him. Curse him. Something. But words wouldn't come.

"Don't worry, Luke. The airport will be fine without you. Maybe even better. A forest needs a wildfire every once in a while to keep it healthy. Just takes someone with the balls to light it!" He slid his helmet over his head and gave me a thumbs up. Then he jumped.

Bastard.

I stared at the open doorway for only a moment, then turned around in the aisle. An excruciating process. The path to the flight deck seemed to have lengthened. I mustered all of my remaining energy and I began to crawl, the icy wind clawing at my back.

Forward.

But the floor was quicksand and my arms were concrete.

My vision narrowed to just the single path to the cockpit. I clutched at the base of a seat, pulled, straining. My lungs wouldn't seem to fill. Move your body, Luke. Come on. Another foot. Darkness hovered around the edges of my vision.

My mind screamed for me to fight. Crawl. But the tunnel of light I was crawling toward had narrowed to a pinprick. Air and light. That's all I wanted. But the air wouldn't come. And as I lay with my face on the carpet, the light slowly went out.

THIRTY-SEVEN

PURSUIT

THE COLD WAS BACK. The smell of plastic. Engine noise. Wind roaring. But muffled. Infinite black faded ever so slightly to gray. Then a hint of pink.

Light.

My eyelids fluttered open for half a second and shut again. An image now danced on the inside of my eyelids. A backlit silhouette. Long hair blowing in the wind.

"Just breathe, Luke." Muffled. A world away.

Better not be an angel.

I was going to be pissed if I was dead.

But I had it coming.

My skin hurt. A stabbing in my limbs like needles. An inferno in my veins.

I opened my eyes again.

Sierra peered down at me. She pulled the oxygen mask from my face, took two deep inhales herself, then put the mask back on me. I gulped at the air this time, my arms spasming back to life, clawing at the mask, pulling the air deep into my lungs. When she pulled the mask away the next time, my words finally came.

"Brooks. Rigged the plane."

"I know." She took another breath, then put the mask back over my face. "I got the passenger oxygen system back online, but I need your help. We need to move Chase. And we have to get that door closed to re-pressurize."

I nodded, saving my breath.

"You. How?" I finally asked while she used the mask again.

She seemed to understand my question.

"Told you I was a good actress." She gave me a sly grin. "If Brooks followed my channel better, he'd have known I did the Shaw Air Force Base pressurization chamber six months ago. Plus I summited Mount Whitney last summer."

"You faked being passed out."

"I guarantee I'm not the first girl to fake her way out of a bad night with Brooks. For the record, if you want to last at high altitude, take shallower breaths and don't exert yourself. No one in my high-altitude training ever mentioned it as a good time to start a fistfight. You should have lost faster. My faking was getting awfully close to reality."

It hurt too much to laugh. But my muscles were waking up. I got to an elbow. Then my feet. Sierra helped. The panel that had covered the cargo area hung open. Chase's unconscious body was still stuffed inside.

Sierra helped me drag him out and lay him on the floor. He still had a pulse, but it was weak. He was shivering.

"Put him on the oxygen while I get this door shut," I said. I activated the retraction mechanism on the cargo door. It struggled against the wind and the suction of the air flowing past it, but I was able to haul on it by hand once it was close and get it latched. From here, the pressurization would have a chance to work again.

"We need to get him to a hospital," Sierra said as I moved

forward past her. She had donned a second passenger oxygen mask and had a palm pressed against Chase's clammy skin.

"We need to get back first," I replied. "Brooks isn't done. He said 'four' of us."

"Four?" Sierra did the quick math. "Who else? Oh shit. Nina?"

I nodded. "With us dead, she's his last loose thread. I think Brooks is going to kill her."

I climbed into the flight deck and donned the pilot's oxygen mask when I got seated. I breathed deeply and stayed still, using only my eyes to scan the instruments. The plane was still on a course headed out over the Atlantic. Night was falling outside, the lights of east coast cities illuminated below. My vision became clearer, colors brighter. Specks of light in the sky showed airplanes headed north toward Jacksonville or south toward Miami.

When I finally felt like my body was recovered enough to fly, I disengaged the autopilot and got us turned around and aimed for the West Coast, then I optimized the pressurization controls and the heater. Eventually my skin warmed and my fingers returned to their full range of motion. The slow drop in cabin altitude would eventually help us acclimate back to a higher pressure.

I worked the radio. Brooks had us on a track to St. Augustine at just shy of eighteen thousand feet. It was just below Class A airspace, high enough to make us hypoxic, but still low enough that he could jump. I got on with Jacksonville approach to cancel whatever flight plan he'd asked for, and turned VFR direct to Albert Whitted.

ATC obliged.

As I reset the heading on the autopilot, I considered trying to relay our problems through the radio. But how do you explain to

ATC that you need to stop a rogue pilot from committing a murder on the other side of the state?

Where was he right now? I watched the moving map of the GPS and found my answer. The little blip of Brook's Cirrus SR22T appeared on the screen. His plane's N number was visible as he departed a small private airstrip near Lake George.

If I could see him, he'd eventually see us too. Especially if we flew right up on him. Despite his best efforts to kill us, he'd accidentally gifted us a faster plane. In a race back to Albert Whitted, we were going to win.

I turned in my seat and yelled to the back. "Are you getting any kind of cell service?"

"No!" Sierra shouted back. She moved forward to talk to me.

"How's our patient?"

"I don't know," she replied. "He tried to say something. But he's all drugged up. I can't make out what it was."

"We need to warn Nina what Brooks is up to. I'm going to drop us to a lower altitude and see if we can pick up a cell signal. Try calling her. If we can't get ahold of her, I'll need you to call the Saint Pete Police and see if they can locate her."

"I'll try. What are you going to do?"

"I'm going to follow Brooks." I nosed the plane over and descended.

As soon as my phone showed a bar of reception, I sent a text message to Reese.

>>> SOS. Nina Yee is in danger. Jason Brooks is going to hurt her. We need to find her ASAP.

I pressed send. Then I copied the message. I sent it to Tyson too. Then Rip.

I added. "Spread the word."

Then I returned my attention to the moving map of the GPS and the little blip of Brooks's Cirrus. Except it had vanished.

Shit.

Brooks had disabled his transponder.

He'd already seen us.

I should have disabled our outgoing signal before I'd turned around.

Was Brooks still headed for Saint Petersburg or was he going to make a run for it?

I turned and shouted to the cabin. "Did you get ahold of Nina?"

Sierra shook her head. "She won't pick up."

Damn.

I pushed the throttle full forward, and the PT-6 turboprop responded with a surge of acceleration. We were at a lower altitude now and sucking down fuel at an unreasonable rate. It made me check the gauges.

The digital readouts showed our fuel quantity was low. Brooks had planned for this plane to run out of fuel over the Atlantic, not make a round trip. With the quantity we had left, we might make the West Coast again, but not at this power setting. I reduced power and swore. Stopping for fuel would give Brooks enough time to outrun us.

I had to be smart.

My left eye was swelling. I fingered the bruise and flinched. "Use your head for more than a damned punching bag, Luke," I muttered.

What was Brooks going to do? If he flew back to Clearwater, where we'd departed from, he'd know he was expected. Same with Albert Whitted. Whatever his original plan was, he would alter it now. But how?

Was it possible he'd give up? Know he had lost? But recalling that cocky grin he'd had on his face before he'd jumped, I doubted it.

If he'd called Nina while he was on the ground, he could have already spun this story in his favor. He could have told her anything.

"We need to get ahold of someone at the airport," I shouted back to Sierra.

"I'm trying." A few moments later she came up to the flight deck. "Nobody can find Nina. Enrique just went by her place. She wasn't home."

"Shit. Is anyone at the airport right now?"

"I'll find out." She took a look at my face and came back a moment later with a cold drink from the cooler.

"Thanks." I held it to my eye.

As the minutes dragged on, my worries grew. There was no sign of Brooks' plane on the moving map and in the growing dark, there was no good way to spot him in the air. Even if he had his lights on, which I doubted, the distances were too great.

I was headed southwest but with no real heading. I was flying blind.

Finally my phone buzzed. It was Diana. Sierra had started a group chat.

"Nina's car is at the airport. But no sign of her."

"Check the planes," I texted back.

But they wouldn't need to check all of them. Nina was only comfortable flying a few planes in the fleet. On a hunch, I pulled up FlightAware and typed in the full registration number for Six Two Delta, the online rental plane. The page took forever to load with my poor connection, but finally it appeared on screen. The plane had recently departed Albert Whitted Airport and flown south. It looked to be in the pattern at Venice Municipal.

Found her.

I typed the word "Venice" into the group chat, and hit send.

Then I turned on course, checked my fuel gauges, and swore some more. It was going to be close. But I was on my way.

Be smart Nina. Don't you dare die.

THIRTY-EIGHT
VENICE

VENICE MUNICIPAL AIRPORT sits on the western coast of Florida about 43 nautical miles south of Saint Petersburg. The short distance makes for a scenic lunch destination on a casual Saturday. Tonight, I was just hoping to make it in one piece. Had I been in a Cessna 182 or something with a manual fuel selector, I would have been running on one tank and timing how long it lasted, so that I knew exactly how much time to expect out of the second side. But the PC-12 has an automatic fuel-balancing system that uses pumps to keep the fuel load even all the time. When I was out of fuel, there would be no reserve.

So I traded some of my precious fuel for altitude again, taking us back out of cell phone signal, but reducing our drag with the slightly thinner atmosphere. I didn't have a lot of flying time in a PC-12 so I adjusted my power settings for maximum fuel economy at cruise per the plane's operating manual and said a prayer it would be enough. We weren't traveling at max speed, but we were still cruising faster than Brook's Cirrus. It was hard to say if we'd overtaken him already since I had no idea where he was. I'd turned my transponder off before turning on course toward Venice. My last track had me pointed toward Clearwater, so with any luck, Brooks would figure we were headed there and we'd have the element of surprise.

Nerve-wracking minutes ticked by as we flew over the darkened landscape of Central Florida while trying not to hit anybody, and we finally approached the coast. The lights of Tampa Bay shone brightly. Tampa at the top of the bay, St. Petersburg on the peninsula, and to the south, Sarasota. I could even make out the lights of the Skyway Bridge that connected Pinellas County to points south.

The flight had been long enough for doubts to creep in. Was I headed the right place? I didn't know for sure if Nina was even the one who took Six Two Delta to Venice. It could have been some other student pilot.

But I had to trust my gut. Forty-three miles wasn't long enough to be logged as a night cross-country flight for an average student pilot's training. You needed to go at least fifty, and you typically didn't linger long on the ground. Six Two Delta hadn't departed again, so whoever took the plane there went for a reason other than landing practice. If it was Nina, what was she thinking?

Venice Municipal came into view out the window with my fuel gauges solidly in the red. The low fuel annunciator light glowed brightly. I was grateful for the extra altitude I'd gained.

Especially when the engine quit.

It's an eerie feeling when a plane's engine goes silent. Your body becomes accustomed to the frequency vibration an engine outputs, even vibrations as subtle as those from a PT-6 turboprop. The quiet sets your skin prickling.

But the silence was broken by warning horns. The master caution light glared in my vision.

"Luke?" Sierra shouted from the back.

"Get buckled!" I shouted back. "We're landing!"

Landing was a generous term for it. We were a seven-thousand-pound glider now. Good news was, as gliders went, you can do worse than a PC-12. At 110 knots it boasted a glide ratio of nearly 16:1, meaning for every thousand feet of altitude I lost, we could glide a little over two and a half nautical miles. From my current altitude of ten thousand feet, I could theoretically make it thirty miles. Venice Municipal was twenty. But that didn't factor in any turns. It was going to be close.

I tuned to the local UNICOM frequency and advised any traffic that I was engine out and inbound for landing. Then I glued my attention to the airspeed indicator, making sure I didn't deviate off my target descent rate. Sierra climbed into the flight deck with me.

"I'm going to buckle in up here with you if you don't mind. Please tell me you have a plan."

I pointed out the window to where the approach lights of the Venice Airport blinked near the darkness of the gulf.

"One plan. We'll make it. How's Chase?"

"I got him into a seat. It was hard. But I think he's improving. He sort of sat himself up before he passed out again."

"We'll get him help as soon as we land."

Then we lapsed into silence. Landing a plane with no engine is theoretically no harder than landing with an engine, but you only get one shot at it. I made shallow turns and lined up for Runway 23. The wind was favoring Runway 5 for departures, but I didn't want a headwind. In this case, I preferred a tailwind to extend my glide. It was only a problem when someone in a Piper Archer called on the radio that they were taking Runway 5 for departure.

"Aircraft departing Venice, I am on a three-mile final for Runway 23 with an engine out," I said.

"Aircraft calling Venice, Venice is using Runway 5," the irritated voice called back.

I mashed the push to talk switch harder this time and growled into the radio. "Maybe you didn't hear the 'engine out' part. I am now two-mile final for Runway 23 ENGINE OUT. Please clear the runway!"

That did the trick. The other plane acknowledged.

Thank God.

I lined up on the centerline for Runway 23 and dropped the landing gear.

The thing most new pilots get wrong when planning an emergency landing on a runway is that they aim for the same spot they normally do, the threshold. But I was of the opinion that if I was going to misjudge a landing glide, I'd rather skid into the grass at the far end of the runway doing ten knots than come up short doing a hundred knots. So I aimed for the middle.

Sierra murmured something encouraging about my descent angle, but tightened her seat belt anyway.

I put some flaps out. We were going to make the runway, though I was cutting it closer than I planned. With both the landing gear and the flaps down we sank fast. Down down down, flare and . . . the tires chirped on the asphalt. Main wheels then the nose. We were on the ground and still rolling. I'd come in hot a thousand feet into the runway and the Taxiway Bravo sign was coming up fast. A little too fast. I wasn't going to make that turn. But off to the right I spotted the ramp I wanted and there was only one way I was getting there.

"Hang on," I said, and swerved the plane off the runway between the runway edge lights.

"Oh geeze," Sierra blurted out and gripped the edge of her seat as I took the aircraft off-roading through the grass at the edge of the runway. I cut across the apron, my landing lights shining a path ahead and helping me dodge the metal taxiway edge lights. We careened over Taxiway Echo and back into the grass on the far side. Our momentum slowed, but we had just enough to rock us through the shallow grass runoff ditch and back up onto the pavement of the Taxiway Bravo ramp. The plane rolled to a stop near a few aircraft on tie-down in front of the T-hangars. I finally tapped the brakes belatedly for good measure.

"There," I said. "No problem, right?"

Sierra looked over and finally exhaled. "You're the one who gets to explain this parking job."

I pulled my headset from my head and tossed it aside. "Any landing you walk away from is a good one. Let's go find Nina."

THIRTY-NINE
AIRPORT RODEO

THERE WERE ROUGHLY fifteen hangars scattered between us and the main terminal ramp. It was a long walk. When the landing lights of an airplane glowed off the final approach end of Runway 5, I broke into a jog.

Shit. Brooks was landing.

"Nina!" I shouted toward the distant ramp. "Are you here!"

"Luke, wait!" Sierra shouted. She'd been trying to keep pace beside me but slowed to a stop. "Chase. What if Brooks goes after him?"

We'd checked Chase briefly before exiting the plane. He'd been showing signs of coming around, even muttering a few words, but was still incoherent. Sierra had a good point. If Brooks was coming here to snip loose ends, there was nothing to stop him from putting a bullet in Chase while he sat prone in a seat. It was admirable that Sierra wanted to stay with him, but her being there just gave Brooks two loose ends to snip at once.

"Get the police on the phone, and EMS. If they show up fast enough, we'll be okay. We closed the door to the Pilatus. The lights are out. If we're lucky, Brooks won't know Chase is still in there."

We continued on, Sierra dialing 911 as we jogged, me searching ahead for Six Two Delta.

"Luke!" Sierra shouted again. She pointed through a gap between hangars where Brooks's Cirrus blasted down one of the taxiways at high speed.

Shit. He was going to beat us. I sprinted for the main ramp. I cut across the grass and raced onto Taxiway Alpha.

The darkness obscured the planes on tie-down. And half the planes on the ramp were high-wing Cessnas. Six Two Delta, wherever it was, blended in with the crowd. Finally, I spotted a figure in the darkness, the faint glow of a phone screen near her face.

"Nina!" I waved as I ran toward her. But Brooks made the turn onto the ramp with his Cirrus directly behind me and gunned the engine. The three-bladed propeller pitched to a high whine as the plane launched toward me. He was going to run me down with the prop.

I cut sideways, dodging his kamikaze plane attack and dove to the asphalt, rolling beneath the long wing of the Cirrus as the plane roared over me. Brooks blasted by, and I clambered to my feet, brushing gravel from the skin of my scraped elbows. The bastard had nearly diced me. I took off at a sprint after him. Nina was standing near her rental plane, a duffel bag slung over her shoulder. Brooks screeched to a stop beside where she was standing and popped open the passenger door. His arm waved as he gestured for Nina to climb aboard.

"Nina! Don't!" I shouted. But she was already sliding around back of the wing to climb up the step.

"He's going to kill you!" I shouted.

She couldn't hear me over the sound of the engine. She glanced back and saw me though, as I waved desperately for her to stop. But she was on the wing. Brooks started moving before she was even in. I was running full tilt now, arms pumping, but slower than I could usually run, my chest aching. The prop wash from the Cirrus blasted me as Brooks turned the plane for a taxiway centerline. Where was he headed? The runway? It was a straight shot all the way down Taxiway Alpha. He could hit the end and blast off on Runway 13 with a single left turn. But not if I caught him.

I was in reach of the aircraft's elevator. I had one shot before he accelerated out of reach. I mustered all the energy I had left and leapt onto the tail.

Cirrus makes a goddamn aerodynamic airplane. There was nothing to hold onto other than the leading edge of the horizontal stabilizer. The flat horizontal surface of the tail was carbon fiber composite without so much as a rivet to create drag. The only thing that could possibly slow that thing down now was me.

My two-hundred and twenty pound frame flopping over the tail did a fair job of tipping the balance of the aircraft. The plane roared, nose-high, the engine fighting against my weight as Brooks used forward thrust to compensate for my unhelpful drag. The bad news was he was still rolling, and gaining speed. My feet were dancing on the ground behind me, but the toes of my work boots bouncing off the pavement were doing little to stop his forward momentum. Even if I swung around and planted my feet on the other side, there was no way I could fight a 315 horsepower engine with my feet. I needed a better plan.

I glanced behind me. Sierra was back there on the taxiway, her figure growing smaller. She threw her hands up. She had her phone out. But help was going to come too late.

Think, Luke, think.

What I wouldn't give for my Sig right now. I'd blow those tires in a heartbeat. But I didn't have that option. All I had was my body weight and the fact that I was lying on the elevator. I could feel Brooks straining to move it beneath my hips. It was a stalemate. If Brooks tried to get airborne with me still holding on and forcing the elevator down, he'd never get off the ground, or he'd stall the aircraft on takeoff and likely kill us all. And he knew it. Somewhere between here and the runway, he was going to have to stop the plane and get rid of me.

My guess was he was going to shoot me.

But I had a plan too. And a Swiss Army knife. Could I slash the tires before he climbed out and lined up a shot? I dug into my pocket with one hand and removed the knife. I held on tightly to the horizontal stabilizer with my other hand and used my teeth to pull the blade out.

We were nearing the end of the taxiway. The engine revved twice. He was trying to scare me off. A game of chicken. I bit the the blunt end of my knife with my teeth and hung on with both hands. Then I felt my hands getting wet. And slippery.

The bastard was deploying the leading edge anti-icing fluid. The alcohol-based TKS fluid wicked from tiny holes in the stabilizer's leading edge, coating the surface and making it slicker than a fish.

He took the turn onto the runway at high speed, trying to dislodge me with centrifugal force. And it would have worked, but I plunged the blade of my pocketknife deep into the composite core of the stabilizer and held on. I slipped around the edge of the elevator, temporarily taking my weight off it, but as the plane straightened out on the runway, I fought my way back, getting a leg over the control surface again. Brooks slammed the elevator into my knee repeatedly, trying to dislodge me, but I was in this now. If he was going to try to take off, he'd have to do it the hard way.

And he tried. At full power, the propeller blasted so much air that I couldn't keep my eyes open. The turbocharged engine surged, and the plane picked up speed. We rocketed down the runway with Brooks trying to get the nose up. My weight was helping him there, but with the elevator jammed in the position it was, the tail kept forcing the nose down. The faster we went, the more the aerodynamics worked in my favor—if you can call bucking down the runway like a bull rider at a rodeo any kind of win. The plane almost flew, the nose coming off the ground momentarily, but then it porpoised on the runway as the tail slammed the front wheel back to the ground.

We rocked up and down twice like that before the engine noise abated. Brooks slammed the throttle back and braked hard on the runway. The tires skidded, smoking with burned rubber. Brooks was mad now. And when the gull door on the pilot side of the aircraft flew up, he was right behind it. He rose to his full height with my pistol in his hand.

"Boy, you are just one stubborn bastard, aren't you!" Then he aimed the gun and fired.

FORTY
INCURSION

NINA SCREAMED.

I might have screamed too if I hadn't been so busy not getting shot. I was off the stabilizer now, running forward, ducking low to stay out of view of Brooks. I rolled under the right wing with my knife still in my hand. The first thing I did under there was try to slash a tire. I stabbed beneath the wheel fairing at the exposed sidewall, but the blade of my Swiss Army knife bounced off, barely leaving a mark in the dense rubber. I stabbed it again. Failed. Swore. I'd only managed to nick my own fingers with the blade when it tried to fold up on me.

I pulled another attachment from the knife. It had an awl. Something I'd only used on rare occasions to puncture extra holes through leather belts. Tonight I held the knife clenched in my palm so that the pointed metal tip of the awl protruded about an inch through the closed fingers of my fist. Then I punched that tire. Hard. Kept punching. It made tiny puncture holes. But damned if that did anything to deflate it. The holes were too shallow to reach the tube inside. I needed a bigger knife, and Brooks was walking around the back of the airplane.

The engine was still running. The propeller spun in an arc of death to my right.

"Nowhere to run, Luke!" Brooks shouted. "Just you, me, and the runway." He was holding my Sig Sauer with two hands, one cupped beneath the grip. I was in front of the right wing now and popped up far enough to have a look but ducked again as he aimed and fired. The bullet ricocheted off the asphalt of the runway.

But then a rumble reached my ears. Two bright lights in the sky above shone down on us from the airplane that was descending for the runway. Not just any plane. My plane, *Tropic Angel*. Its twin radials roared as it flew overhead, buzzing our position at high power and then climbing up and away again.

The cavalry had arrived. But there wasn't enough runway here for landing. My father and whoever else was aboard would have to go around and land on the other runway. They'd arrive too late.

And Brooks knew it. He fired at me again and started walking forward, unhurried.

I scrambled on hands and knees under the rumbling engine of the Cirrus, hot exhaust blasting me in the ear as I rolled beneath the aircraft. Then I leapt up onto the left wing, scrambled around the still open pilot's door and jumped into the cockpit. I reached up and closed the door behind me.

"Hi, Nina," I said. "Good to see ya." She shrank into the passenger seat beside me.

"What are you doing!"

"Hey!" Brooks shouted just before I got the door latched. The engine was still running. I made a move to gun the engine and leave Brooks behind in the prop wash like he'd done to me, but the parking brake was still on and he was too fast. By the time I'd found the brake and released it, he'd had time to run around the back of the airplane and leap up onto the wing. He held onto the door latch with one hand while he pointed the gun at my head with the other. At ten inches, he wasn't likely to miss.

"I don't want to put bullet holes in my own plane," he shouted through the Plexiglas. "But I will if you don't get out here right now!"

I pulled my hands away from the throttle and the control stick and held them high.

"Now open this goddamn door!" Brooks shouted. He eased back a step, eyes burning into me. Maybe he was worried my elbows were bleeding on his fancy upholstery. If so, he was going to hate what I had in mind next.

I turned to Nina. "You know one reason these airplanes cost so much?" I closed all but one finger of my right hand into a fist and pointed to the ceiling of the aircraft with my index finger. Her eyes followed my gesture to the handle above my head for the ballistic parachute.

"No," she murmured when the realization hit her.

But I already had both hands on the lever and pulled down in one swift motion.

I have to hand it to Cirrus. When they build a rocket-propelled parachute system, they don't mess around. In a catastrophic in-flight emergency, deploying the chute can save your life and lower the entire plane safely to the ground. But I figured it could *keep* the plane on the ground too.

The moment I engaged the handle, the rocket exploded out of the roof of the fuselage at a forty-five degree angle to the rear, rocking the entire airplane several feet ahead. If Brooks hadn't lost his footing from the deafening blast and our surge forward, he certainly would have when the parachute's cradle straps came bursting out of the wing roots.

I had the fuel mixture control pulled and the door open a moment later. Then I was out, leaping to the ground and not stopping till I'd reached Brooks. The plane's engine sputtered to a stop behind me. Brooks was just trying to climb back to his feet when I reared back to clock him with a right cross. I wanted to knock some of those pearly whites of his straight down his throat. Brooks flinched. But I checked my swing. Barely.

"I'm feeling pretty well-oxygenated now, Brooks," I said. "If you're ready to go another round, you'll make my day."

Brooks lowered the arm he'd put up to defend himself and glared at me. But he didn't get up. I suspect he didn't like his chances in a fair fight. I didn't blame him.

"It's over," I said, nodding my head toward the distant fence line at the edge of the airport where red-and-blue emergency lights were flashing. The Venice first-responders had found the scene, though they still hadn't found their way out to the runway yet.

Brooks gave me a smile. His bright white teeth showed once more in the flashing of his tail strobe. "You got me, Luke. Nice job. But you might be premature on thinking it's over."

He tilted his chin up, pointing.

I turned around to find Nina Yee had exited the aircraft. And she'd picked up my gun. Now she was aiming it at me.

FORTY-ONE
RUNWAY CLOSED

"NINA. BE CAREFUL WITH THAT," I said.

Nina's eyes glistened with tears.

"Why?" she moaned. "Why couldn't you just leave it alone!"

Her hand was shaking.

The red-and-white parachute from Brooks's Cirrus wafted up and down in the breeze, half inflated behind us.

"I don't think you want to hurt anyone," I said.

"You don't think I could? Would you say that if *he* still had the gun? You're such a goddamn sexist."

We weren't alone anymore. Sierra had commandeered a golf cart from somewhere and rolled up to find us. "Nina, are you okay?"

"Stay away!" Nina shouted, pointing the gun toward her.

"Whoa, whoa! Hey!" I said. "No one doubts your seriousness. We came here to help you."

Behind Sierra, several more figures appeared from the darkness. My father, Frank, plus Rip, Tyson, and Reese. Reese had her favorite Kimber pistol in her hand and held it aimed at Nina.

"What's the situation, Cap?" she asked.

"Trying to deescalate," I said.

A second plane had landed too and didn't bother to roll to the ramp. It stopped and shut down on the nearby Taxiway Delta. A Cessna 182. The occupants climbed out. It was Gabby Turpin and Diana Longoria.

In the far distance, EMTs had found their way to the Pilatus.

"How many damned people did you bring?" Nina asked. She waved the gun back and forth. Mostly aiming at Reese now. "Nobody come any closer!"

Everyone stayed where they were.

"We heard you needed help," Dr. Turpin said as she approached. "We're not here to hurt you."

Nina laughed. A bitter sound. She looked to Brooks. "Are you getting up yet, or what?"

But Brooks stayed on the ground. "Look behind you," he said. "My plane's toast. Thanks to this shithead. I'll be sending you a bill for that by the way," he said to me.

"Gonna try to sue me from prison? Pretty sure those last lights I saw come down the road were cops, not ambulances."

Brooks finally got to his feet and brushed himself off. He turned to Nina. "Fun's over, kid. We're gonna have to postpone that romantic getaway I promised you."

"That's it?" Nina said. "I can't believe this. For once I get with a guy who can actually help me get ahead in my career, and he immediately bails? Typical."

"I don't know that I'd exactly call this a relationship," Brooks said. "Fun fling, yes. But dating Chase's sloppy seconds? You had to know this wasn't going to last."

Nina's face fell. She lowered the gun, and her lip quivered. But when I took a cautious step forward, she raised it again. Except she didn't aim it at me this time. She aimed it at her own temple.

"Whoa whoa whoa," I said.

"Don't do that, Nina," Sierra pleaded. "Please. Be careful."

"You say that. But you wouldn't if you knew," Nina said. The tears brimmed in her eyes. "It wasn't him who posted that video of you two on the boat. It was me. Did you know that? I locked you out of your account. I'm the one that sent the video around. All of that was me."

"It's okay," Sierra replied. "You probably didn't mean it to be such a big deal."

"I did." She wiped her cheek with the back of her hand. "And it felt damned good. For once you were brought down with the rest of us."

"Nina," I said. "He might have talked you into posting that video to disgrace me and Sierra. I know he was after Bud's job. And maybe you saw him getting the examiner role as your only solution for passing your exams. But I know you aren't the one who spiked Sierra's drink with ketamine, and you aren't the one who killed Bud."

Nina's brow furrowed. "Nobody killed Bud. He just died."

"Is that what Brooks told you?" I asked. "The other day when I said I was looking for Chase. I figured you were going to call him and tip him off. But you called Brooks instead, didn't you? Just like the night you failed your checkride. Did Brooks tell you he was coming back to see Bud that night?"

Nina's resolve seemed to waver. She looked at Brooks.

"He killed Bud and tried to frame Chase for it," I continued. "He used you to set me up and eliminate his competition for the examiner slot. And tonight he tried to kill all four of us to cover it up."

"Nina, don't tell them anything," Brooks replied. "That's what lawyers are for. I've got a great one. We'll be fine."

"If he says he'll protect you, he's lying," I said. "Whatever he promised you, he didn't plan to deliver. You were just a pawn he was using. But you don't have to be."

Nina glared at Brooks and shook her head. But her grip tightened on the pistol, still pressing it to her temple, as if she could use it to excise the pain. "I just wanted a chance at what you all already have," she whispered. "I just wanted to be a damned pilot. Is that so bad?" Another tear ran down her cheek. "But there's no way I'll ever get there. Not now."

"Nina." Dr. Turpin's calm voice cut through the stillness. "If you look at the other pilots here, none of us got where we are by cutting corners. But that's not to say we didn't have help. Trying to cheat the system and take a shortcut is never the right choice, and that's on you. But not seeing that one of our community was desperate for help?" She pressed a hand over her heart. "That's on us. When this is all over, and we get this situation resolved, and you own whatever you did and take responsibility for it, you can come fly with me. My 182 needs to run more. We can take it up whenever you want."

"I'd go up too," Diana said. "I'm not an instructor, but I can fly with you and help you build time. I need more hours too."

"I'd fly with you," Tyson said. "I found a little 150 I'mma try to fix up. We could fly that when I get it running right."

"I can fly with you," Rip said. "Maybe do some aerobatics."

"And me," Sierra said. "I'll fly with you too."

Nina stared back at Sierra. "*You* would? After all this?"

"Us girls need to stick together," Sierra said.

Nina couldn't hold her tears back any longer then. She sobbed. The pistol fell to her side. Then she dropped it to the runway. Dr. Turpin moved in and took Nina into her arms. Diana and Sierra stepped forward too, encircling her and rubbing her shoulders.

Brooks rolled his eyes. "Somebody sing fucking Kumbaya already."

"Don't worry," I said. "Nobody wants to fly with you anymore."

The police arrived then. Several squad cars.

When the first uniforms approached, Brooks tried to interject his version of things. "My property has been vandalized, officers." He pointed to his airplane. "You'll want to log that."

The officer in charge put her hand up. "Please keep it down for a minute. We'll have a chance to take everyone's stories."

"I've got some footage that will make things easier," Sierra said, holding up her Insta 360 Go. "Especially the part from inside the Pilatus when Brooks tried to kill us." She dangled the tiny camera on her finger for Brooks. "Amazing what they can capture when you let them run."

"Goddamn influencers," Brooks muttered. "Just once, try doing something without recording it."

"I'm not recording this," she said, and slowly extended her middle finger.

It took a while for the cops to sort it out. But they secured our weapons and took testimony from everyone there. It made for a late night. Brooks was mirandized and arrested with probable cause for felony assault, kidnapping, and attempted murder. He was now also a suspect in the death of Bud Truman and would eventually face numerous drug-related charges for the ketamine druggings and harm to Chase. Brooks was separated from us early, and we saw him loaded into a squad car from a distance.

They transported Chase to Sarasota Memorial Hospital. He'd evidently started talking by the time they got him there. He'd asked for Nina. But Nina went to another hospital for a mandatory psych evaluation after her attempted self-harm. She seemed in better spirits as she'd left though. And she wouldn't be without visitors.

The cops took my Sig Sauer into evidence, and I wouldn't see it again for a while. But Reese got her pistol back and was cut loose early. She hung around though, since *Tropic Angel* was our shared ride home. My entire crew had stayed. Diana and Gabby Turpin too.

"Thank you for coming tonight," I said to Diana. "I think it made a world of difference for Nina to see so many people show up for her."

"She's one of our own," Diana replied. "Of course we came. And for you. I'm sorry I was so hard on you. I was dragging my past into it and that's never fair."

"Did I earn my way back into your circle of trust yet?"

"Maybe," she said. "Barely." But she said it with a grin.

"I'll take it." I checked my watch, then showed the time to Sierra. "You missed your live broadcast to your followers. How are they going to handle that?"

"It's okay. I'm a tease, right? That's what we do. I'll get them a video eventually. Looks like it will be even more dramatic than they expected."

"Didn't the police take your SD card?"

"They let me copy all the good stuff off it first." She held up her phone. "Just the shot of you deploying a Cirrus chute on a runway will be content gold. Can you imagine the internet commenters getting their teeth into that one? I'm going to make up a really silly reason why you did it too. It'll probably break the algorithm."

"They'll feast like piranhas."

"For fifteen minutes. Then we'll all be forgotten."

"I don't know. I found the night pretty memorable," I said. I hooked a thumb toward *Tropic Angel*. "You still interested in logging some muti-engine seaplane time?"

Sierra smiled. "Sure. Let's go home."

FORTY-TWO
BREATHE EASY

WHEN MIKE GONZALEZ showed up at Hangar 4 a day later, he took in the sight of the Stearman that was there getting an oil change and rubbed a hand along the wing.

"It's amazing that a plane made in 1941 can still look this good. They sure knew how to build them."

"They're making pretty high-quality stuff these days too, though," I offered. "You ever try to stab your way through a Cirrus tire lately? Damned near impenetrable."

Mike raised an eyebrow. "Should I ask why you'd know that?"

"Probably not."

"The office sent me out as a follow-up. I feel like we're about to have a lively conversation."

He knew a lot of the facts already. News about Brooks had spread around the airfield fast. Details were still fuzzy about the truth of Bud's death. We'd broken that news privately to Amelia, but the drama surrounding Brooks trying to murder Sierra and Chase and me in the Pilatus was plenty juicy enough to keep the rumor mill happy.

"Sounds like Brooks had offered to promote Chase to his bosses as a first officer in his corporate gig," Mike said. "But it was all a ploy to get Chase to give up his new hangar space. I suppose the company will be looking for two new pilots now."

"I saw Eric this morning. He's a stickler for the rules, but he said in this circumstance, he's comfortable skipping down the hangar waiting list to the next name."

"Anyone we know?"

"I didn't ask. I just hope whoever it is will enjoy the view. What's going to happen to Nina?"

Mike cringed. "Good question. Her private pilot certificate is likely going to be revoked. We take falsification of records very seriously, especially with intent. She'll have to earn her way back. She'll be unable to try for another certificate for at least a year. But after that? We'll see. The road's not permanently closed for her. Her instructor, on the other hand, he's going to have a tougher go. Starting over from scratch all the way back to the instructor level will take a lot more work. That's if he avoids accessory charges in the murder attempt on Rip and Hank. Even if he does, you'd better believe he'll face a lot more scrutiny. And a longer wait time."

"I think his students will be better off without him."

"The world's going to need more drone pilots. Maybe he can deliver packages."

"You'd want him flying a drone to your house?" I asked.

"Not my house. Yours though. That I'd be fine with. You think Nina had any idea what Brooks was up to? The murder plot? Or Chase? Seems like he was awfully involved to be completely unaware."

"It's in the hands of the St. Pete detective bureau now," I said. "They reopened Bud's case as a homicide. We'll have to see what else they dig up."

Mike took in the view of the city skyline and sighed. "All of this still leaves a vacancy in my pilot examiner pool." He brushed a hand through his hair. "Might be a bit of a hard sell, but I'm willing to go back to bat for you at the office if you're still interested."

"You can't be that desperate," I said.

"Turns out your ethics weren't as questionable as many believed."

I stuck my hands in my pants pockets. "I appreciate the offer, Mike. But I think I'll pass. I've spent enough time in the public eye lately. I'd like to go back to just maintaining what I've got. Running Archangel is more than enough work to keep me busy."

"All right. I'll go back to searching then."

"Why don't you start your search out there?" I pointed to the ramp where two women were walking around Bayside's Beech Baron.

Mike shielded his eyes from the sun and peered out. "Sierra Noble?"

"She's got an ATP. She's a multi-engine instructor. I think you'd be hard-pressed to find a pilot with the variety of flying experience she's managed to attain."

Mike squinted. "Awfully young though, isn't she?"

"Is there a reg somewhere that says a pilot examiner has to be some crusty old dude?"

"None that I've run across."

"And Bud liked her."

Mike nodded. "I'm going to give that some consideration. Thanks."

"Speaking of pilot training," I added. "I was thinking you might want to put on a local seminar about the benefits of high-altitude endorsements for general aviation pilots. Maybe recognizing the effects of hypoxia? I'd attend. Turns out that knowledge comes in handier than you'd think."

FORTY-THREE

MEMORIAL

THEY HELD THE "CELEBRATION OF LIFE" for Bud Truman at his hangar on Taxiway Charlie. It was at sunset to avoid the heat, and the skyline of the city was aglow with light from the high-rises. Attendance was well beyond the estimate, so the ladies from the planning committee sent line guys scurrying for extra chairs last minute. But when people kept showing up, they gave up and just let people stand.

It seemed Buford "Bud" Truman's life had touched too many people at the airport to be accurately counted. Some were former applicants who had come to him for exams. Others were fellow pilots from his airline years. Many were simply friends—and a few people he'd known who also enjoyed sitting around their hangars in lawn chairs taking in the peaceful views.

My entire crew attended, even Cassidy, who had caught a jump seat to Clearwater last minute to make the ceremony. She saved me a folding chair in the back. Diana was there too. So was Dr. Turpin. A huge contingent of the Bayside employees showed as well.

Cassidy crossed her legs next to me as the minister said some words about our hopes for Bud in the afterlife. When the minister's sermon dragged on to the point of redundancy, and it was clear he was showing a little too much enthusiasm with the crowd's size, Cassidy leaned over and whispered in my ear. "So how did your date with Diana go?" Her eyes had wandered across the aisle to where Diana was sitting, looking fetching in a fitted black dress.

"What did you hear?"

"I heard you pummeled a guy."

"That's a stretch. I nearly lost that fight."

"Is that why you didn't get a second date?"

"It's more complicated than that. But good news is, I've punched fewer people this week."

"What about her?" she gestured to where Sierra was sitting between Enrique and Hank and Maddie Martin. "Saw you two made some sparks online."

"Don't tell me you saw that video too."

"Of course I did. What's her story?"

"Sierra is only attracted to me when you deprive her brain of oxygen."

"Right," Cassidy nodded. "Been there."

I elbowed her. She smirked.

"Sierra will fly farther without a guy like me weighing her down. I've learned that if your relationship is like a seaplane, you want to be a propeller, not the anchor."

"*You've* learned that?"

Someone shushed us.

Cassidy waited an appropriate amount of time till the shusher wasn't paying attention and leaned back over. "Are you going to try again? With Diana? Quitters never prosper."

"That's cheaters."

"What?"

"That never prosper. Cheaters. Quitters never win, and winners never quit."

"I'm shocked you didn't get a second date with that first-rate knowledge of clichés."

The shusher turned and shushed us again. Cassidy and I bowed our heads piously as the minister led a prayer.

Then he called on friends and relatives to say a few words. No one jumped to go first.

Cassidy piped up. "He'll do it." She pointed to me. "Right here. Luke Angel would like to say something."

I shook my head and muttered at her. "You know I hate giving speeches."

"Funny. I *do* know that," Cassidy replied with a cheery smile. "Go get 'em, Tiger."

I made my way up from the back of the group to the microphone with only a few audible murmurs from the audience. The minister stepped aside.

Bud's daughter Amelia gave me a nod from the front row next to her husband. Eric Feldman, the FBO manager, was beside them, with several city employees and our local district rep. Mike Gonzalez and a few other FAA inspectors had shown up too and were hovering in the back. Many of the people watching me I didn't know, but there were plenty I recognized, most of them people I interacted with every day.

I hadn't prepared anything, so for a moment I worried I might blank entirely and stammer something unintelligible. But I was facing Bud's hangar now—his wall of aircraft paraphernalia and mementos he'd saved. And I could picture the place without any of the crowd in the way, just Bud, sitting there in his tattered lawn chair staring out at the sky. And picturing him that way made it easier. We'd had conversations out here on this taxiway plenty of times.

"We nicknamed this row of hangars 'Skyline Boulevard,'" I

said as a start. "For obvious reasons. Pretty sure it was Bud that came up with it. I think he might even have made a sign somewhere on that back wall." I pointed. A few people turned to look.

"Bud loved this place. This view. We had a lot of good talks after hours. Him the wise one, me just wishing I could be as cool as him someday. But I will say, the last time we ever spoke, we disagreed on something. Not an argument per se, but a difference of opinion." I scratched idly at the stubble on my face, then realized I was doing it and quit. "He could be a stubborn guy at times. Bud once described himself as 'a mule wearing cement shoes in a tar pit' with how stuck in his ways he could be."

A few chuckles came from his former colleagues. And Amelia gave a begrudging nod.

"Funny how some of us can get that way. I'm guilty myself." I met Cassidy's eye from the back of the crowd.

"The last night we talked, Bud was worried about the state of the world. He wondered if this new generation would take care of this place the same way his had. He worried they were too focused on themselves to take their jobs seriously. Because one thing Bud and I did agree on was that we're not the owners of these airplanes or airports any more than we are owners of the sky. We're caretakers. Guardians of a legacy passed down from generations of aviators who came before us. Some of them even flew in our same planes. But we figure that if we do our jobs right, then someone else will be flying them long after we're gone."

I shifted my feet and stuck one hand in my pants pocket and looked out at faces staring back at me. "But I think in this one case, Bud would be happy to be proven wrong about his fears. And if he's up there right now watching us, I'd like to think he's satisfied. Because when I look at this group that showed up tonight, there are a few aging faces, even the ones who don't like to admit it. Like this guy." I pointed to Hank, and he chortled.

"But I see a lot of youthful faces too. And I don't see people too stuck on themselves to care about others. I see people who showed up. And the future of aviation looks pretty bright, if you ask me."

Sierra peered back at me from the second row and nodded. Tyson lifted his chin a little higher.

"I'm going to miss Bud Truman," I said. "He was a superb pilot and an even better friend. And if we all meet again on the far side of the horizon, I hope he saves a lawn chair for me. Because I guarantee he's got himself another hell of a view."

I handed the microphone back to the minister amid a smattering of applause. Then I walked over and shook Amelia's hand. She thanked me and wiped a tear from her eye with a handkerchief. A few others got up to speak then too. And when the time came, a controller up in the tower flashed a light. I knew they'd sent a clearance on the radio too.

Bud's RV-8 came streaking in from the western sky. Rip was at the controls, and he shot a trail of smoke out as he blazed down the runway for a low approach. The little plane buzzed the airfield in a final salute to our absent pilot, then shot upward, banking hard left and climbing skyward. We all watched it turn west once more, around the far side of the glittering skyline, headed out toward the beach and the last of the fading twilight sky. We watched in silence, and in the end, all that was visible was the speck of the plane's tail nav light blending in with the newly twinkling stars.

FORTY-FOUR

EPILOGUE

FRIDAY MORNING, I closed the shop and gave my crew the day off. Sierra Noble sat in the co-pilot seat of *Tropic Angel,* with the engines running.

"I can't believe this thing has actual roll-down windows like a car," she said, sticking her hand out.

"No school like the old school," I said.

Sierra had mounted one of her 360-degree cameras to the bow cleat again, and another camera hung inside the windshield recording our movements. We'd run through the preflight checklist together and were nearly ready for departure.

I turned and called back down the aisle. "The captain would like all passengers to take their seats for taxi and takeoff."

"Easier said than done!" Diana shouted back, the puppy in her arms resisting being returned to its carrier. Three other puppies were also loose, romping around the back of the cabin, while Reese and Tyson tried to wrangle them.

"Looks like they already spilled a couple of their water bowls," Sierra pointed out.

"No worries. It's a seaplane. It's designed to get wet."

Murphy looked on from the divan, panting happily, as if he had personally fathered these rambunctious puppies. Reese had one dog tucked under her arm like a football. "I think Oreo might need a friend," she said. "What happens if none of them make it to the next shelter? Like if they all end up at my house."

Sierra and I gave each other a knowing look and smiled.

It was a gorgeous day to be flying in Florida. It was hot, and loud, and a thunderstorm was already building on the far side of the bay, but we had a mission.

The tower cleared us to taxi to Runway 7. Sierra handled the throttles, setting the big Wasp engines rumbling with a throaty roar.

"I could get used to this," Sierra said as the seaplane lifted free of the runway and climbed.

"I was thinking I could try a new business tagline," I said. "Archangel Aviation. It's for the dogs."

Sierra laughed. "Maybe you should stick to flying, and I'll manage the social media taglines." She turned us on course with a broad grin on her face.

Later that night, when I was back aboard the boat, I saw that same smile had made the montage video she posted of the flight for her social media accounts. Thanks to her popularity and her tagging Sky Bridge Pet Rescue in the post, over half the dogs we'd transported already had new homes pending.

The skydive video was gone from her profile page. Also the splash-in at Egmont Key. All the former mentions of me were deleted with them. Archangel was already sinking back below radar. But Sierra's honest post about what had happened to her at the bar inspired three other women from airfields on the east coast to come forward about hazy nights they'd spent with a "Puppy Pilot with a Pilatus." Jason Brooks II may have hoped he'd faded from their memories, but he would hear their names again in court.

I scrolled through the comments on Sierra's latest video. She'd rebranded. Her account profile now read: Beach Sierra: Living Grounded. Flying High.

I watched her pet rescue video from *Tropic Angel* one more time, her relaxed easy smile on display. She looked lighter. And that made me smile too. I hit the like button.

Then I tabbed over to my profile. I admired my one cat photo, then scrolled down the profile page to the button that said "Delete Account."

"Are you sure?" it asked. I pressed YES. Then, I tossed my phone onto the sofa cushion beside me and picked up my paperback.

Flipping a few pages and locating the one where I'd left off, I saw Spenser and Hawk were once more neck-deep in trouble. I readjusted the pillow behind my back to get comfortable. I had no idea how they were going to get out of this one.

But like any good mystery series, I couldn't wait to see what happened next.

Ready for more of Archangel Aviation?

Be sure to download the hilarious bonus chapter featuring Luke's second date with Diana. You'll also get the bonus, behind-the-scenes details about the making of TROPIC ENVY and be able to receive the bi-monthly newsletter. Be the first to know about new books in the series.

Get your bonus.
https://BookHip.com/HWMKSTF

You can also follow Nate Van Coops on Amazon, Audible, and his social media pages. Learn more and even pick up your own Archangel Aviation T-shirts and other gear at:

https://nathanvancoops.com

ACKNOWLEDGMENTS

Thanks for taking another flight with Archangel Aviation!

I hope you've enjoyed the ride.

This was a fun one to write! Want to learn more about the real-life inspirations behind the world of TROPIC ENVY? Be sure to pick up the bonus material that includes photos, behind-the-scenes looks at the airplanes in the book and some real-life characters who helped inspire this story. Even the true origins of dance break! Also meet several of the aviation content creators making the aviation community a better place.

I'm thrilled that these books have been met by such a strong response from the community. Each week I receive emails from readers who have had their lives touched by aviation for the better and have enjoyed following Luke's adventures. I try to respond to every email as time permits, so thanks for taking the time to say hello.

Reviews are the lifeblood of a series so if you've enjoyed this book, kindly leave a review on the platform you purchased it from. I read every one.

Luke's penchant for finding trouble will continue. If you want to keep hanging out with me in the meantime, I write biweekly newsletters that include what's going on at Albert Whitted Airport, flying adventures with my family, and of course, book news. You can join at natevancoops.com or by picking up any of the books' bonus epilogues.

Thanks to my beta team, the TYPE PROS, who are my brave test pilots. A captain is nothing without a crew and this crew is amazing. Each one of you makes my books fly higher.

Thank you specifically to Marilyn Bourdeau, Julie DeStefano, Mark Hale, Judy Eiler, Bill LeBus, Claire Manger, Yvonne Mitchell, Ginelle Blanch, Elaine Davis, Sarah Van Coops-Bush, Marc Brown, Laura Donnelly and Bethany Cousins.

Special thanks to Walt Driggers who was kind enough to show me around Bayfront Tower, and let me dream up a murder in a hangar like his on Taxiway Charlie. His historical knowledge and support of Albert Whitted Airport played a key part in the plotting of this novel.

Thanks also to FAA Inspector Rohn Cash with the Tampa FSDO for fielding my fictional scenarios and helping me keep the novel's pilot deviations and FAA responses within the ballpark of plausibility.

Sam Ranscht, Acelyn McKernan, Cheryl Hollon, Dovev Weaver, thanks for being my co-working friends at COHatch. You make the day-to-day writing so much fun!

And to my writer friends, Lucy Score, Alan Lee, Cissy Mecca, James Blatch, Boo Walker, T. Ellery Hodges, Avery Maxwell, and Tina Gallagher. Our virtual water cooler chats keep me motivated and inspired. Also a big thanks to the Tropical Authors group for always floating each other's boats.

Thank you Scott Brick for using your tremendous talent to bring these thrillers to life in audio. I like these books, but they're even better when you read them.

To Stephanie, Piper, and Morgan, I've had a lot of occupations over the years but "Dad" is my favorite job title. I love you.

-NVC

ABOUT THE AUTHOR

NATE VAN COOPS is a commercial pilot, mechanic, and certified flight instructor in St. Petersburg, Florida. His addictions to tacos and pickle ball wage a war for supremacy daily. When not writing, or flying at his favorite airport, you'll find him e-biking around St. Pete with his wife and kids. He also writes science fiction books under the name Nathan Van Coops. Learn more at natevancoops.com.

To inquire about the availability of film or television rights, send email to: inquiries@nathanvancoops.com